I0689286

# *the*
# memory
# tree

## glenn haybittle

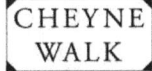
CHEYNE
WALK

Published by Cheyne Walk 2017

Copyright © Glenn Haybittle 2017

*This book is a work of fiction and, except in the case of historical fact, any resemblance to actual persons, living or dead, is purely coincidental.*

All right reserved. Without limiting the rights under copyright reserved above, no part of this publication may be reproduced, stored in or introduced into a retreival system, or transmitted, in any form or by any means (electronic, mechanical, photocopying, recording or otherwise), without the prior written permission of both the copyright owner and the publisher of the book.

The moral right of the author has been asserted.

Published by Cheyne Walk

www.cheynewalk.co

ISBN-13: 978-0 9932863-5-3

I was standing on the highest mountain of them all, and round about beneath me was the whole hoop of the world.

And while I stood there I saw more than I can tell and I understood more than I saw; for I was seeing in a sacred manner the shapes of all things in the spirit, and the shape of all shapes as they must live together like one being.

And I saw that the sacred hoop of my people was one of many hoops that made one circle, wide as daylight and as starlight, and in the centre grew one mighty flowering tree to shelter all children of one mother and one father.

Black Elk.

# Part One

## 2084

### 1

Alowa and Nya enter Suite 911. Suite 911 repeats every other executive suite in the dome. Everything streamlined, recessed, encoded, computer-plotted. Inside, three adolescent boys in hygiene suits are watching media streaming of *History*. Alowa's heart quickens as she dares a glance at the exotic images on the wall. Women with beaded hair in bright painted clothes dancing beneath the moon and stars to a pulsing drum. A pulsing drum that enters Alowa's bloodflow as a kind of entreaty. It's all she can do not to sway her body in time to the hypnotic rhythm of the drum. The hypnotic heartbeat rhythm of the drum. She wants to respond to a memory of a dance in her feet, in her hips and in the muscles of her legs.

Access to streaming of *History* is denied all cash neutrals.

*The things I have thought. Gone. The things I have seen. Gone. The things I have done. Gone. My face in the glass.*

"How may we be of service?" asks Nya.

Alowa feels a prickling wet patch developing beneath her armpits. She has no memory of any of these executive sons. But she has a bad feeling. An agitated pulse in a vein somewhere in her body. In her head she names the boys A, B and C.

Boy B, who has hair the colour of egg yolk, asks, "Are they immigrants?"

Boy A says, "You are so naïve, Hal."

"Well, are they?"

"You tell me."

Boy A looks into Alowa's eyes. "Which one do we choose?"

"Why not both?"

"Because how are we going to explain the disappearance of two chattels?"

Boy C speaks for the first time. "If it comes to that how are we going to explain the disappearance of one chattel?"

"It was your idea." Boy A swipes his wrist. The dancing women vanish from the wall. Replaced by grainy monochrome footage of nature into which acrylic colour begins to bleed. The camera stalks over trees and bushes. Trees and bushes dusted in white powder. Alowa tries to remember what this white powder is called. She has the knowledge somewhere in her neural archives but cannot access it. *The things I have thought. Gone. My face in the glass.*

Then the camera zooms in on three animals. Alowa does not recognise them except as animals but the nonchalance and restrained power of their movements is mesmerising.

"There are the lions," says Boy A. "About a hundred yards from the chute exit."

Alowa catches Boy C staring at her legs, the naked zone above her red vinyl boots and below her red vinyl skirt.

"So, which one is it to be? Which one are we going to remove from the database?"

"How about eeny, meeny, miney, moe?"

Alowa's neck muscles stiffen inside her Unity collar.

"I say the less attractive of the two," says Boy A.

It's wrong to wish with all her neural circuitry that Nya is the least attractive but Alowa's skin prickles hot and cold with the shame of this wish.

Boy A scans Alowa's face and then looks at Nya. "In that case, this one."

"Okay," says Boy C. "You get her feet."

Boy A squats down in front of Nya. "You are programmed to obey my commands," he tells her. Nya, Alowa can tell, is caught between a natural impulse to struggle and the sacred Unity pledge of obedience. Boys B and C help Boy A bring Nya down. Alowa stands wishing she were invisible. The boys pick her friend Nya up by her feet and shoulders. Nya pleads with them not to do this. She looks at Alowa. There is nothing in Alowa's memory she can draw upon to help her through this ordeal. *The things I have thought. Gone.* The way her friend Nya looks at her makes Alowa's collar chaff at the skin at the back of her neck. It makes her skin bristle with too much sensitivity. Like when the overseer cuts her nails or hair. She watches the boys activate the emergency exit chute in the wall. Watches them carry Nya there. Watches them force her head inside the oblong hole. Then shove the rest of her body into the portal until finally her twitching feet in the red vinyl boots disappear too. Her friend Nya's cry of alarm is more full-blooded than any noise Alowa has ever heard but it quickly becomes thin and is finally sucked away like a hygiene flush. The boys have all turned to look at the grainy footage of outside on the wall. They have forgotten about her. They have forgotten about Alowa.

Alowa watches the film. Nya tumbles out of a gash in the wall and lies in a crumpled heap. Alowa is relieved to see Nya get to her feet. Alowa feels her friend's indecision in her own muscles. Alowa feels more inside her friend's body than inside her own. Except she feels guilt. Like a sludge sucking at her thoughts.

The camera pans out. The animals have been alerted. They begin moving stealthily towards Nya. Fanning out in a semi-circle as if this is something they have discussed and settled on as the best plan of action.

Boy A says, "What would you do if you were her now?"
Boy B says, "Try and get back in the chute?"
Boy A says, "You'd just slide back down into their jaws."
Boy C says, "I'd climb a tree."

Boy B says, "Can lions not climb trees?"

Boy A says, "You're so naïve, Hal."

Alowa has been watching the animals move towards Nya. She sees the expression she knows is on her own face on her friend Nya's face. She is startled by how vividly she is imagining herself into Nya's body, into Nya's mind. It's as if they are one and the same person. That's how her heartbeat is experiencing the moment.

The animals are all crouched down low in the powdered white scrub. Watching Nya. Alowa isn't sure if Nya can see them. The tension down there is fed up into Alowa's own body as if she, Nya and the beasts are all wired into the same circuitry.

Then one of the lions nonchalantly lets itself be seen by Nya. Nya edges away from it, towards the two crouched down in the grass to her right. When the more brazen of the beasts breaks into a canter Nya runs, straight into the ambush. One of the animals jumps up onto her shoulders and brings her to the ground. Alowa turns away just as a splash of blood spatters the gleam of white powder on the ground.

Alowa acts before thinking. Something she has never done before in memory. She slaps Boy A in the face. For a moment he is too stunned to react. She too is rooted to the spot by incredulity. She has committed the cardinal sin. Then she is being wrestled to the ground. She too is shoved into the chute. Her body shuttled down through a black void by a force she has no knowledge of or power to resist.

When she gets to her feet everything is more bright and strange than dreams. It is the first time she can remember being outside. Her first time under the sky. Her breath visible on the chill air is one wonder. The scent of the earth is another wonder. *The things I have thought. Gone. The things I have seen. Gone. The things I have done. Gone. My face in the glass.* The lions are about fifteen feet away. Feeding on her friend Nya. Alowa sees Nya's unseeing eyes are wide open. All three animals look up at her. Alowa feels everything within quickening and everything without slowing down. As if a Unity needle has entered her vein. Adrenalin surges into her muscles. But Alowa doesn't move. Despite the wild throbbing pulse in her veins. She pretends she is invisible. She pretends she is erasing herself in smoke. An image that has mysteriously streamed into her mind. She looks down at the trail of her friend Nya's blood. She remembers what Boy B said. *I'd climb a tree.* The animals have returned to feeding. She edges towards the nearest tree. The novel crunch and slide of a surface taking an imprint of her footsteps. The first branch of the nearest tree is beyond the reach of her hands even if she stands on tiptoes. But there is a vine wreathed around the crooked trunk. Alowa reaches up for a tendril and hangs suspended for a moment. Testing its strength to support her weight. And then she hears a noise. Except it isn't really a noise. More like the silence heightening to a new pitch. More like a displacement of the air. But she suddenly feels something magnetised to her with murderous intent.

The animal with burning eyes is padding towards her. She heaves herself up. Her heart is pushing through her chest. The beast is no more than six feet away from her. Its smell reaches her at the same time she hears its breathing. It makes a deep ferocious noise that resounds in the chill air. It's the most powerful and frightening noise Alowa's body has ever had to withstand.

Alowa sits pinioned in the crook of the branch. She is so cold her thoughts seem to be floating away from her body. Floating up towards a solitary silver point visible through the grey haemorrhage of sky. For the first time it occurs to her that her thoughts might be more durable than her body.

Inside the UniCorp dome where Alowa dispenses her good will the temperature is always the same. Alowa has never experienced cold. She doesn't understand how it thieves inside her body and then begins to take her body away.

The beast is still down there. Avoiding eye contact. It exerts a pulsating allure. Never has anything demanded so much space in Alowa's mind. There is no room for anything else. Alowa thinks that if she talks to the animal it might change its mind about her. Understand she deserves sympathy, that she is a loyal dispenser of good will. She tells it she bears it no ill will for eating her friend Nya, though this, of course, is a lie. It is the first lie Alowa can ever remember telling. She finds it doesn't distress her to tell a lie as much as the overseer led her to believe it would. She tells the animal, with a note of indignation that is also new to her, that there is more to her than just calories. "I have a heart," she says. "I have feelings." The beast yawns while she speaks to it and she looks down into its bloodstained mouth with the deadly curving canines. Otherwise it prowls back and forth around the tree, ignoring everything she says. Then it reaches up for her. Rests its two front paws on the trunk of the tree. Primeval claws. Drool ebbing out from its mouth. Its smell catching at the back of her throat. For a moment she thinks it is going to climb up the trunk.

Another flurry of white starflakes begin falling down. They settle on her eyelashes. She licks at them as they slide down onto her lips. Soon she can no longer see even the coloured neon logos of the domes. The animal pads off. As if these wet white flakes carry some kind of menace. Or perhaps it is trying to trick her into climbing down? Alowa wonders if the overseers will come looking for her. The tracking chip in her collar will tell them where she is. Or perhaps they will think the lions have eaten her, like they ate her friend Nya.

Soon there is no longer any feeling in her body and she is no longer aware of where her limbs stop and the tree begins. Everything seems to go out of focus. The world becomes a smell. A thick pungent earthy smell that flickers light into Alowa's mind, a guttering image.

*Look how beautiful the flames are, Alowa. Look how beautiful my naked body is, Alowa. Are you looking at my naked body? I'm dancing towards you.*

The light bleeds away. The image of the naked boy fades. Alowa knows she has to move or the cold will kill her. *I have a heart. I have feelings. My face in the glass.* She climbs down from the tree. Smoke seems to lift off the black swell of the trees and foliage. She feels the darkness enter her. And then extend her out into the surrounding silence. As if it is a medium that allows her to flow out into it. Alowa strains her eyes into the shadows. Her ears pricked like a night creature in peril. Her skin tells her the lions are awake. Her skin tells her the lions are aware of her presence. Her skin tells her that the lions are listening to her fear. The wild throbbing pulse in her veins. She pictures the lions about eight hundred yards away, over to her right. Crouched down in the long grass. She pictures them forming into a hunting party. Working as a team. Noses lifted. To catch her scent. To sniff out her fear. Three lionesses.

The dry bracken dusted with white flakes beneath her feet crackles. Shadow unfurls from her like smoke. *Look how beautiful the flames are, Alowa. Look how beautiful my naked body is, Alowa. Are you looking at my naked body? I'm dancing towards you.* The memory edges towards her and then wanes. A blurred image she can't bring into focus. She feels the presence and smell of the smoke. The smoke seems to envelop her. Making her limbs feel lighter and lighter. The memory freezes her to the spot. Even when she senses a crackle of current move just beneath the surface of the earth. Over to her right. She thinks she senses the black grass sway. Something she feels rather than sees. She hears the rustle of agitated foliage. She still has the sensation of being shrouded in smoke. Her instinct is to run. But she remains a statue. She feels the muscles in her abdomen contract, her blood thicken like melted candle wax in her veins. Then a black shadow bolts out into her field of vision. A living creature scared out of its wits. Behind it is an explosion of power that comes surging towards her. The lioness appears within six feet of her. Both a whirlwind blur and the most vivid thing she has ever seen. It charges by her. Ignoring her, as if she is invisible. As if she is shrouded in smoke, as if she smells not of skin and blood but of smoke.

# 2

"You passed out. Hypothermia. Lucky we found you. Me, Spoon and Bolt were out scavenging. In the lion park. We carried you here. I took off your Unity collar. So they won't know where you are. They'll think the lions got you."

Alowa has just woken up. Her mind a torpor of cloudy sediment. Her blood anticipating the kickstart of morning medication – the o-zone capsule. Her hand goes to her neck. The collar is an echo there. Still there but gone. *The collar is your identity. Without it, you are a fugitive and will be terminated.* Her heartrate increases. Her skin flushes. The absence of her collar floods her with fear. *The things I have thought. Gone. The things I have seen. Gone. The things I have done. Gone.* She sits up. There are noises above her. Like an irregular heartbeat. High up over her head. A boy is kneeling by her side. For a moment she thinks he is the boy she saw taking off his clothes in the smoke. The boy she still can't remember. This boy is wearing a black hood that covers his face except his nose and mouth. He has blackened teeth and a spittle of saliva on his lower lip.

She throws off the piece of plastic sheeting covering her. She jumps to her feet. She bows. "How may I serve you?" she says uncertainly.

"You don't have to serve me. We are all equals here. No masters, no slaves." He pats her arm, as if seeking to guide her to embrace the kindness in his eyes.

"Where am I?"

"District 17 of the reservation. My name is Digger. I'm a

hacker. That's a secret I've told you. To build trust." The boy removes his hood and leans forward into the light of the fire. His skin is like the delicate wrinkled white petals of a flower. "Don't worry. I don't have the sickness. You must be used to well-nourished people. Working in one of the domes. I'm afraid that isn't the case here. We're all starved. We're cash neutrals. What's more, they say all us cash neutrals are medicated to keep us compliant and the medication damages the ecology of our minds. We lose our long term memory. That's why we've stopped eating their rations here. We grow and catch our own. On the roof is where we grow our nutrients. Hidden from the spy drones. They say all our most important memories are stored in our bodies and with the right training and discipline we can retrieve them all."

"Can I ask you a question?"

"Of course."

"Am I an immigrant?"

"I don't know. You might be. I don't mind, even if you are."

"What is an immigrant?"

"It's slang for a bioengineered facsimile of a human being. You know, an individual whose neuropaths are plotted by computer chips. Or something like that. Apparently you have to understand consciousness as information. Once it's been understood as information, encoded as ones and zeroes, it can be archived and uploaded. I've never seen an immigrant. At least not to my knowledge. There was a girl where I worked who was accused of being an immigrant but I don't think she was. I think it was just my co-workers being cruel again."

"How can you tell an immigrant from a normal person?"

"I don't know. I guess it's a feeling they give you of something not quite being right."

"Do I give you that feeling?"

"No. I like you."

"Thank you."

"Tell me what it was like working for The Black Snake."

"The Black Snake?"

"UniCorp. It's what we call them here in the reservation. They fucked up the whole world. They are a freemasonry of the rich and powerful. A complicit and elite minority of greedy power-crazed executives. For decades they sponsored and organised terrorism and hazardous environmental projects that caused catastrophic natural disasters. And when they had whipped up enough fear and division and poverty they took over. One by one sovereign countries were replaced by militarised authoritarian states. All run by UniCorp. And that's what we have now. The ethos of UniCorp is short term gain at the expense of long term consequence. Short term memory at the expense of any kind of detailed overview. Obviously they've erased your memory. I'm curious to know what it's like to be on the inside."

Alowa has no idea what he's talking about. *The things I have thought. Gone. The things I have seen. Gone. The things I have done. Gone.* Her ignorance leaves her without a voice.

"My ignorance leaves me without a voice," she says.

"That was their weapon. Ignorance. One consequence of ignorance is that it misdirects anger. This is what our ancestors did. They blamed people in the same boat for their dwindling autonomy. They fought among themselves. Our ancestors have a lot to answer for. But you shouldn't blame yourself. They've obviously tampered with you."

"Can I go outside? I've never been outside. Except when the lions ate my friend."

"Of course. But go into the backyard. It's dangerous out in the district. We need to verse you in its customs before we let you out there on your own."

Outside a powdery mist shrouds a long high-walled enclosure. In the near distance she can see flames. She walks towards them. An old man is standing by a mound of burning leaves. He is ushering the smoke up into his face. He is a wizened old man blackened with dirt. Wearing loose scarecrow clothes. His filthy breeches have clotted paint stains. Bright greens and reds. The sleeves of his coat are so large they look like black wings when he lifts his arms. He is an old man until he smiles when he seems to become much younger.

"Greetings," she says. It's what she has been trained to say to strangers whose authority is ambivalent.

"Hello Alowa. I'm glad the lionesses liked you."

"They ate my friend Nya."

"Sometimes we have to part company with our friends. It's the only way the next part of the story can begin."

"Do you live here with Digger?"

"You can call me the janitor, Alowa. The smoke brought you here. I think you know that even if you don't recognise me yet. I am to remain a secret to everyone else. You're never to talk to anyone else about the things I say to you. I'm going to help you recover your memories. To do this I'm going to teach you how to enter your dreams and manipulate them. Because there is a dance inside you, Alowa. And you have to learn this dance again. Be quiet for a moment and tell me what you hear."

Alowa does as she's told.

"I can hear a distant ringing in my ears."

"They did this to you, Alowa. They anaesthetised you. It's what they do. That tone you hear in your ears is the sound of you sleeping. The sleeper in you needs to awaken. Your mind is nothing at present but a running stream of text updates, Alowa. Isn't that so? You've lost all your pictures. Come closer. Let the smoke envelop you." The old man begins to make bewitching moments of dance among the smoke. A wind arrives and lifts some of the burning leaves high into the air. Fiery red sparks dance in the air. The leaves float and swirl about in the air. The old man is studying Alowa closely. Alowa is mesmerised by the dance of the sparks and the leaves.

"Now sit down here by the smoke."

He is fanning the smoke towards her. It makes her cough and then it makes her drowsy. Her eyelids flutter. Her head slumps forward.

She is close to moving water. Salt on her lips. This is how the dream begins. A man in a surgical mask wields a primitive knife. He draws a line with the blade across her arm. Bubbles of blood emerge and run into a hot trickle towards her elbow. Cruel-eyed dirty white birds hover and fight and screech. Then she is in the water. She has to swim to the opposite bank. A grandstand of spectators behind her. A low hum of excited anticipation. A drone low in the sky overhead. There are about fifty other swimmers in the water. It surprises her that she knows how to swim. She enjoys the sensation of marrying her body and her will. Her body obeying commands she doesn't need to think about. Her breaststrokes become ever more fluent. She has never felt so gracefully in possession of her body, so exalted in it. Then something flashes across her field of vision. A war party of nagging patrolling fins in the water. She is aware of a disturbance to her left. The water kicks up into a froth, a spiral of turbulence. She catches a glimpse of a huge powerful grey beast and the flailing arms of a swimmer disappearing beneath the agitated surface. A thin red dye seeps up onto the surface of the water, pooling and becoming thicker. Then the nightmare vision rushes into her eyes. Turns her inside out. The beast shimmying up towards her. Huge snout, mouth open, razor teeth and the small skewering black eyes. About three times her size. It is rising up through the water towards her. She has the sense of an implacable deadly will streamlining straight for her. She panics. She turns in the water. Begins swimming away from it. But it is even more frightening to feel its swift power and not to be able to see it. All of a sudden she no longer has control of her legs. She is swallowing water. She is being tugged at, shaken, dragged down into the depths of the water. Every physical pain she has ever known, every terror, suddenly converges on her and is magnified.

Her tongue is still crusted with the terror when she is jostled awake. The janitor is sitting against an old wall. Polishing a battered blackened pot. He tells her to sit down cross-legged on the grass opposite him.

"At the moment you are sitting with your back to the entire world," he says. "This makes you very vulnerable."

Alowa notices a fly on the grass. It seems to be watching her. But as soon as it has her attention it begins turning in circles and then cleaning itself. Then it suddenly vanishes yet she does not see it fly off. She hears it buzzing close to her ear. It appears on the grass again. It repeats this pattern of behaviour several times. Suddenly vanishing and buzzing in her left ear. It never lands in quite the same place, as though staking out new territory. It draws her attention to the surrounding grass and bracken. She sees a fallen pink petal, a forked twig, a drop of dew suspended on the tip of a blade of grass.

"The fly is increasing your capacity for wonder," says the janitor. "You've had a dream, haven't you?"

Alowa tells him about the dream.

The old man smiles. Except his teeth are different. They are animal teeth. More sharp and curved and unevenly spaced, more cruel than she remembers them before. Alowa's nostrils flare with fright. She jumps to her feet, poised to run away. Except the steady gaze of the janitor's eyes holds her still, as if she is caught in a web. She pictures an intricacy of intersecting silver threads, encircling her as if measuring her for a new uniform. The bark of a tree leaves its print on her palm when she leans against it for support.

"Sharks don't really like humans," he says. He smiles and his teeth are human teeth again. "They don't like our taste. Usually they will take a bite and then swim off repulsed. The problem is, that bite can be fatal. A shark accumulates its power through inspiring fear. It moves swiftly and silently, drawing to itself only that which is essential to its task. You will have to send the fear it inspires back to it. You will dream this dream again. Next time you have to enter the dream awake to change it. You have to be simultaneously inside and outside the dream. When you begin to dream look down at your feet. You must find your feet in the dream. Only by registering your feet will you be able to manipulate the dream. Because otherwise the dream will happen exactly as it foretells. The beast you saw is called a great white shark. To enter *History* you will have to swim the gauntlet of the sharks. I have seen this in a vision."

"You're frightening me."

"Our bodies like fear as much as they like laughter. And perhaps they like sadness best of all. Soon I will teach you how to summon a dream ally. We have to wait until it's dark. Agreements have to be made in the dark for them to be binding. Your dream ally will help you defeat the shark. You and your dream ally will have an argument. Every impassioned argument revives memories. The dream ally will teach you a warrior song."

"I never want to see that beast again."

"Tough shit," he says and laughs. He begins stamping rhythmically on the ground as if coaxing her to dance with him. A gust of wind blows a moving circle of leaves around him as he dances. He shifts his weight gracefully from one foot to the other and moves forward and backward in little jumps. She is hypnotised by the lightness with which his feet skip over the ground. Her own body mimics his movements in imagination. He sings as he dances. A throaty impassioned chant. "You do this dance then climb this tree. You climb down and do the dance again. You do this until sweat has brought the smell of your sex out. Your dream ally will be attracted to the smell between your thighs."

Alowa can feel the ghost of the dance in her limbs and muscles, prompting her to enact it. While she dances she is disappointed the leaves don't form a moving circle around her as they did when the old man danced.

"Okay, let me smell you." He kneels down in front of Alowa and sniffs at her crotch. He breathes in deeply and makes a comic show of deriving great pleasure from the odour. His laughter is like a young boy's. Alowa too can smell herself and it is a new source of wonder in her.

"I am not moving my lips but I am talking to you. In your dreams you will learn what you know. In your dreams you will know who you are. In your dreams they will try to catch you. In your dreams you will defeat them. I will be the one who brings you your dreams."

# 3

"Where's the old man today?"

"What old man? What are you talking about?"

"The old man. He told me he was the janitor."

"Either they really messed with your mind or you're playing us for fools."

Alowa is outside with Mona. Mona is one of the other cash neutrals who lives with Digger. Mona doesn't like Alowa. *"How do we know she isn't a spy? She just mysteriously arrives here. The waif. The romancer. The damsel in distress."* Alowa walks the reservation streets with Mona. Through the smog and pollution and drizzle. Through the labyrinth of ruined tenements, the windswept junctions. Underneath the tagged overpasses. The façade of buildings missing, rooms exposed. Wires tangled in the masonry. Trees mutilated. Dead leaves strewn over the rubble and ashes in the streets. Through the smog and pollution and drizzle that makes Alowa's eyes sore. Stepping over the rubble and garbage. Avoiding eye contact. Bewildered at the chaos and deprivation everywhere. She tells Mona how clean and hygienic everything was inside the dome. She is pleased she can remember the dome and her friend Nya. Mona isn't interested in anything Alowa says. Mona is unkind to her at every opportunity. "You don't need to know where we're going. You don't need to know anything. Don't ask me questions. In fact, don't open your mouth. Don't open your mouth and we'll get on fine."

Mona wears a rucksack. Inside are her memories. Everyone

wears a rucksack. Everyone has memories except her. Alowa walks behind Mona. *They anaesthetised you.* Alowa has been given new clothes to wear. Clothes whose textures against her skin are foreign and unsettling. Clothes that secrete the smell of strangers. The absence of the familiar is both liberating and frightening. Her new clothes, the foreign way they touch her skin, want to change how she is accustomed to experiencing herself. She is excited by the broadening outlook of the person who lives in her head. *The things I have thought. The things I have seen. The things I have done. My face in the glass.*

There are fires in blackened metal drums. Slush and mud underfoot. The sound of drones up in the sky. People pushing wire trolleys with squeaking wheels. Children crying. Mothers calling. Men mumbling. Fallen-world voices. Fallen-world faces. Everyone wearing endtime clothes. Her fingertips tingle with the cold.

A metal bird descends overhead. The noise it makes jars the joints in her body. The whirring blades fluster her hair, suck the air from her lungs. Scraps of parchment and debris fly up into a duststorm. Mona stops and together they watch the drop of boxes. They are lowered into a square formed by security teams with peak caps and grubby yellow and blue armbands. Mona for once reluctantly answers her questions. They are UniCorp boxes of rations and nutrients that the workforce will carry to the local altarhouses where the two daily meals are served.

In a shanty market Mona walks on ahead. Pushing her way through the crowd. As if she is embarrassed to be seen with Alowa. The smell of burning wood, roasting nuts. Alowa finds it difficult to keep Mona in sight. She doesn't like brushing against these dirty people. She does not want to touch or be touched. Filthy yellow sheeting rustling overhead. A boy stops in front of Alowa. He looks at Alowa wide-eyed. He alarms her. Her heart thumps as if she has just finished running. He has a bruise under his eye and recent cuts on his cheek. A tide mark of ingrained dirt around his neck. He has filthy bandages on both hands.

His long nailed fingertips poking out. He flips off his hood. He has dishevelled white hair. A padded jacket, trouser legs torn in flapping shreds.

"Alowa," he says. "We thought we would never see you again. How did you get back here? Are you a fugitive," he says, lowering his voice and looking anxiously around.

She has no recollection of the boy talking to her. *The things I have thought. Gone. The things I have seen. Gone. The things I have done. Gone. My face in the glass.*

"You don't remember me, do you? What have they done to you? Blue. I'm Blue, Alowa. A friend of Solstice. We were all on work detail together. Surely you haven't forgotten Solstice. You two were soulmates. Solstice still has your memories. You gave them to him before they took you away. Wait till I tell him I've seen you. He'll be over the moon."

*He knows who I am. I am a memory for him. He knows who I am.*

"I've got to go, Alowa. But can you be here tomorrow at the same time? Just after the rations drop. I'll tell Solstice to meet you here and bring your memories. It looks like you need them. Tomorrow, here, after the rations drop. Can you remember that at least? Shall I write it on your wrist?" She lets him take her wrist. He writes **Solstice** there in black chalk. Following the line of her vein. Mona appears just as he is completing the **e**. Mona tugs at her arm and throws the boy a disgusted look before dragging Alowa away.

"Was he your contact?"

"His name is Blue. He said he knows me."

"But you, of course, don't remember. You don't remember anything. Do you remember my name, Alowa? Do you remember that I don't like you and I don't trust you? Who is Solstice?"

"He said Solstice has my memories."

"Is Solstice a fellowship agent, Alowa? If there's a raid tonight I will make sure you're terminated within seven sleeps. I've told the necessary people about you. They're checking you out in the databases."

*He knows who I am. I am a memory for him. He knows who I am.*

# 4

Alowa notices a fly on the grass. It seems to be watching her. *The fly is increasing your capacity for wonder.* But as soon as it has her attention it begins turning in circles and then cleaning itself. Then it suddenly vanishes yet she does not see it fly off. She hears it buzzing close to her ear. She is close to moving water. She notices the fins before the man in the surgical mask cuts her arm. The nagging fine-tuned patrolling of hungry sharks. She knows the man in the surgical mask is going to cut her before she sees him. It no longer surprises her she knows how to swim. *When you begin to dream look down at your feet. You must find your feet in the dream. Only by registering your feet will you be able to manipulate the dream.* No matter how hard she tries she can't find her feet. She is aware of a disturbance to her left. The water kicks up into a froth, a spiral of turbulence. She catches a glimpse of the huge powerful grey beast, the great white shark, and watches the flailing arms of a swimmer disappearing beneath the agitated surface. A thin red dye seeps up onto the surface of the water, pooling and becoming thicker. Then the nightmare vision rushes into her eyes. The beast shimmying up towards her. Huge snout, mouth open, razor teeth and small skewering black eyes. *You must find your feet in the dream.* It is rising up through the water towards her. She has the sense of an implacable deadly will streamlining straight for her. She panics. She turns in the water. Begins swimming away from it. But it is even more frightening to feel its swift power and not to be able to see it. All of a sudden she no longer has control of her legs. She is swallowing water. She is being tugged down into the depths of the water. Every physical pain she has ever known, every terror suddenly converges on her and is magnified.

The dream is almost exactly the same the second time Alowa dreams it.

"This is because you can't remember the song your dream ally taught you. Tonight we will have to summon the dream ally again. You will have to wrestle the form it takes to the ground and compel it to teach you your warrior song." For the briefest of moments his eyes are black and staring, just like the expressionless malevolence of the eyes of the beast in the water. Then his eyes are kind and encouraging again.

"What does the dream ally look like?"

"It depends. You chose to see it as a bat. Tonight maybe you will choose to see it in another form. A long dead ancestor in a decayed state for example."

"Can it hurt me?"

"It can tear you to ribbons if it feels like it. It might even demand a sexual favour from you," he says and winks at her.

She is always hurt when he makes fun of her. She pulls the sleeves of the garment she wears over her hands and screws her hands into fists.

"You have to slow down your relationship with the world. You're always in a hurry to return to the stream of text in your head."

Alowa is beginning to feel dizzy with hunger. He has not allowed her to eat, except for roots and nettles he keeps making her chew.

"What did that boy mean when he said Solstice has my memories? He said Solstice was my soulmate. What does that mean?"

"It means you're connected by a songline. And the song you share has a dance and the dance, when performed, will trigger a hidden power you have encrypted into your circuitry."

Alowa looks at the handsome lines on his face. The mud

crust on his boots. Then there's a displacement in the air, a subtle shift in the ambient atmosphere, a heightening of awareness. The janitor extends his arm and looks up at the sky. Alowa feels a scream rise up inside her as a black bird, the flapping of its large silvered wings like a disturbance deep down in her being, suddenly descends and lands on the janitor's extended arm. For a moment the bird looks her in the eye. She has to defend herself against the hard piercing gleam in the bird's eyes. It forces her to recoil, to find something solid within herself to hold on to. *The things I have seen. Gone.*

"Say hello to Esawa, Alowa."

The bird has a string of painted teeth around its neck.

"That's yours," says the janitor. "But you have to wrestle it from your dream ally. It's a sacred ankle bracelet of painted elk teeth. You can store your memories in those teeth."

The bird gives Alowa another piercing knowing look before it flies off.

"Now listen, Alowa. I know you like Digger but he's deceiving you. Digger is a UniCorp watcher. But we must make him think he's still in possession of his secret. The UniCorp fellowship want to find Mitakuye Oyasin in *History*. They send watchers disguised as cash neutrals into *History* and Digger is one of these watchers."

"Who is Mitakuye Oyasin?"

"She was my colleague. You might say she's your ancestor. But she has many faces. She is a very slippery customer. Many people seek Mitakuye Oyasin in *History* but very few find her. Only those she wants to find her. Soon you will be arrested. You will be deported into *History*. As long as you make it past the sharks. All of you in the house will be arrested. Digger has arranged this. It's Digger's task to find Mitakuye Oyasin in *History*. He thinks Bolt will lead him to her. It's Bolt he's watching. But Bolt is an innocent. Digger has got his wires crossed. It's you he should be watching. Your task will be to find Solstice. Now then, take off all your clothes and lie down on the ground.

I will close my eyes if you don't want me to see you naked."

"Why are you whispering?"

"So as to keep your body one step ahead of you."

His broad smile reassures her. She feels protected by it. She takes off her clothes. She lies down on the ground. He begins massaging a red paste into her feet. The red paste has a powerful sour smell, like rotting fruit. A warm tingle in the soles of her feet snakes up her legs and settles in her naval and at the base of her spine. She begins to taste the air. Begins to identify and breathe in the individual scents of the plants and trees around her.

He lodges a stone between each of her toes. "Don't forget, when you begin to dream, look down at your feet. You must find your feet in the dream. Only by registering your feet will you be able to manipulate the dream."

A fly begins buzzing in her ear. She watches it trace out a geometric pattern on the air. As if following invisible lines and between the lines are spaces it cannot enter. She feels more and more drowsy. Slips down into a space beneath one heartbeat and another. The fly adds modifications to the geometrical lines it is spinning on the air. She begins to see these lines as a network of crisscrossing white threads, on either side of which are rolling banks of green smoke. She hears a rustling to her left. She has the distinct feeling she is being stalked. The underwater beast with the black staring eyes circling her. She hears the same rustling but this time behind her. She is floating in deep water. *You must find your feet in the dream.* She can't though move her head. Instead she floats upwards. She sees herself down below. She commands herself to look at her feet. But she can't see her feet. Her body is like a pool of warm gold floating on waves of darkness. The fly adds modifications to the geometrical lines it is spinning on the air. Festooning the air with a webbing of silver filigree. For a moment she feels as though she is rolling through an infinity of black space. *You will encounter a shadow being and you have to wrestle it to the ground and force it to sing you your warrior song.* A greenish mist arises around her, dampening her clothes, moving along with her as she floats. There is a winged silhouette, appearing and disappearing among the rolling banks of green fog. As if the fly has grown in size. It's like white flakes are falling in front of her eyes. A transparent silvered grid of webbing billows over everything. Accumulating and dispensing energy. Alowa thinks the silhouette might be the bird. Esawa. The silhouette makes its own light. It is defined by liquid silver lights, joined together by crisscrossing silver threads. Red embers spit and spill around the silhouette. The silhouette pulls at the matrix of silver threads. A flood of blue light breaks over her. Alowa experiences it as a blow to the chest. For the first time she notices her feet. There is a tiny red spider on her foot. When it moves it trails in its wake a black ink that tattoos her skin. Painted images move beneath her lids but her concentration cannot hold them in place and they fade. She watches the spider quickly scurry around her left ankle. It circles her ankle seven times. *Painted elk teeth from a sacred dream.* The voice whispers close to her ear. It is the voice of the silhouette that makes its own light. There is turbulence in the air around her. A great swirling of concentrated energy. Alowa glimpses the beast with the black staring eyes rising up through water. A piercing cry opens up a void inside her. Then she is wrestling with something slippery and leathery, suffocated by a foul stench. A burning sensation at the top of her head begins to reveal a chanting in her mind. Alowa chants the individual notes in sequence.

When she wakes up she is wearing the ankle bracelet of painted elk teeth.

# 5

*How old do you think this wall is, Alowa? How long ago was it built? Long enough for someone to have been murdered against its stones? Look at me pressing my palms to this wall. Feeding its history into my blood. Look at me, Alowa.*

The last time she saw Solstice. The only time she remembers Solstice.

*Look at me, Alowa. What's this I'm holding? Do you recognise it? This is a scroll. A printout. A rotting parchment bond. Look Alowa. I'm going to burn it. It is going to be my burnt offering.*

The last time she saw Solstice. The only time she remembers Solstice.

*Look at the flames, Alowa. Aren't they beautiful? Look at the smoke. I'm dancing in the smoke, Alowa.*

The last time she saw Solstice. The only time she remembers Solstice.

*I'm going to strip naked for you, Alowa. I want you to look closely at my naked body. I want you to tell me if I'm still in my pure state.*

*I'm not looking.*

*I'm taking off my clothes, Alowa.*

*I'm not looking.*

*Have I ever told you how much it hurt that you didn't choose me, Alowa? Have I ever told you how much damage it did to me that you chose boring reliable Sak over me?*

*We'll never be infant bearers anyway. So what does it matter?*

*I've taken off my overalls, Alowa.*

*My eyes are closed.*

*Undergarments, gone. Burning on the pyre. Look how beautiful the flames are, Alowa. Look how beautiful my naked body is, Alowa.*

The last time she saw Solstice. The only time she remembers Solstice.

*Are you looking at my naked body, Alowa? I'm dancing towards you. Do you remember this dance?*

She looks at his naked body.

*Here I am, Alowa. Dancing naked on the winter snow.*

Alowa has remembered the last time she saw Solstice. She remembers nothing else about him. She sees his naked body but not the dance it performed. She fingers a red tooth on the elk teeth bracelet. She wills the memory of Solstice into the painted tooth. *Every memory leaves a different weight in the mind and body, Alowa.*

"What's that?"

It's Digger and as usual his voice is kindly and confiding. *I know you like Digger but he's deceiving you. Digger is a UniCorp watcher. But we must make him think he's still in possession of his secret.*

Alowa has never seen the janitor anywhere except in the backyard. Neither Digger nor Mona nor anyone else in the house appear to know of his existence. It's an anomaly that troubles her. She decides to take a risk. "The janitor gave it to me," she says. "To help me remember."

"Who is the janitor?"

"A man I met."

"I'd like to meet him. When are you going to see him again?"

"I don't know. He just appears."

"Where does he appear?"

"In the yard."

Digger looks at her askance. As if he thinks she might be trying to trick him.

"The yard here?"

"Yes."

"That's impossible. Are you sure you're not dreaming him?"

"I might be dreaming him. My dreams are getting more vivid."

"That's because you're no longer imbibing UniCorp chemicals. Did Bolt introduce you to the janitor?"

"No. I haven't spoken with Bolt."

"I hear you met someone who recognised you yesterday and you're meeting him today," he says.

Alowa has to hide her surprise that he knows this. She looks down at the zipped bag she sleeps in and caresses the red Solstice tooth on her bracelet. *I'm dancing in the smoke, Alowa.*

"Sorry. Mona told me. I didn't know you wanted it to be a secret."

"It's not a secret. It's just that it upset me a little."

"I hope he helps you remember who you are."

"Thank you, Digger. I have to leave now."

"Good luck."

Alowa wonders if it's because she has no memory that she also has no means of knowing if Digger is deceiving her. He appears the kindest person of all the people in the house. Kinder even than Nya. It pleases her that she hasn't forgotten Nya. It pleases her that she remembers the way to the shanty market. *The things I have thought. Not quite gone. The things I have seen. Not quite gone. The things I have done. Not quite gone. My face in the glass. Changing.*

She arrives at the market before the rations drop has taken place. She walks through a swirl of steam and smoke. She stands by a table of shrine relics. She knows they are shrine relics because the man selling the items keeps shouting out the words. She doesn't know what shrine relics are though. There are strings of coloured beads, carved wooden figurines, crosses, bleached and painted bones, scrolls of parchment, pieces of coloured rock.

"I can see you like that. That's a sacred medicine bundle,

smuggled out of *History*. Because I like you, you can have it for ten tokens."

"I don't have any tokens."

The man stares into her eyes. "No tokens? Clear off then! You're an immigrant, aren't you? Get away from my goods. You ought to be deprogrammed."

The words hurt her. The words make her legs sag. She is still upset when the boy Blue appears. His thin face blackened by grime. "You remembered? I was afraid you wouldn't. But I've got some bad news. Solstice didn't return home last night. We're all really worried. He went tagging in District 26. Never came back. You have to pass through some dangerous districts to get to District 26. The bloodrunners. The hackers. The death cults. Who knows what might have happened to him. I looked for your memories but he must have them in his rucksack." The boy is breathless with the urgency to impart drama. He keeps looking over his shoulder.

"Am I an immigrant?"

"Ssssh. Do you want to get us monitored?"

"I'm sorry," she says.

"How can any of us know that? No one's memory stretches back that far. To our origins. You could come back with me, if you want? We could talk there."

"I can't." The janitor has told her she will be arrested tonight. In the middle of the night.

# 6

The pile of dead leaves on the rooftop burns. The circle of footprints in the snow around the fire belongs to Solstice. He is dancing around the burning pyre of dead leaves. In his blue overalls. In his plimsolls. In his red coat. Dirt ingrained in the seams of his face and hands.

"Every night I build a fire for you, Alowa. Every night I dance on the rooftop for you. Look at the flames, Alowa. Aren't they beautiful? Look at the smoke. I'm dancing in the smoke, Alowa."

When he has finished dancing he sits cross-legged at the edge of the rooftop. He is studying the surroundings through a pair of rusted binoculars. A thin covering of snow, like white gold filigree in the smoky moonlight, has restored innocence to the blackened rubble of buildings within the reservation perimeter walls. But it is beyond the walls that interests Solstice, the floodlit entertainment palace and the three glowing domes, as inaccessible as knowledge of his birth. Alowa, he knows, is inside one of those domes. He draws out a map of what he sees in the snow with his mittened fingers, imagining himself out there.

"Thought is constantly striving to become body, isn't it, Solstice?"

Startled, Solstice drops the binoculars. He swivels round to see the face of the man who has spoken. Dreading the crisp black uniform, the heavy boots and red insignia of the HASAF. But it is not a member of the Health and Security Alarm forces. It is an old man in a long fur-collared coat leaning on a rake. His face like a sculpture of a holy man in red clay. His white hair shaved close to the scalp. Solstice looks at the cracked leather gloves he wears, as old and weathered as the man himself. But despite all the furrows in the man's face he has piercing young dark eyes.

"I've returned to remind you of the dance, Solstice. I'm pleased you've remembered the dance. I taught you the dance. I taught you everything you began your journey with, Solstice. Now you need to find Alowa."

The old man grins. As if he has said something funny. Solstice grins too because there's something infectious about the man's wide smile. Then Solstice recognises him as the janitor.

"You're the janitor," he says, his eyes widening. The janitor at DSOS Holdings and Leisure Inc. where he and Alowa had been on the same work detail before she was taken away. The janitor had always been kind to him and Alowa. Had always taken a special interest in them both. He doesn't though remember him teaching the dance he has just danced.

He notices the janitor is wearing a blue and silver thimble on a chain around his neck. It's like some memory object from prehistory. Its beautiful contrasts of washed out colour. Solstice can't take his eyes off it.

A wind arrives and lifts some leaves in the air. Solstice watches through a spray of snow a golden leaf trace an elegant pattern on the air and then attach itself to his dungarees. When he looks around the old man has gone.

It's only a dream. But when he wakes up he is enveloped in the old man's atmosphere. It's like a sadness but with both beauty and a hint of mischief swirling about in it. And any appearance of Alowa in his dreams, even if only the mention of her name, always makes him both sad and hopeful. He still has her memories, along with his own, in his rucksack. He and Alowa had inadvertently discovered the dead janitor's body. How many years ago? The lifeless body of the old janitor was slumped on the floor. Why had they entered the room? Something had pulled them both inside. They hadn't discussed entering. They had simply slid back the door.

There was a spider on the old man's hand. Solstice had the feeling the spider was looking at him. He had the feeling the spider was the janitor looking at him. He told Alowa he had never seen a spider before. Neither had she. But they both knew immediately it was spider and that spiders spin webs. They looked around and saw the web directly above the old man's lifeless head. The old man was dead but the web seemed strangely alive. Like plaited filaments of suspended energy.

Solstice empties his rucksack onto the floor. For once all his wonder and curiosity isn't centred on the red bundle that holds Alowa's memories, the red bundle he has never opened. It's his own memories that he is excited by. Among the array of scattered objects that all possess a charge of mystery there it is - the thimble on a chain the janitor was wearing around his neck in his dream. Or an exact replica of that thimble. His heartbeat quickens with wonder. No matter how hard he tries he cannot remember its significance or its origins. The same is true of all his memory objects. He picks up the thimble and puts it around his neck. He slips it beneath his vest when he hears approaching voices. The weight and wonder of it resting in the small hollow of his chest wall subtly changes the way he feels about himself. He becomes more mysterious to himself.

Solstice sleeps on the floor of Unit 80Z. The partially gutted and scorched building is half way up a tilted street of eviscerated buildings. At night the building shifts and creaks inside its frame. His room, musty with dust and webs, has a stained glass window that is only partially broken. He is woken most mornings by motes patterning shafts of coloured light. About twelve other people sleep in the building, all GIs. Solstice has never been able to find out what exactly is meant by genetically inferior.

In the basement he and his housemates are given the assignment for the day. His assignment is District 26. He is given the code and the gesso. A tiny pink stub today. He reads the code. *Kin-Y is closer than you think.* The supervisor reminds him to bring back some code. Sometimes he talks in secret with Blue, his friend, about the meaning of these codes. Neither he nor Blue understand the purpose of tagging walls in other districts with code. So many secrets he isn't privy to. Isn't trusted with. Solstice has no secrets of his own. Unless it's how much he misses Alowa.

There is a more lively pulse in the reservation streets because there was a HASAF collaring operation yesterday. People taken away, never to be seen again. No one knows what happens to them. They disappear into *History*. The snow has mostly turned to slush in District 13. Orange and green plastic waste wraps trampled into the blackening mire. Solstice is proud of his thimble. Finally he has a secret. It remains hidden under his vest, inside his red coat. But it gives him a feeling of power in his body. A feeling of being singled out. The ghostly presence of the janitor in his thoughts imparts a sense of wellbeing he finds difficult to explain. He knows the janitor was a font of knowledge. That he answered lots of the questions Solstice has never been able to ask anyone else. Except he can't recall a single conversation they shared.

Solstice sets off from the altarhouse after lunch. He has Alowa's memories in his rucksack along with his own memories. *Never leave home without your memories.* He has memorised the route indicated on the tiny map he was given. He will be venturing into areas of the reservation he has always avoided. He tries to put out of mind the horror stories of intimidation and violence he has heard. There is black slush underfoot and the prickling stir of smog in the air. Before long he has the feeling there is someone in the shadows behind him. Someone stalking him. Only barely eluding his eyes. His thoughts lack anchorage, his fear grows. Memory can sponge up fear. But his memories don't extend back very far. Something they put in the rations destroys your memory cells. They don't want cash neutrals having access to long term memory. Someone said that. Once upon a time. He can remember this.

District 24 is a predominantly elders area - scarecrow people, prophets, endtimers, grime on their faces, grime beneath their fingernails, grime on their threadbare watermarked robes. They shuffle through the ramshackle shanty town dilapidation of the district, eyes averted, wary of connection, except the occasional destitute begging for surplus. Tarps, with their mildew stench, bulge and crack in the icy wind, making a noise like a body being pummelled with repeated blows. Outdoor metal stairways hang off their stanchions. Boards tacked over every window space. Steam rises from vent holes. There are fires at the corners. A drone hovering silently overhead. Over the ruined courtyards and compounds and viaducts, the shuttle spaces and cannibalised warehouses. A bright orange beam in the grey drizzle. Every expanse of corrugated iron and concrete is tagged by oSSo, the hackers of District 6. Solstice keeps looking over his shoulder, the feeling he is being stalked never appeased. When he turns a corner he faces the entrance to an underground tunnel. On either side the high walls are spiked with razor wire. There is no way round it.

There is the ghost of a wind in the tunnel. There are spectral echoes. The yellow recessed lights splutter on and off, as if splicing the visual world into frames, each with an unsettling pause. And each time the light returns it is like being naked again, it is like being stripped down to the rudiments of his being. Up ahead is a terminal. And the spraypainted shuttle that no longer moves. Every so often he crushes a syringe underfoot.

Solstice brings some saliva up into his mouth and swallows it. It's a reassurance of sorts, a confirmation that he still recognises himself. Even though his saliva is beginning to taste different. To taste of spiralling fear. He has strayed too far towards the picketed precinct and someone notices him. A group of dog soldiers, trespassers, addicts, deviants and med pimps, all hooded, all marked, sitting on crates with legs splayed, shoulders loose, advertising ease and entitlement. Here they come, stepping over the debris, ambling through the flotsam and jetsam. Nine of them. Both sexes. The team leader wields some kind of spray canister. He's wearing a skullcap. His statement jewellery, a cluster of nose rings. There's something misaligned about his face. His facial muscles triggered into a constant volatile twitch. He has the cruellest face Solstice has ever seen. No point in making any kind of appeal here. He motions Solstice to climb up onto the platform. Solstice is primed to run, his blood thin and pumping. But he doesn't run. He tries a smile. He tries diplomacy. Knowing how futile the decision is even in the midst of executing it.

"I want your bag and all your clothes."

Solstice looks down at his red coat, his black leggings, his scuffed and ragged plimsolls.

"Yeah, take off your fucking clothes." This one is wearing some kind of latex surgical mask. His hair brushed back into greased spikes. Mucus leaking from his damaged red nose.

Solstice doesn't want to take off his clothes. It's the last thing he wants to do. Apart from the humiliation, how long will he last in the reservation without his clothes?

Out of the corner of his eye he sees the metalled fist coming but it still takes him by surprise. The fist smashes into the bone beneath his left eye. The full force of a body's strength in the blow. It knocks him to the ground.

"Get up, snitch. Who told you you could chill down there?"

Solstice struggles to his feet. He is careful not to look anyone in the eye. They are all looking at him. Waiting. Waiting for another excuse to hit him. He presses his hands together. He keeps his eyes lowered. No one speaks. They are all looking at him. Waiting. Waiting for another excuse to hit him again. He presses his nails into his palm. The same youth punches him hard in the face again. Knocks him down again.

"You thinking there might be a way out of this, snitch? There's no way out of this. This is the end of the line. This is the endzone."

Solstice lays curled up, staring at the grubby crème tiles of the tunnel's arched roof. One of the females coughs up some blood. Spits it out down beside his head. A foamed pinkish slither pullulating with imagined toxins.

"You need to cut this bloodrag, Enko."

"Not so fast. Everyone needs to take a deep breath here."

Solstice looks up. A beautiful blonde girl in a shiny black catsuit and combat boots. Hair piled up into a beehive. No statement jewellery but a self-assurance in her eyes that stills everything. She holds no firearm and yet has the respectful attention of the team.

"This boy here is one of my people," she says. "Call him an eye-witness if you like."

"One of your people, is it? I hope you've got the product. We're all getting jittery here. We're all getting impatient for the product. We're getting impatient for the chemicals." Misaligned Face both slurs and spits out words like things that bring a bad taste to his mouth.

"Chems will be here tomorrow. And this boy here is part of the set-up. He has leverage with the source. He's the bridge. Without him there's just an abyss."

"What the fuck is an abyss?"

"You tell me. It's something I see when I look into your eyes. We've had an update. What we are about to lay our hands on is an amulet of chemical engineering that will provide memory rushes from before you were born. We're talking Adam and Eve. We're talking Big Bang. It's still in its testing stages. UniCorp is testing it on primates. Word is, they start talking. Picture that. A monkey holding a conversation." The girl winks at Misaligned Face.

"Tomorrow then."

The girl takes Solstice by the hand and leads him around the detritus towards the exit.

"Thanks," says Solstice.

"You don't have any power. Those guys think they have power. Delusions are just another form of drug addiction. Wouldn't you say? What's your favourite delusion?"

"I don't know."

"I already have you down as a romantic. But what you need are some combat boots."

"So you're a chem trafficker?"

"As far as they're concerned. As far as you're concerned I work for the Kelp."

The Kelp is a terrorist organisation. UniCorp blames everything bad that happens on the Kelp.

"Have you been following me?" he asks.

"There's a plot afoot. Power needs plots because plots are secret until they unfold and the most gratifying kind of power is holding onto an explosive secret. And here am I handing you an explosive secret. Now I have to blindfold you. You don't mind, do you?"

"I have to do my daily tag."

"We can do that later."

She winks at him. Then she pulls out a pair of black panties and waves them under his nose.

"Your blindfold. All I've got I'm afraid. You're about to be initiated into the one secret that can't be downloaded. We'll need to do a DNA synopsis. What's your choice of donation, blood or semen?"

# 7

The girl who has blindfolded Solstice and steered him up two flights of metal stairs, turned him in several circles when they emerged above ground, is called Eyria-O. She has become more beautiful now he can no longer see her. More intimidating, too. Beautiful women have a habit of making Solstice feel he still has a long journey ahead of him before he becomes a grown man. But the doubts prickling him about Eyria-O are different. He has the feeling that there's something not quite aligned about Eyria-O. As if her humanity has a crust over it.

*A woman should have a mood she filters through to you.*

Once or twice he has heard sniggering. He knows how ridiculous he must look with a pair of black panties tied across his eyes.

"Is this really necessary?" he says.

"Nearly there. Supposing I told you that I've met Kin-Y in person. Leader of the Kelp. Most wanted man in history. There's no known image of Kin-Y, right? But I can put a face on him. I know exactly what he looks like because his features are what I see before I go to sleep at night. Supposing I told you I'm taking you to see the most wanted man in history."

"You're taking me to meet Kin-Y?"

"I'm taking you to meet your destiny."

Now and again he hears the monotone drudgery of a prophet or an endtimer delivering warnings above the shouts and cackles of the market stall traders. There is a smell of fried onions and paprika and coriander. There are more sniggers. Rotting matter bursts, squelches and slides beneath his feet. He pictures drainage bags splitting and spewing stains over his plimsolls. Up above a spy chopper sprays shards of decibels down onto the street. There's a smoky drizzle and a powdery chemistry smell that tickles his throat. *Our DNA goes through countless damaging events every day.* Eyria-O turns him round in circles a few more times before finally announcing that they have reached their destination. She leads him up wooden stairs. He stubs his foot on a loosened nail.

"Who have we here?"

"A potential new recruit?" replies Eyria-O to the gruff male voice.

"Hello potential new recruit. How many people would you say are in this room?"

Solstice has a sense in the blackout of there being no more than five people in the room. But there could quite easily be twenty. Or just three. Essentially he is more concerned with the mood. That he can trust whoever is in this room not to do him physical harm.

"I don't know," he says.

"So Eyria-O's panties aren't transparent." This is a different voice. A scoured and hardened voice, lawless with ragged loose stitching. Solstice puts a mocking unkind face to it and immediately feels a little less safe.

"Let me tell you what intel we have on you. Solstice 0747: a GI cash neutral, formerly a barcoder at DSOS Holdings and Leisure Inc., confidante of fellow cash neutral and DSOS worker Alowa 0092, since employed as a dispenser in dome #104. Newsfeed activity: At 17.00, 20.12.77 Alowa 0092 and Solstice 0747 stumbled upon the dead body of the DSOS janitor, Aubyn 0974. Cause of death: still unknown despite rigorous prolonged analysis by YTC forensic teams. Infra-red analysis revealed Alowa 0092 was wearing a shirt decorated with symbols underneath her clothes. Decryption officers unable to ascertain what purpose or significance these symbols might have. This shirt is now in the possession of Solstice 0747. Both 0747 and 0092 are considered grade 3 subversive. On no account are either 0747 or 0092 to be drafted into edition #7 of *History*, the liquidation of the Sa'i Tor Shyela tribe."

Solstice wants to ask how this voice got hold of one of his memories.

"I've seen footage of you and the girl and the dead body. You talk in whispers about spiders and webs. What was that all about?"

"I can't remember. I think there was a spider in the room."

"Any idea why they don't want you participating in the liquidation of the Sa'i Tor Shyela tribe? That began this week. Great fun so far. Though despicable of course. I think it has something to do with this shirt. What's the meaning of this shirt, Solstice?"

"I don't know. I never saw it. I never saw Alowa in her underclothes."

"But you would have liked to. I can tell by the tone of your voice. I'm going to look at the shirt, Solstice."

"You can't delve into Alowa's memories."

"Why is that?"

"It isn't ethical."

This makes everyone in the room laugh. Solstice now knows there are three people in the room, besides himself. He senses someone move up behind him. Someone unfastening his rucksack.

"Don't worry. I'll put it back. I just want to see."

Solstice pictures the man taking Alowa's memories from his rucksack. The weight and texture and feel of the red bundle is one of the most familiar sensations his own hands know.

"What do these symbols mean? They look like Sa'i Tor Shyela symbols to me."

"I don't know. I've never seen the shirt. I've never opened Alowa's memories."

"You don't know much, do you? Not surprising, grade 3 subversive is small fry. How would you like to move up to grade 1?

Eyria believes you have potential. Can you keep a secret, potential new recruit? The temptation to betray a secret, always breathing its hot breath in your ear. Isn't that so? Her Holy Eminence, the Observer is not exactly on our side in the struggle. But neither is she exactly against us. In fact, she says a lot of things we want to hear. So we don't want her life meter terminated. Supposing I was to tell you we aim to save the observer from a Fellowship assassination plot? Would you want to save her?"

"I hardly know anything about her."

"Well, we want to save her. Let me ask you the million dollar question. Do you believe I'm Kin-Y?"

Solstice would expect Kin-Y to be more softly spoken. He doesn't know why. Perhaps he thinks all wise people have no need to raise their voices. The voice telling him it belongs to Kin-Y has no restraint in it. No suggestion of a withheld music. It is the voice of someone jostled by doubts and conflicts and, above all, vanities. Or so Solstice feels. Also he feels no real awe in the presence of this voice. The voice of the most wanted person in the world. He feels on edge and far too vulnerable but this is largely because he's in a strange room with a pair of black panties tied round his head. And he is still unsettled by the blood or semen question.

"Stretch out your hand."

Solstice does as he's told. His hands are astir with heightened sensitivity in the pitch dark. His hand makes contact with something metallic. "What is it?"

"Find the trigger."

*A firearm.*

"Here, let me guide you."

Something tells him he should not touch the trigger. But he has never handled a firearm and he is curious. He curls his fingers around the metal grip. His finger pulsing on the trigger, like a bee settling onto an anther's pollen. The trigger is slick with his own sweat.

"Just so you know. That we're deadly serious about what

we're doing here. We'd like you to help. Okay, take him away now, Eyria."

"You can give me my panties back now," says Eyria-O after she has turned him in several circles and walked him another half mile.

Solstice unties the blindfold and hands Eyria-O back her panties.

"What does it feel like to have met the most wanted person in the world?" she asks.

"Who was the other person in the room?"

"You could see through my panties?"

"No."

"Probably better you don't know his name. Come to think of it, do I even know his name?"

"Have you seen the footage of me and Alowa?"

"You've got the hots for her, haven't you? I do believe I'm jealous."

Solstice notices Misaligned Face is sitting on some steps with his fellow trespassers. Misaligned Face brands the air between them with a coded gesture of malevolent augury. Eyria-O wags her finger at him with a loose smile.

"Does he work for you?"

"Are you kidding? He sells highs and memory rushes. Just another trespasser. Just another TP."

"And yet he slinks back into the shadows the moment you appear."

"Must be my menacing charisma."

They cross a waterway. Plastic bobbing about in the scurf and scum, in the rainbow slicks of grease and oil. A bird embalmed in black muck flapping its wings in vain. A rations chopper hovering nearby. A ghostly orange beam tunnelling through the grey drizzle. And above, the vain struggle of the winter sun to fight through the dirty cloud of the heavy winter sky.

"This is our building here."

He follows her into a thickening smell of damp and rodent

activity. The room is like a miniature citadel of book towers. Books stacked in tottering piles on the colour-quenched rugs against every wall. Every book has the same title - *The Genetic Prognosis and the Fall of Culture.*

"Not something I'd want to read," he says.

"Or anyone else by the look."

But he likes the musty smell of old parchment and he likes running his fingers over the typescript. He has heard rumours that there are books in District 14. But he has never been sent there.

Rust comes off on his hand when he grips the wire meshing screening an old elevator shaft.

"Looks like more stairs."

"They'll remind you where your muscles are. We're about to be briefed."

On the top floor they enter a large storeroom. There's a smell in the room of leakage. Everything smudged with prints, everything hairline fractured, everything stained with leaking effluents. The man in charge of this briefing is introduced to him as ML. He has a gnawed narrow face with volatile bushy eyebrows. He keeps scratching his upper arm. As if it's some sort of code. ML keeps scratching his upper arm and his eyebrows shift up in a suspicious arc. ML says,

"Hello Eyria and welcome Solstice." He introduces Solstice to each of the seven people in the storeroom. One of them is Mylos. Solstice recognises him as the terrorist wanted for blowing up a UniCorp culture dome. Mylos is the second most wanted man in the world. Mylos is dressed in army fatigues, a utility cap and dark glasses. He rubs together his hands as though soaping them in water.

"And this is our family immigrant. Vevra -O109."

Solstice has never knowingly seen an android in the flesh before. He stares at her as if she is an angel. Vevra-O109 looks like Botticelli's Venus, destroyed in the terrorist attack. Except she's wearing clothes. A black pvc micro skirt and a snowwhite sweater. Her hair, or perhaps it's her neck, smells of a dream coupling. She doesn't respond to any of the jibes of the five virile men.

"Our new recruit is evidently taken with Vevra. Hey, Vevra, show our new recruit some interest," says another of the five men in the room.

"I'd rather see her do a cartwheel. Do a cartwheel, Vevra-O," says a man called Ray who wears huge mirror glasses.

"Vevra's clearly been put on pause. Can we not activate her? I've got a question for her."

"Go ahead."

"Vevra-O?"

"Here I am," says Vevra-O with a coquettish wet smile. Vevra-O's voice has a husky breathless quality as though she has just broken off some act of physical exertion.

"My question is this. How sexy is chest hair?"

"Much more important in determining levels of desire is the way a man's hair sits on his head, Ray."

Guffaws from the virile men. Ray doesn't have any hair on his head.

"Let's talk business," says ML. He scratches his upper arm. "What we've got here is, in part, a mainline exercise. And, in part, a corporation assassination."

ML brushes his hand over his handheld device and a grid of luminous lines fills the room. The lines almost immediately spawn a 3D virtual sim. Buildings and roads and a plaza in wet acrylic colours. A motorcade arrives and then the holograph freezes.

"The target has a paper bag over his head."

"Our little joke. All the world's a stage, Ray. You want me to take the paper bag off the head, Ray?"

"I'm not sure. Why don't you tell me?"

ML swipes his handheld device. The paper bag disappears from the head of the figure in the black car. It is an image of Ray sitting in the back seat of the leading car. There is another chorus of virile guffawing.

"Your codename for this op, Ray, is Ruby. You got that? Ruby."

"You're asking me to assassinate myself? Or is today national get a rise out of Ray day and no one told me?"

"Okay, can we get serious now? In actual fact this will be an exercise to find out how effectively history has been erased. Intelligence tells us they're setting up the reconstruction of some history frames. One of the seminal events that brought about the abolition of national sovereignty as a political modus operandi. One of the seminal events that paved the way for UniCorp to establish its hegemony."

"Do I know what hegemony means? What does hegemony mean, Vevra-O?"

"The predominant influence, as of a state, region or group, over another or others, Ray."

"Now how about performing a cartwheel?"

"You don't inspire me to perform cartwheels, Ray."

"Now I know for a fact that I love you, Vevra-O," says Mylos.

"The motorcade arrives in Artery 911. They position one team here. Another team here. And the third team here. A perfect isosceles triangle. It's all a question of control. The driver will slow down here. The driver is one of their team and trusts them not to hit him. He trusts them to shoot straight. Each shooter will have time to get off three shots. See this guy standing on the grass verge here. He will be punching his fist in the air. Like an angry protestor. When he stops punching the air it means the target is terminated and the shooters can stop shooting. If this doesn't happen the driver will stop the car before the underpass."

"This is virtual or this is real?"

"Let's just say it's both. Meaning, as far as we can predict, it will become part of the game. The bleachers are probably taking care of the fallguy. Some cash neutral. Who knows who he is? He's probably in deep sleep somewhere. He'll have a handler who will keep nudging him deeper and deeper into culpability. No doubt the bleachers are beginning now to sprinkle his trail with incriminating evidence. Cast him as borderline unhinged and a sympathiser of the Kelp. What are you thinking here, Solstice?"

"I thought you were the Kelp."

Someone sniggers.

"Yeah, that's us," says Mylos, slapping him hard on the shoulder.

"Don't believe the rumours that UniCorp founded the Kelp. That they sponsor us. That they control us. All poppycock, Solstice. Once upon a time everything was in the hands of the gods; later it was called fate; nowadays everything is determined by secret conspiracies. And that's the truth of the matter."

"All hand held devices will be confiscated and then contaminated in the Fellowship labs. All witnesses will be recruited into *History*. Perhaps even all suspects. The investigation might be carried out in *History*. Turn it all into entertainment. What have I forgotten? They will leave enough clues to implicate themselves. Why? Because that too is part of the game. The part they most enjoy. It's their way of advertising their invulnerability. Any questions?"

# 8

Eyria-O has blindfolded Solstice again with her black panties. She guides him through a dust storm. Tarps flapping, doors swinging on rusted hinges, glass crunching beneath his feet. When they enter a building she guides him down some stairs. There is a mounting smell of leaf mould and damp stone.

"Okay, we've arrived," she says. And then she gives him a lingering wet kiss on the mouth. "Now I've bewitched you," she says, removing her underwear from his head. "How does that feel? To be in my power?"

"Are you an immigrant as well?"

Eyria-O looks at him with shock-horror. "Do you know that's the absolute worst insult you can throw at any female? You know that, right?"

Solstice feels put in his place. He looks back at her sheepishly. He offers a tight hard-fought smile that begs charity.

"I've a mind to shed my clothes. I've a mind to stand before you naked. In fact that's just what I'm going to do, Solstice 007 or whatever your damn suffix is." She begins angrily peeling off her catsuit. She is naked underneath. Her body is sleek, hairless and evenly coloured, like an avatar. She grabs hold of his hand. His hand with the dirt beneath the fingernails. Presses his hand between her legs and clamps it there.

"Does that feel like a dehydrated plastic pussy to you?"

"No," he admits, though, of course, his hands have never before known contact with this part of a female's anatomy. He has dreamed of it. Dreamed of doing this with Alowa. And now he feels a bit guilty, a bit seedy, as if he has betrayed a bond he shared with her. With Alowa.

"Now put your fingers in your mouth. Put your fingers in your mouth and tell me you taste silicone. You taste assembly line. Okay, you've got your fingers in your mouth. What do you taste? I'll tell you what you taste. You taste ocean. That's what you taste."

"I've never tasted the ocean."

"Of course you've never tasted the ocean because you're a pliable cash neutral with zero security clearance. You might even be an immigrant yourself. A half breed. Come to think of it, you probably are. You want to stay a nodding head, a flesh puppet, be my guest. Do you know if you weren't contaminated I might show you what you're missing?"

"What do you mean, contaminated?"

"Haven't you ever wondered?"

"Wondered what?"

"Why you never get excited down there?"

She presses his hand between her legs again. "Look at you," she says, nodding down at his groin. "Where's the activity? Where's the tower? Nothing." She takes hold of his soft male organ through the cloth of his leggings. "Nothing. Do you think that's natural?"

"I don't know."

"It's not natural, Solstice. It's not natural because they've tampered with you. That's what we're offering you, Solstice. We can decontaminate you. We can enable it so you get excited down there. Or do you want to go back out there and hang with the trespassers?"

"No. That's not what I want."

"Come on then. I'm afraid you'll be kept under guard for a day or two. Until we're sure you are who you say you are."

"Who else could I be?"

"You tell me. Shall I tell you a secret? I like your smell. Females most prefer the body odour of males who are most different from them genetically. Did you know that?"

Solstice is in a small bare basement room without windows. There is nothing in the room except a battered old suitcase. There are four fat mosquitoes on the white stucco wall. They have a gloating satiated air. Solstice stealthily swivels, arranges his body into combat position. He moves his extended palm slowly towards them. With an aggressive grunt he slaps his hand hard against the wall. An eggshell crack appears in the white stucco. One of the mosquitoes buzzes in his ear before flitting off. Solstice, taking the provocation personally, gives chase, repeatedly clapping his hands in mid-air as he strides across the room. His calf then cramps up and he lets out a howl of distress. *Dehydration.* He hops on one foot for a bit, moaning pitifully. The mosquito pages him again. He swipes at it and the pain in his leg takes a sharper bite.

He explores the suitcase. It is stuffed with sour-smelling clothes and trinkets and mysterious objects, like someone's memories. He pulls out an old games console. It's dead of course. The red button fails to light up any connection. He sits against the wall. He remembers the thimble and pulls it out and prises open the lid. As he does so he notices a green light appears on the games console. He is not used to things working and is still more surprised when a spray of light emerges from the console. Six feet away a lone pixelated figure takes form on the wall. It disappears for a moment as if losing connection, and then returns with startling clarity. A small three dimensional young girl. The backdrop is vaguer, a heatmap of silver, blue and grey outlines that fuses off into darkness. Solstice wonders if this is streaming of *History*. As if something in the thimble has connected him to the Source. She wears a short fringed skirt, fur boots and carries a bow with a sheaf of arrows over her shoulder and a knife in her belt. Typescript informs him her name is Zima Scribes. A message appears informing him she has five lives. Solstice hits the forward arrow key on the console and Zima walks with the stumbling determination of a newly escaped prisoner. The world around her begins to take shape. A landscape of snow. The scene as if intimately lit by firelight. There are a few other avatars lurking around. The gaze of all the avatars is strangely intent, almost chemically heightened. Every figure looks around, up at the sky, down at the ground with a kind of dumbstruck delighted awe. He notices a motionless man sculpted into the snow and white mist. In an unnatural contorted pose. Both hands suspended in mid-air as if plucking at the strings of an invisible musical instrument. He moves Zima closer. Suddenly her limbs are flailing as if she is falling from a great height.

**You have four lives remaining.**

He watches Zima clamber up to her feet and dust herself down. Nearby there is a lone figure standing on a spur of rock. An old woman with long grey hair. Detailed and highly defined. Solstice knows she is just a projected configuration of pixels and that as such should have no emotional charge but he immediately senses a heightened vitality about her. She stands with her legs spread. Her long grey hair flapping as if a strong wind is blasting across the virtual landscape. She gently but intently rubs the base of her left thumb with her right thumb. She does this for at least a minute. Then she suddenly thrusts out both arms four times in quick darting movements. Emitting a feline hissing noise. The audio startles him. Her arms make a swishing noise. He can hear it.

Zima stands still. Watching her. Watching closely. Mesmerised.

The old grey-haired avatar presses her two middle fingers against her thumb and pulls back her index and little finger to make a kind of horn. Her wrist pulled back. She extends her arms up towards the sky. Then, with her fingers still forming antlers, she traces a circle in front of her and a circle behind her. She does this four times. Silent now. Then she does the thrusting movement again. Four times with the feline hiss. The sharp intake of breath.

"Now you do it."

Solstice's body lurches back in bloodthumping bewilderment.

He hears the words rasped out like sea over shingle inside his head. The avatar has addressed him from inside his own head.

"How did you do that?" he says aloud in the empty room.

"Step up onto the rock and do what I did."

He moves Zima onto the spur of rock. His fingers still jittery from the shock of hearing the rasping haunting voice inside his head. As soon as she standing on the rock his avatar begins rubbing the base of her left thumb with her right thumb. Of her own volition. She rubs the base of her left thumb with her right thumb with her legs astride and her knees bent. Of her own volition. Stretches out her arms and crosses them in front of her and lifts them into the air. Of her own volition. He begins to feel an invigorating tingle on his skin, all the way down the length of his spine. Once again he feels weirded out. He watches the woman whisper something in Zima's ear.

"I've been waiting for you to come," he hears her say inside his own head.

Solstice jumps back in alarm again. He looks around the empty room as if expecting to find himself the victim of some kind of practical joke.

The woman presses something into Zima's hand. He feels the contact on his own hand. And then the presence of something sitting in his palm. For a moment he has the sensation he is holding a small damp pebble.

"How are you doing this?"

With lightning fast movement the woman snatches at Zima's hand. He watches her take the pebble from Zima's hand and hold it out for Zima to see. The feel of the pebble in his hand has gone too.

Solstice hears someone outside the door. He quickly stuffs the console into his rucksack. Eyria-O enters carrying a tray. "Time for some calories," she says.

Solstice wants her to leave. But Eyria-O stands her ground. "I'm not leaving until I see you consume all your calories," she says.

There is an ache in Solstice's body to get Zima back on the spur of rock. To watch her rub the base of her left thumb with her right thumb with her legs astride and her knees bent. To watch her stretch out her arms and cross them in front of her and lift them into the air. The physical imprint of the exercise is still in his body, like the most sensitive part of his nakedness.

## 9

**You have three lives remaining.**

Solstice has just watched his avatar Zima splatter into a starburst of acrylic blood. He was looking for the old grey-haired woman avatar inside the game but instead three figures in riot gear converged on Zima and atomised her with heavy artillery.

**You have one life remaining.**

As soon as he gets the resurrected Zima to her feet she is ambushed again by the same three figures in riot gear. Her entire upper body bursts in a nail polish red fireball.

Solstice curses the figures in riot gear. "You've cheated me out of a life," he says aloud to the wall. "And anyway, how's she supposed to fight that kind of firepower with a bow and arrow?" He hears the quickfire clatter of typing from inside the console and then text appears.

"Every animal has about the same number of heartbeats per lifetime. An elephant lives longer than a mouse but its pulse rate is so much slower that, measured in heartbeats, they both live lives of the same length. Would you rather live the life of an elephant or a mouse?"

The old grey-haired woman with the yellow and brown parchment skin is standing on her rock with a grin on her face.

"What's your name?" Solstice types out on the keypad.

The old woman avatar gives Zima a hearty thwack between the shoulder blades. A surprisingly realistic animation for such rudimentary old fashioned software. Solstice, kneeling on the brick floor, is startled as he feels a slight jolt between his own shoulder blades.

"Why don't I call you Solstice and you call me Mitakuye Oyasin."

Solstice feels dizzy even though he is kneeling on solid ground. *How does she know my name?* It's like a bird has entered his mind and is crashing about trying to find an exit. He looks around the room for an explanation. Trying to convince himself this must be part of the game Eyria-O and her clan are playing with him.

"Do a forward roll on the grass," says the woman. The words appear on the screen as if she's talking to Zima but Solstice has the unnerving sensation that the old woman avatar is staring out at him. That she can see him kneeling on the brick floor.

Mitakuye Oyasin performs the act herself. Again Solstice is impressed by the animation. He decides the person operating the avatar must have some kind of sophisticated animation override. The old woman performs the forward roll with the bewitching authentic agility of a young gymnast.

"Your turn, Zima," she says.

Zima falters jauntily into some synthetic shrubbery. Solstice furiously punches the four arrow keys on the console but can't restore to Zima any freedom of movement. For a moment he loses sight of her. There is nothing on the screen but a vacuum of monochrome colour as if this is the visual moment of death in this world.

"You're a real drain on my energy, do you know that, Solstice? You have no *woksape*, no *unsiiciyapi*, no *woohitike* and no *wowicake*. No wisdom, no humility, no bravery and no truth."

"How do you know my name?"

"Think of yourself as a programme, Solstice. Not a very good one. You can be hacked into. In your case it's a piece of cake hacking into you because you've haven't been updated for so long."

Solstice sees there are evanescent gold bands flickering around her body. They seem to form a web for a moment and then slowly unfurl into a random pattern. Again she gives Zima a slap between the shoulder blades. Again Solstice feels the blow in his own body except this time it is more powerful and knocks him off balance.

"How the hell do you do that?"

Mitakuye Oyasin's features fall into a comically fake expression of contrition. Then she performs a back flip and lands squatting on her haunches, a fierce burning light in her eyes, like a wild cat about to spring. Then she laughs.

"Come with me," she says.

She seems to have control of Zima now. Zima walks without any help from his fingers on the touchpad. Solstice watches the two avatars stroll along a riverbank where vines snake around the trunks of huge trees and twisted gnarled roots have pushed up to the surface of the earth. He thinks he can feel the terrain beneath Zima's feet on the soles of his own feet. The squelching of the mud and leaf mould, the hard ridges of the stones and roots. Now and again he thinks he can feel the sun on his arms and the back of his head. He can't remember the last time he felt the warmth of the sun on his skin.

"How old do you think I am?"

Solstice hears the voice inside his head. All his ideas are at sea now, bobbing about and menaced by a hunting circle of fins.

"Did you hear me? You look like you've seen a ghost."

"Please tell me how you're doing this," he says aloud. "Otherwise I think I'm going to lose my mind."

"Your mind is worthless in its present set-up. The mind of an imbecile."

The old woman avatar imitates an imbecile. Crossing her eyes and covering her top lip with her bottom lip. Then she begins taking off her clothes. It is a seductive piece of theatre the way she removes her clothes. Solstice can't help admiring the spectacle. The shimmying wriggle of her hips as she lets her skirt fall to the ground. The simmering intensity in her green eyes. She suggests everything she wants will come of its own accord. The naked body of the old woman is youthful. No slumping or gathering in folds of excess flesh, no crosshatchings of wrinkles. It is a beautiful body, shorn of hair and uniform in its bronzed pigment. Her breasts are firm and jaunty. She now knocks Zima to the ground and lies on top of her. She makes lewd thrusting motions. Solstice feels a warm weight pressing down on his groin. And then it happens. For the first time in his life Solstice feels the stirring of blood in his loins produce an erection. He tugs down his leggings to look at it and at the same time, for reasons unknown to him, is forming a picture of the flurry of activity in his neural corridors - the ferrying of electrical signals, the synthesis of clandestine proteins, the overspill of avant-garde chemicals. This new trick of his body is spellbinding. The sensation is both empowering and a new source of vulnerability. He wishes Alowa was here to see it. *Look, Alowa. It's a miracle. Like an annunciation. Is it beautiful or ugly? What do you think?* He himself can't make up his mind.

He notices Mitakuye Oyasin is crouching down at the river's edge. She begins filling a pipe with some red and black flakes she takes from a gourd around her neck.

"Now you crouch down here," she says to Zima, patting the ground in front of her. She tells Zima to close her eyes. Solstice finds his own eyes close. When he tries to open them he cannot. His eyes are closed but he can still see Mitakuye Oyasin blowing the smoke into Zima's face. The thick pungent smoke clings to his face. It tickles his throat and immediately makes him feel light-headed and then nauseous. Then he is violently sick.

"Wash your face in the river," Mitakuye Oyasin tells Zima. He sees Zima too has vomited.

Solstice feels too weak to manoeuvre Zima to the river and is further stupefied as he watches her walk over to the riverbank of her own accord. He watches Zima, autonomous again, peer down at her reflection in the water. Except it is not her reflection in the water; it is his own reflection. The shock of seeing his own face in the virtual trickery of the computer game makes him retch again. When he returns to the visuals Zima is still gazing down at her reflection in the water. Except it's her face that is reflected in the water. The old woman, still naked, has the face of Alowa.

"Alowa, is that you?"

Once again he hears Mitakuye Oyasin's rasping mischievous voice in his head. "I have been killed but I did not die. You will be killed but you will die. That is the difference between you and I. Unless you dream yourself into my dream."

# 10

Eyria-O has taken Solstice to the book depository in District 2. Outside the window a small crowd has gathered down in the plaza. Her Holy Eminence the Observer is due to arrive in her motorcade in less than two hours.

"You know what to do if anything goes wrong?" says Eyria-O.

Solstice knows without a shadow of a doubt that Eyria-O is going to betray him. He just can't work out the narrative the betrayal will take.

"Meet you in the picture house," he says.

"Give me your wrist. We need you to have reception."

He holds out his wrist and Eyria-O makes it momentary glow green and gold by pressing down her thumb there.

"What's that?"

"I'm activating the Source within you. For an hour or so."

"I didn't know I had access to the Source within," he says.

"Didn't I tell you I'd restore all your powers to you? Now you need to tell me you're still under my spell. Because I'm not convinced. When I look into your eyes I do not see bewitchment." She grabs hold of his genitals through his leggings and gives them a squeeze. Nothing happens down there. Nothing stirs. "And until I see bewitchment I can't help you. You'll remain limp and futile. I have to go now. You stay at this window here until the motorcade has left District 2. And keep your eyes peeled. Especially down there behind that picket fence. If you see anything suspicious lean out of the window and gesture to where the problem is. Our agents will then do what they can."

He watches Eyria-O leave the building from the sixth floor window. She crosses the road and walks alongside the grassy knoll towards the overpass. Misaligned Face is down there with his team. Eyria-O acknowledges his presence with the faintest flick of the head.

He takes a deep breath. He tells himself to calm down. His instinct is to get out of this building now. Until he thinks of Misaligned Face and all the poisons out there. He finally reasons he will have a better chance of outwitting them if he is initially seen to comply with what they expect. Except he isn't too sure who he means by them. So he shows himself at the window and waits. And while he waits he experiments with the Source. He wants to watch streaming of *History*. But he can't connect. The virtual glowing touchpad on his wrist is unresponsive to his fingers. Instead he pulls out the games console from his rucksack.

The woman, Mitakuye Oyasin as she calls herself, appears on the wall under the window, sitting cross-legged by a fire. The smoke spirals up towards the sky like a rope. She tosses a few more sticks into the flames and embers flare up and sparks spray. Solstice can smell singed cloth. He looks down at a tiny burning red circle on his dungarees beneath his red coat. The unreality of what his senses tell him grips him by the throat and makes him feel he is on the verge of choking. Then, when he looks down at his dungarees again, there is nothing, no sign of charred cloth, no smell of burning. He tells himself his overwrought nerves are causing him to hallucinate.

"You're back then. Can't keep away from me, eh? Do you want to solve the mystery of my vagina, Solstice?" When she stands up her shadow thrown by the flames is enormous and for a moment is the beautifully etched outline of a bird of prey. "Come on," she says. All her speech appears as old world text. "We need to get away from this place. We're being stalked."

Solstice is about to type out "By who?" into the text box when he hears the old woman say,

"Your death."

She looks out of the painted light of the virtual world, out at him. She says nothing. Just stands there staring out at him. Her gaze pulls at Solstice like a tide. A flurry of electrical connections seem to light him up from within. For a moment he feels as though he is about to take shape as his avatar, about to be sucked into the virtual world. There is something about the expression on her face that sweeps a sad nostalgic mood through Solstice. Perhaps because he knows his life is in danger he has a pining to know who made him. His early history. His life prior to the Re-education Programme. She is still staring out at him, the intensity of her gaze seeming to cross worlds. He notices Zima is back in the snowfield. The old man is still frozen into the snow. Both hands suspended in mid-air as if plucking at the strings of an invisible musical instrument. Solstice knows his face.

"Touch his forehead."

Solstice watches Zima touch the old man's forehead. The moment she touches it he feels a jolt of energy course through his body, warming his blood, unravelling a knotted thread within him. Then it arrives. A memory of the old man. He raked leaves into piles, set fire to them and danced in the smoke. Solstice realises Alowa was with him. She too saw the old man dance in the smoke. He can't believe it. He knew Alowa much further back in time. Except they looked the same age. They didn't look like children. They looked like young adults when they should have looked like children. Solstice is overwhelmed by the longing to tell Alowa. To remind her. *Alowa, we knew each other when we were children. Except we weren't children. We heard the same voice calling when we were children. Except we weren't children. We were fully grown. How is that possible, Alowa?* The old man comes better into focus. He remembers now that the old man gave Alowa a shirt. A beautiful shirt with symbols painted on it. The shirt the man calling himself Kin-Y took from his rucksack, the shirt that is one of Alowa's memories. And he also realises this old man was the janitor at DSOS Holdings and Leisure Inc. He remembers again the day he and Alowa had inadvertently discovered the dead janitor's body. The lifeless body of the old janitor was slumped on the floor. He remembers the spider on the old man's hand. The feeling the spider was looking at him. The feeling the spider was the janitor looking at him.

"What are you waiting for? You look like you've seen a ghost," says the old woman.

"Who is Kin-Y?"

"Just another UniCorp joke. Why are you dwelling on irrelevancies? Nothing you do has been verified in the realm of dreaming. And until you learn how to enter your dreams you'll be missing more than half of your circuitry. You are now in mortal danger. I can see your death breathing on your neck at this very moment."

Solstice feels a chill at the back of his neck. He feels as if all the weight in his body has melted into slush.

"As unbelievable as this might sound, you are of my lineage. I played a part in your creation. I have a duty to share my knowledge with you."

"Are we roleplaying?"

"Nothing can happen in the ordinary world until it has been dreamed. Soon you will experience the deepest dream you have ever had. Maybe it will kill you. You are being lured into a trap. So what you have to do is reverse the paradigm. You have to stalk the stalkers."

"How do I do that?"

"I'm preparing you."

"How?"

"I'm preparing you to meet me. I'm preparing you to meet your maker again."

Not for the first time Solstice thinks her graceful swaying way of walking is unrealistic for a woman of her age. He is fascinated by the delicate way she curls her fingers.

"I appear old to you because that's how you like to see wisdom," she says. "As something wrinkled and grey-haired."

"How do you do that? How do you read my mind like that?"

The shadows of birds flit over the ground close to where Solstice's avatar walks but he can see no birds in the digitalised sky.

"We're going to the winter camp of the Sa'i Tor Shyela. There you will remember who you are and where you came from. And you will share the secret of what you know. We all dream a dream in the mother's womb, which we then forget. The Sa'i Tor Shyela reclaim the dream by means of the vision quest. We all share each other's dreams. At the moment you are the dream I'm dreaming. I've pulled you into my dream. Soon I will be the dream you are dreaming. Soon you will pull me into your dream."

Zima follows the woman avatar to the summit of a ridge. Down below in the valley, in a thick swirl of snow, is a large village of tepees.

Solstice senses the excitement growing outside. He goes to the sixth floor window just in time to see the motorcade heading towards him.

# 11

UniCorp agents arrive in the middle of the night. As the janitor told her they would. They are masked and heavily padded. They make far more noise than is necessary. They point weapons. They shout and break things. They shine torches in Alowa's face. They tell her to get out of her zippered bag. She looks down at the string of painted teeth twined around her ankle. It is the first time Alowa can ever remember feeling love for anything that belongs to her. She is frightened the men in masks will take it away from her. *The things I have owned. Gone.* They gather all the occupants of the house in one room. Mona shouts back and they hit her. They shout back louder and knock her to the floor. Bolt looks as frightened as she feels. There is no sign of the janitor. Alowa studies Digger's face. *I know you like Digger but he's deceiving you.* When she catches his eye he looks away. *Digger thinks you're an innocent. That's why you won't be allowed automatically into* History. *That's why you'll be made to participate in the lottery. They don't see you as crucial in any way to finding Mitakuye Oyasin. They see you as expendable, Alowa.*

The militarised police make her kneel on the floor. One of them holds a syringe. They put tape over her mouth. A hood over her head. *They see you as expendable, Alowa.* Someone manhandles her. She feels a pressure and a prickle on her arm, like a feeding insect. Her body is invaded by a foreign agent. A heaviness takes possession of her limbs. One thought begins collapsing into another. The pictures she sees pale and semi-transparent. She is hauled outside. She can hear a mechanical heartbeat. She thinks it is one of the flying metal birds she saw dropping rations and nutrients. A wash of light explodes through her blindfold. She is enveloped in dust and noise. The air is sucked from her lungs. She no longer understands what is happening to her. *My face in the glass. Gone.*

She awakes alone in a white cubed cell. The cell expands and shrinks. The ceiling rises and falls. *Adrift in lost time. The connection between my mind and body. Severed.* There's a red eye on the opposite wall. The attention to hygiene, the absence of shadow, the watching red eye reminds her of her life as a dispenser in the dome. When memory returns the cell solidifies. The walls and ceiling stop fluctuating. When she tries to get up it's like an invisible opponent wants to push her back down. Her legs sag beneath her when she stands. She is dizzy and feels nauseous. She feels distant from herself. *The things I have thought. Gone. The things I have seen. Gone. The things I have done. Gone. My face in the glass.* She wonders where the janitor is. His absence seems to be the hollow pit in her being that is making her feel nauseous. She needs him to explain what is happening. She sits down on her bunk. She sits down to stop the dizziness. She caresses the elk teeth twined around her ankle. *I'm taking off my clothes, Alowa.* She gets to her feet. She paces back and forth. She is intimidated by the watching red eye. As she was in the dome. *Solstice still has your memories. You gave them to him before they took you away.*

When she wakes again, sweat pooled under her armpits, sweat cold and sticking her clothes to her skin, she has dreamed the same dream again. The shark attacked. The shark dragged her under the water. *Stare it in the eye and sing your death song. If it comes too close jab it in the eye with your fingers pressed tightly together like this. Your dream ally has made you a gift of a sacred objects from the spirit world. The red elk bracelet. It will give you power.* She can't remember the death song. No matter how far back into the darkness of her mind she wills herself she cannot remember the song.

A guard enters the cubicle. She bows to him. She can't help herself. Despite her new clothes the routine of her life as a dispenser is still a stubborn memory in her muscles. Especially the geisha position of readiness. He tells her she has been entered into the Lottery. He looks at her with sympathy.

She is escorted underground. She sits with raised knees in the underground shuttle. There is computerised panelling above the windows. Streaming images of commodities for sale and teachings of the observer. An obituary for the observer. An image of Her Holy Eminence's assassin. *I'm going to strip naked for you, Alowa. I want you to look closely at my naked body.* Alowa recognises him. Her whole body seems to light up and glow with the volatile secret knowledge she now possesses. *Are you looking at my naked body, Alowa? I'm dancing towards you. Do you remember this dance?* For a while she feels far too visible, as if picked out by spotlights. For a while she thinks someone will come to arrest her. An accomplice to the crime.

The shuttle drills through the recessed orange lights of an eternal tunnel. Her memory too seems lit by these faint recessed orange lights. She catches glimpses of blurred puzzling details that quickly vanish as if a candle is blown out.

Opposite her is a boy. A boy with beautiful glowing black skin. He tells her she has nice eyes. The two guards laugh. The two guards poke fun at the boy. One of the guards tells the other guard he has nice eyes. The other guard snorts out laughter. The boy shrinks and the glow leaves his beautiful black skin.

Every time Alowa empties her mind it quickly fills with a huge high definition image of the shark showing her its teeth. And her heart is a hostile presence in her body, hot and palpitating.

It all happens exactly as in her dream. She is one of a group of contestants led in single file to the moving water. She is taking note of the flowers. She is taking note of herself taking note of the flowers. It's like she is separated into two people. The flowers are explaining themselves to her. The white petals, suffused with pink, open on a cluster of golden arching stamens. The buds are grey-purple, the lobes of the spotted lip a dark passionate purple. The anthers are bright with uncollected pollen. She is close to moving water. Salt on her lips. She moves down the line. The flowers are explaining themselves to her. Salt on her lips. A man in a surgical mask wields a primitive knife. He draws a line with the blade across her arm. Bubbles of blood emerge and run into a hot trickle towards her elbow. She watches herself being cut by the blade. Salt on her lips.

Cruel-eyed dirty white birds hover and fight and screech. Alowa wades into the water. The water tugs at her legs. Alowa begins swimming. Because this is what she has been ordered to do. By officials in white coats. At the same time she floats up into the air from where she watches herself swimming. The Alowa she watches is enjoying the sensation of moving fluently through the water. The Alowa she watches feels gracefully in possession of her body, exalted in it. The Alowa she watches is still unaware of the war party of fins in the water. For the watching Alowa the image of the shark pushes everything else out of her mind. It is as if the shark is inside her head, behind her eyes, straining to get at her. Her heart is hammering in her chest. Impeding the natural resources of her body. She notices the boy who told her she has nice eyes. He was not part of her dream. He is struggling. He keeps swallowing water. She can't remember the song she needs to sing. This does not concern her much. She has little belief a song will stop the beasts patrolling the depths of the water. There are about fifty contestants in the water. Each has been cut and trails a dribble of blood. She is half way to the opposite bank when the attacks begin. She sees out of the corner of her eye other contestants vanish in a froth of turbulence. Spreading slicks of pink blood on the water. Now and then she spots a grey fin. Strength is leaving her and she begins spluttering and floundering. The opposite bank recedes into a more remote distance. The light begins to fail. Her head reels. Everything becomes pale and semi-transparent. She slips into a realm of shadows and smoke. The bracelet is a flurry of energy around her ankle. She sees the janitor. His mouth opens on animal teeth. She has the sense of him raking leaves in her mind. The leaves are lifted into the air and swirl around there in a mesmerising dance. The song she learned begins to whisper itself into her ear. Then she is aware of a surge of force beneath her. She sees the shark. Looking up at her out of the corner of its black eye. Its shimmying movement sends vibrations jarring through her. It performs a sharp turn and lunges up at her. The song is like a distant echo in her mind. She locks eye contact with it for a moment. The next thing she knows she is drifting above the water again. She is watching the shark bite down into her leg. Except it is not her leg. It is the leg of the janitor. The old man is looking at her with a fierce cold expression in his eyes. His blood pooling around his head on the surface of the choppy water. The song in her head floods through her entire body. It consumes her.

Next thing she knows she is crawling over solid ground. She is coughing up water. Officials in white coats and masks wrap her in a crinkled sheet of silver and congratulate her. She checks she is still wearing the ankle bracelet before passing out.


Thirteen Hosts sit in a semicircle around Alowa in a forsaken echoing room with watermarks and peeling plaster on the walls. Crisp yellowing graphs and charts pinned to the walls. A filthy white surgical coat hanging from a nail on the door. The floor underfoot makes a sound like breaking eggshells when she enters the room. The Hosts are dressed identically in dark suits, crisp white shirts and black ties. They all wear an identical mask. An elaborate beaked mask made of animal hide and black crow feathers.

"The story is about to begin. Your story. The stories we will tell are already hunting us."

Alowa tries not to listen to the pulse of her own heart.

"You have the opportunity now to become a culture asset for the rest of your life."

"There are no movement restrictions in *History*. You can go wherever you choose. You can befriend whoever you choose. Though some say there is a destiny that shapes our ends rough hew them how we will."

Alowa senses a smile pass along the row of masked faces as the woman says this, a smile of superior knowledge.

"What happens in *History* will become your memories. It's our memories that teach us who we are."

"We all have a specific task within *History*. It's up to you to discover your task."

"You will be given a map. The map indicates safe havens within *History*."

"Safe havens, relatively speaking."

There's a note of amusement in the voice when it says the words *relatively speaking*, an amusement which she feels is passed around the semicircle of people watching her.

"However, safe havens are often bereft of mystery. And it's only the discovery of what previously has always been mysterious that grants us power and status within *History*."

"The safe havens are stockade fortresses. The mysteries are to be found and solved in Ȟe Sápa. The Black Hills."

"But where there's mystery, there's also danger."

"As a cash neutral your mating clearance was level zero. These restrictions are now lifted. You may mate with whoever you please. You are obliged to mate with at least one person of either sex within seventy-three sleeps of your entrance."

"You can be eliminated from *History* at any time. Eliminations occur on a regular basis. Therefore it is important to entertain your viewing audience at all times."

"There are many perils in *History* but there are also many bonuses."

"Alowa, are you ready to enter *History*?"

The voices are mesmerising, like a sequence of blood bubbles from a spliced finger. Alowa realises one of the Hosts hasn't spoken. She looks over at this figure. He holds out a scroll to her. The feel of it in her hand triggers a memory. *Look at me, Alowa. What's this I'm holding? Do you recognise it? This is a scroll. A print out. A rotting parchment bond. Something you sent me once. Look Alowa. I'm going to burn it. It is going to be my burnt offering."*

After she takes the scroll she is told to leave. The scroll is a map.

## 12

Alowa is still wearing the red elk teeth ankle bracelet. The girl in the costumes department complimented her on it while tattooing the inside of her thigh. She told Alowa the red cross topped with a blue triangle is a Runic symbol for heritage and that it might save or end her life inside *History*. She has been given a long heavy grey skirt, thigh-length woollen stockings and boots with laces to wear. Her black hair has been pinned up inside a grey bonnet. She has learnt so many new words in such a short period of time. *Bonnet, bloomers, buffalo, runic, oxen.* She has searched among all the contestants for the janitor. She doesn't want to believe he died to save her. She doesn't want to believe she will never see him again. Without him she feels all the weights in her body have dissolved, that she is all alone in the world. *Adrift in lost time.*

She stands now by a wagon with a team of four oxen. Two men, who have been designated as her companions, are arguing about who is going to take the reins. Wilf wears a floppy broad-rimmed brown hat, a red flannel shirt, trousers reinforced with deerskin patches tucked into high scuffed leather boots. He has a pistol tucked into his belt. Alowa has noticed his gaze wanders every time she talks to him. Slate, who is much younger, wears a beaver hat and holds a rifle.

"I have the necessary experience. What do you have? I bet you don't even have body hair. This is a man's job. Tell Slate this is a man's job, Alowa."

Wilf climbs up onto the wagon and takes the reins. Slate

pulls him down by the leg and they roll about in the dust. An official of the Environment Ministry walks over and separates them. He designates Wilf as the driver and Slate as whip holder. Alowa sits between them. They have to wait for the official of the Environment Ministry to tell them they can begin their journey. Alowa has never seen such a large sky. She has never seen so much open space. There isn't a single building in sight. Everyone is excited about the landscape and the sky. A landscape of the past, they call it. A once-upon-a-time landscape.

"How long are you going to sit in a sulk for?" says Wilf with a broad smile in his voice.

Slate doesn't answer.

"What about those Hosts, eh? Those masks gave me the creeps. Did they give you a specific task, Alowa? My task is to acquire ivory tusks. They said the possession of these tusks would grant me status and power. I'm not sure I want to kill elephants. Not that I've ever seen one. Strange looking animals. They said the elephants are sacred to a large tribe of bloodthirsty savages. Gives me a shiver just thinking about them. The blood-thirsty savages, I mean."

The wagon is filled with sacks of food supplies. They have been warned they might be attacked. *Supplies are scarce in History.*

"So what's your story, Alowa?"

*Not to know who I am. Not to know where I have been. Not to know what I have seen.*

"I was a dispenser."

"What the hell is that?"

"Every day repeats the day before."

"Tell me about it."

Alowa decides to take Wilf at his word even though his eyes don't show much interest. "Well, we were electric shocked awake in the Pod. Then it was medication, hygiene and grooming. Then the daily shift in the Cuisine. After that, calisthenics and errand duty. Finally we were on standby for special requests. Only the special requests provided any change in the repetition of days."

"Special requests? Does special requests mean what I think it means?"

"What do you think it means?"

He lowers his voice to a whisper: "Sexual favours?"

"Only with my three entitled patrons."

"Oh, look you here! Slate has come out of his sulk. Slate's interest is suddenly aroused. What were these three patrons like?"

"I don't want to remember them."

"That bad, eh?"

"I like the animals," says Alowa.

"First time I've ever seen oxen. The only animals I ever saw where I lived were rats. Rats and dogs. I don't think though that they are real animals. Immigrants, I reckon."

The hated word. *Not to know who I am. Not to know where I have been. Not to know what I have seen.*

While they are waiting four more wagons appear behind them with more contestants. Digger, Bolt and Mona are among these contestants. Digger tries to hide his bewilderment at seeing her. He recovers his equilibrium quickly.

*They see you as expendable, Alowa.*

"You made it! I'm so happy. I was lucky. I didn't have to swim through the sharks. Nor did Mona. Exciting, isn't it? By the way, did you manage to meet your friend Solstice? Didn't you say he had your memories?"

"No. He wasn't there when I went to meet him. His friend said he had vanished."

"You know the guy who killed Her Holy Eminence is called Solstice? Quite a coincidence, no?"

"I don't know."

"I feel a bit bereft without my memories. The Hosts took everyone's memories. I wonder why they did that. Anyway, that means we're equals now."

Instructions are given to set off. The oxen refuse to move.

Slate whips them. Alowa doesn't like the zeal with which he thrashes the whip over the reddening backs of the animals.

"Those sharks, eh?" says Wilf. "I wonder how many contestants got eaten. Natural selection, I guess. That's why we had to swim the gauntlet of the sharks. Me, I've always been a good swimmer."

There are five wagons in the train, already begrimed in dust. The wagons gauge out new scars in the landscape. The landscape undulates, barren and hard and rusted. On every horizon is a treeline. And then another treeline. The landscape keeps repeating itself. Alowa feels as lost in physical space as she does in her mind. *The things I have thought. Gone. The things I have seen. Gone. The things I have done. Gone.*

Slate thrashes the oxen until they rear and bellow and their hides are damp with blood and sweat. The noise they make has a mechanical rasp to it. Alowa assures herself her voice does not have this mechanical rasp.

"Where are we on the map?" Wilf keeps asking. Slate doesn't answer and Alowa doesn't know. *Where are we on the map? Where are we on the map?*

The bellowing of the cattle, the rattling of the wagons, the shouting and cursing of the rugged men all make it difficult for Alowa to think clearly. The sun, though behind a greasy film, is hot in her eyes, on her shoulders, on her thighs. Whenever she is on the verge of remembering something there is another physical jolt or another searing crack of a whip. Neither can she quite forget that there is an invisible audience watching her. Sometimes it feels like they can hear her thoughts. And she remembers she is probably being watched and stops thinking her thoughts.

Alowa sees everything through a cloud of dust. The seat of the wagon is hard; the oxen are stubborn; the rutted trail so full of bumps that by the end of the day she aches all over.

At sunset they stop by the side of a stream. The animals are put to pasture. Water collected. And they are ready for the evening meal, eaten around a campfire – salted bacon, beans, dried fruit and coffee from a tin mug. Everyone Alowa meets fascinates her. She studies them closely. Eager to identify traits and reactions similar to her own. To discount the eroding fear that she is an immigrant, something assembled, or at least tampered with, in a laboratory or on a factory floor. She no longer speaks openly about her doubts. She has eavesdropped on a conversation about immigrants. Her understanding is that all immigrants are controlled by UniCorp. As she was employed by UniCorp she came away feeling anything but reassured.

Alowa sits with Wilf, sharing the trunk of a tree as a backrest. Vines loop over the trunk, like nooses. That's how Wilf describes them. His face has been bitten by mosquitoes and is pockmarked with raw swellings. The clotted darkness beyond the fire is full of covert noises. She can sense Wilf is unnerved by them. He keeps cracking his knuckles.

"Can't help thinking of those bloodthirsty savages," he says. "They're out there in the night somewhere. Gives me the creeps to think that. The Hosts told me they tie up prisoners with their own entrails while they're still alive. They know no mercy."

"You're frightening me."

"Sorry. Just letting my imagination run away with me a bit."

The other contestants are sitting around the fire about fifty yards away. Alowa caresses one of the teeth around her ankle. There's a sharp resounding crack off to her right. She hears it above the muffled crackling of the fire. Then what sounds like whispering.

"Did you hear that?"

Alowa nods. The branches of the tree creak overhead. Then there's a rustling noise over to the right again. Someone or something is out there, stalking them. She is sure of it. It's like Wilf's fear has drawn whatever it is out of the darkness. Suddenly there are loud howls, war whoops, and the crack of a rifle firing. Wilf throws his arms around her. Out of the corner of her eye she sees two shadows move towards the fire. It's Snake and Niles, the outriders, the scouts, playing a joke.

Later there is dancing with fiddles and banjos and harmonicas. Alowa taps her foot in time to the rhythm but the music is not a current that flows through her body. She thinks back to the glimpse of *History* she saw before her friend Nya was eaten by the lions – the women with beaded hair in bright painted clothes dancing beneath the moon and stars to a pulsing drum that entered her bloodflow as a kind of entreaty. She wishes there could be music like that, a music more attuned to the natural rhythms of her body, instead of this whooping and frantic music which the men seem to favour. Perhaps because they, the men, have a less evolved sense of rhythm, she thinks, surprising herself at how critical she is becoming now that her memory seems to be functioning better. It is a wonder to her that she is now inside *History*. She wishes she could tell Nya.

Some of the contestants are dancing. Bolt is dancing with Mona. They look like part of the landscape, shadows flitting about in the light of the fire. Then Slate walks over to her and asks her to dance. He stutters his request and she sees the hand he offers her is trembling. She is still angry with him for the cruelty he inflicted on the animals.

"Go on, give him a dance. Perhaps then he might cheer up a bit," says Wilf.

Alowa finds it difficult to say no. She has been trained to be compliant. She allows Slate to take her hand. Slate is wiry and awkward. Like a stranger to his own body. He has no rhythm in his limbs. She notices a label peeks up over the back of his jersey. Alowa wants to tuck it in. Her fingers itch with the desire to tuck it in. Then, all of a sudden, Slate loses control of his body. Alowa has time to notice the bewildered and then furious look on his face before he topples and falls down in a heap on the ground. One of the men has tripped Slate from behind. "My turn," the man says. And he begins whirling Alowa round and round. His name is Snake because he has a tattoo of a snake on his thick neck. He has a bulbous red face and huge hands. "You're going to be my prize," he says. "How about you come to my wagon tonight?"

"I'm not allowed," she says.

"Is that so? And why's that?" When he grins she sees bits of gristle between his teeth.

Before she can reply Mona appears. "We have woman's business to attend to," she says. She takes hold of Alowa's arm and drags her away, towards the darkness beyond the reach of the flames.

"Listen. I had to pretend not to like you. Now I have to look after you. You're in great danger. Your friend Solstice is Solstice 0747, isn't he?"

"I don't know."

"I think you know a lot more than you're telling, Alowa. But I understand why you don't trust me. I think the Sa'i are going to attack us. I think it's their plan to abduct you. I think this might happen tomorrow."

"Who are the Sa'i?"

"Don't you ever pay attention? The bloodthirsty savages."

"Why would they abduct me?"

"Your friend Solstice assassinated the observer. Every security force of UniCorp is looking for him. But he's disappeared."

"I don't understand anything you're saying."

"Okay, I'm going to tell you a secret, Alowa. I'm pleased Solstice assassinated the observer. And do you know why? Because I'm an undercover member of the Kelp. As I'm sure you're aware the Kelp are opposed to UniCorp. We are intent on breaking down the global firewall the Illuminati of UniCorp has downloaded. When was the last time you saw Solstice?"

"I don't remember."

"We're slowly infiltrating *History*. Most of the people here are cash neutrals. But not all. The Sa'i Tor Shyela. They're not cash neutrals, Alowa. They are all UniCorp. They enter *History* for sport. Have you heard of Mitakuye Oyasin? She's their mastermind. Except she's not a person; she's a computer programme. She's quantum generated. To mastermind all the forthcoming carnage. I sense you are sceptical. But ask yourself how she is able to appear and disappear in the blink of an eye. That's what she does, Alowa. Human beings can't do that. Computer programmes though can."

Alowa has no answer to the things Mona is saying. *Who I am. Hiding in my blood, flowing through my veins, pumping in my heart. Never entering my head. Who I am. Hiding in my blood.*

"You haven't a clue what I'm talking about, have you?" Mona laughs. Alowa feels all of Mona's dislike for her return in her laughter. "Never mind. You won't see me again."

# 13

Alowa wakes before anyone else. Snake, the lookout, is asleep with his rifle laid across his lap. Snake gives her the creeps. He came to her wagon last night and Wilf and Slate had to make him leave. "You don't want to make an enemy of me," Snake said before he left.

Alowa wanders away from the wagons. Darkness is draining out of the sky and the earth. Everything seems to quiver with the expectation of light. A ghost mist suspended over the frosted earth. Webs sparkling with beads of dew. Every memory of yesterday as if erased. Everything about to begin again. This is Alowa's favourite time of day. The smell of the earth absorbing the early morning moisture. She has the feeling she is not inside her body but rather hiding somewhere out in the stillness and silence all around her. Poised to break into new life. A breeze blows ripples over the stream and quivers over her skirt.

Alowa settles into a squat behind some bushes. Tense with the expectation of being discovered. She grows impatient with her full bladder. Her mind and her body at war again. When the woman suddenly appears Alowa lets out a scream. She pulls up her one pair of pants without wiping herself. The woman is still there. The bone structure of the woman's face is both severe and delicate. Her eyes shine with an otherworldly light. There are four eagle feathers tied to her long black hair and she wears a necklace of painted teeth and bones. Like the bracelet she herself wears around her ankle. The intensity of the woman's gaze is like the flame of a torch licking at the great hoard of darkness within

Alowa. Then, for no more than a heartbeat, she disappears. She simply isn't there anymore. Alowa is momentarily unsteady on her legs. She stares at the spot from which the woman has been erased. Then she is there again. And Alowa is able to assure herself that the intensity of her stare somehow blinded her to her presence for a moment.

"Who are you?"

She has vanished again. This time she doesn't return. Alowa looks dumbfounded at the empty space where the woman had stood. With a feeling she is being consumed by all the fluids in her body. *But ask yourself how she is able to appear and disappear in the blink of an eye. Human beings can't do that, Alowa. Computer programmes though can.*

When her heartbeat returns to normal she decides it must be some technological trick the Hosts have given to this woman as part of the game. She returns to the wagons just as some contestants are preparing breakfast and some are engaged in yoking the oxen to the wagons. She brushes down her heavy long grey skirt which is caked in dry dirt. Digger comes to meet her.

"Mona disappeared in the middle of the night. Everyone's talking about it. What did Mona say to you last night, Alowa?"

*I know you like Digger but he's deceiving you. Digger is a UniCorp watcher.*

"Lots of things I didn't understand," says Alowa.

"You need to trust me. Otherwise harm is going to come to you. What kind of things?"

*I know you like Digger but he's deceiving you. Digger is a UniCorp watcher.*

"She said we will be attacked today. By savages. And they will take me with them."

"How could she possibly know that? Unless she's a UniCorp agent. This is why you have to trust me, Alowa. Do you still think you are an immigrant?"

"I don't know."

"What about this man you call the janitor. Have you seen him?"

"No."

Snake and Niles walk over. Rifles slung over their shoulders. Swaggering through the tall prairie grass with an air of defying anyone or anything to get in their way. Snake tells Alowa they have discovered something she has to see.

"It's a wounded animal," says Snake.

"Yes. A wounded deer," says Niles.

"Where?"

"Not far. Just over there, behind those bushes."

Alowa shields her eyes from the slanting rays of the low sun. Snake takes her arm and lifts her to her feet. She is glad to be free of Digger's interrogating eyes. But she is more frightened of Snake. Against her better judgement she allows the two men to lead her away from the wagons. Some of the men are washing their shirts and underclothes in the stream.

"Sssshhh," Snake warns her. "Behind that bush over there."

Watched by the two men she creeps up close to the clump of dry bushes. Behind the foliage she sees Slate. He is squatting down on his haunches with his trousers and long johns rolled around his ankles. He is red in the face and his cheeks blown out with a great concentrated effort.

"There you are – a wounded animal," says Snake.

"Quick! Take a picture," says Niles. He pulls his shirt up over his head and bends low as if he is stooping over a camera on a tripod.

The men are doubled up with laughter. Slate meanwhile has quickly pulled up his trousers. He throws Alowa a look of black hatred before walking away. She wants to profess her innocence but he doesn't give her the chance. During the morning's march he ignores her. Changes his habits so as to ignore her. Instead of sitting beside her on the wagon he walks beside a heavily burdened pack mule, often striking it across the back with his stick when he thinks she is looking at him. The animal's eyes mist over. Snake and Niles imitate him at every opportunity, blowing out their cheeks and emitting low painful grunts whenever Alowa is close enough to see.

At lunch Alowa manages to get Slate alone. She employs all her skills as a dispenser of good will. She tells Slate how much she hates Snake and Niles and they become friends again.

Alowa and Slate are sitting squeezed side by side at the front of the wagon. Rattling over the raw blighted landscape. Wilf has the reigns and refuses to relinquish them even for a brief spell. He now has the whip too. Slate has become kinder to the animals. Alowa flatters herself that this is because he no longer wants to upset her. Today they are the middle wagon in the train. Alowa is constantly on the watch. Constantly expecting the train to be attacked. For a moment she thinks she sees the savages on the distant bluffs to the east. A long line of tiny figures etched on the immense sprawl of landscape. But when she blinks they have gone.

"I'd guess we're about here," says Slate, pointing down at a place on the map filmed in dust in his lap. "About three days from Fort Chivington. That's where everyone wants to go. What did the Hosts tell you about the map?"

*The safe havens are stockade fortresses. The mysteries are to be found and solved in He Sápa. The Black Hills.*

"They said there are safe havens and places of mystery."

"Which do you prefer?"

When Alowa tries to imagine what a mystery might be the only answer she can come up with is that it is the buried secret of who she is. *Not to know who I am. Not to know where I have been. Not to know what I have seen.*

"Mystery," she says.

"Me too."

"Safe haven for me," says Wilf.

They pass the bloated carcass of an overworked oxen in a water hole, the litter of old campsites. The rutted trail is strewn with discarded things and rotting foodstuffs. There is a hastily erected grave with a toppled engraved wooden cross. It has been dug up by animals and the bones are bleaching in the tall grass. Snake rides up alongside the wagon. He winks at Alowa. But there is malice in his eyes. Then he rides on ahead to catch up with Niles, his fellow scout.

"Now that Mona has vanished you're the only female among us, Alowa. What do you think happened to her?"

"I don't know."

"The men were talking about you this morning. Slate here told them about your past."

Alowa feels Slate flush and stiffen beside her.

"That you were a dispenser. Snake said only immigrants are dispensers. I wouldn't know because I've never met an immigrant. If you are an immigrant I sure am impressed. But Snake also said that rumour has it the savages in the Black Hills are all immigrants."

The blood thumps in Alowa's arteries but she does not look at Slate, does not let him see how betrayed she feels. *Who I am. Hiding in my blood, flowing through my veins, pumping in my heart. Never entering my head. Who I am. Hiding in my blood.*

The landscape undulates, barren and hard and dry. Alowa keeps expecting the landscape to body forth the savages. The land seems to shimmer in waves, rustling up mirages of figures in the distance. As the day wears on and the shadows lengthen and the temperature drops the expected attackers become more terrifying in her imagination. *The Hosts told me they tie up prisoners with their own entrails while they're still alive.*

Niles and Snake return after vanishing for most of the day. Niles has a woman on the back of his horse. A young woman in torn muddied clothes. There are scratches on her face. Niles tells her to sit next to Alowa on the wagon. The young woman tells Alowa her name is Eyria-O. She tells Alowa she was attacked by a group of savages. She tells Alowa she has seen some terrible things in *History*.

# 14

"Slate has the hots for you."

Eyria-O whispers this in Alowa's ear. The landscape too seems to be whispering. Alowa is sitting with her by a fire. She likes to watch her huge shifting shadow every time she moves. She never recognises herself in her shadow. It's as if her shadow knows secrets about her.

"He's desperate to get inside your bloomers. He watches you the whole time. But he's too shy to make a move. You know you have to mate with someone sooner or later."

Slate has apologised to her for treating the oxen with unwarranted violence. It is the first time anyone has ever humbled themselves to Alowa. She said it didn't matter but when he continued to berate himself she began to feel she has more authority than he does. She likes Slate for granting her this new sense of power but she is also a bit irritated by his meekness, his inability to inspire confidence. She realises she would be able to say no to him. There's a new kind of strength that is both exciting and sad in this newfound ability to say no to someone. As if she has superseded her role as nothing more than a dispenser.

"That man Snake frightens me," Alowa tells Eyria-O.

"He's got the hots for you, too. I ought to hate you. No one notices me with you around."

Massing black clouds drift over the moon. The animals are restless. A wind blows sparks from the fires in gusting showers over the camp. The faces of the unshaven men with bottles in their hands look less kind in the volatile light of the fires. Alowa leans closer to the smoke. Smoke always brings the janitor closer. When she's enveloped in smoke she can see his face again. He becomes a reassuring presence in her thoughts.

"Trouble," says Eyria-O. "He's coming over."

Snake strides over. The way he walks, the way he does everything is like a catwalk display of raw masculine stamina.

"I've been chosen to put you to the test," he says, looking down at Alowa, the look in his narrowed eyes like a drawn knife. "We all want to know if you're a real woman or if you're a filthy stinking immigrant." He pulls Alowa to her feet by the arm. "Let's find us some bushes."

The blood thumps in Alowa's arteries. Panic bolts up into her throat. Her scalp burns. Everyone is looking at her with heightened curiosity.

"Leave her alone."

It's Slate. He is aiming his pistol at Snake. His hand is trembling.

Snake lets go of Alowa's arm and turns to face Slate.

"Or what? You're going to shoot me? Perhaps you're a filthy stinking immigrant as well."

There's a voice inside Alowa that urges Slate to shoot Snake. But Niles, who was cleaning his rifle, who obsessively cleans his rifle, has crept up behind Slate and now knocks the gun from his hand. Snake marches forward and punches Slate in the face. The force of the blow knocks Slate to the ground. He doesn't move. Snake kneels over him and hits him in the face again. Blood spurts out.

"Enough is enough," says Wilf. In his long frock coat and floppy hat. But his voice lacks authority and Snake ignores it. He begins taking off Slate's clothes. He begins with his boots. When he's stripped him naked he throws the clothes on a fire. He drags Slate's naked body towards one of the wagons while making fun of Slate's famine physique. His concave chest, his knobbed knees, the almost supernatural whiteness of his skin, the diminutive size of his genitals. As he is strapping Slate to the wheel of the wagon with a length of rope there is a lacerating flash and crack up in the sky. Everything is momentarily lit up like a revelation. The noise seems to shift the ground on which Alowa stands. She doesn't understand what is happening. There is a grumble of thunder up in the blackening sky. And then another searing and zippering crack of light. In the blazing rod of skyfire Alowa sees how strained and frightened is the expression on her companions' faces. Everyone runs to the wagons as torrential rain begins lashing down. The fires all die. It is pitch black. Alowa stands in the rain.

"We need a knife to cut him free. And some light to see. Come back to the wagon for now, Alowa." Eyria-O puts her arm around Alowa's waist and together they stumble towards the wagons.

# 15

Slate is in the back of the wagon with a fever. When Alowa and Eyria-O cut him free his whole body was shaking. They slept on either side of him in the back of wagon to give him their warmth. Eyria-O made one or two crude jokes and Alowa couldn't help laughing. But mostly they talked about Snake and how much they hated him.

Early in the morning Alowa and Eyria-O went down to the stream to wash. There was no sign of Snake but still Alowa's heart was beating too fast. Like there were beating wings in her chest. The elk teeth rattling around Alowa's ankle was the loudest noise. Eyria-O asked her what it was and Alowa lifted her long skirt that was still wet and showed her. Eyria-O then surprised Alowa by stripping naked. She laughed at all the dust and sand that fell from her underclothes. She encouraged Alowa to do the same. Alowa had never seen another naked female. Discreetly, she studied Eyria-O's naked body. Discreetly she felt Eyria-O studying her naked body. Alowa found many subtle differences. She thought Eyria-O's body was more pleasing to the eye. But she found no major anomaly that might single her out as a half breed, an immigrant. *Who I am. Hiding in my blood, flowing through my veins, pumping in my heart. Never entering my head. Who I am. Hiding in my blood.*

Now she sits with Eyria-O and Wilf at the front of the wagon. Snake and Niles have ridden on ahead again.

"I'm not looking forward to tonight," says Alowa, speaking her fear out loud.

"I won't let him hurt you," says Eyria-O. "After all, we're friends now. Tell me a secret. Then we'll truly be friends."

*Are you looking at my naked body, Alowa? I'm walking towards you.*

Alowa doesn't have to share a secret because a series of echoing cracks come from the other side of the ridge they are climbing.

"Gunshots," says Wilf. The wagons are brought to a halt. All the men ready themselves with their rifles. Digger volunteers to run up to the summit of the ridge. Everyone waits nervously. Alowa presses her hands together. *I think the Sa'i are going to attack us. I think it's their plan to abduct you.*

"It's okay," shouts Digger from the summit. "It's only Snake and Niles."

Down below Snake and Niles are crouched down, cutting free the tusks of the two elephants they have shot. A smaller elephant with only one tiny tusk is hovering close to the animal Niles is carving up with a large knife. He shoos it away. The small animal swings its tail and flaps its ears. It makes a mournful noise. Alowa wants to protect it. Never before has she felt such an urgent enveloping protective instinct. Under her breath she tells the young elephant to go away. She makes imaginary shooing gestures with her hands. The young elephant looks over at her. The gentleness in its eyes makes her even more fearful for its safety. Then she notices Snake has paused in his butchery. He is looking up at her. He lays aside his knife. He picks up his rifle. He takes aim at the baby elephant. He shoots the baby elephant. He shoots it three times. Alowa cries out. Eyria-O cradles Alowa in her arms.

"Poor things," says Eyria-O. "Sometimes I hate men. Nothing better to do than assert their virility at every turn. They don't seem to have an ounce of tenderness or wonder in their body. We're crossing this amazing country which throws open your heart and soul. Everywhere you look deer skipping about, eagles soaring, herds of buffalo grazing in the sun. You'd think it'd inspire a little wonder in these men. Not a bit of it. All they want is to shoot anything that moves. It's as if they can't stand movement. Nothing is allowed to move except them. But you mustn't let Snake to get to you. I know he's a vile man. And the elephants are wonderful creatures. Did you know they have really poor eyesight and they're sort of clumsy but they remember everything they do, everyone they meet and every route they have taken? And they're loyal and protective when they trust you. It's disgusting that they're going to be exterminated."

"I don't understand what's happening here. What is *History*?"

"Entertainment for the entitled. We're nothing but extras. We can't exit the script they've written for us. Only the Sa'i Tor Shyela have any autonomy. They're determined to protect the elephants. The elephants are sacred to the Sa'i Tor Shyela. That's why they're called the Elephant Nation and that's also why they're going to be wiped out soon. The Sa'i Tor Shyela are all immigrants, you know. Every single one. UniCorp created *History* as a colony for them when they began showing signs of autonomy. I wish I was an immigrant. They're better than we are. They have compassion. They have natural feeling. Ironic, isn't it? Your ankle bracelet looks like a Sa'i Tor Shyela memory amulet. Where did you get it?"

*In your dreams you will learn what you know. In your dreams you will know who you are. In your dreams they will try to catch you. In your dreams you will defeat them. I will be the one who brings you your dreams.*

"A man I met gave it to me."

"A man? What was his name?"

*You're never to talk to anyone else about the things I say to you.*

"I never knew his name."

"What did he talk to you about?"

"Can we go back to the wagon? I don't feel well."

Alowa misses her old life as a dispenser. There was a grid then. A coherent supervised routine of expectation. She is frightened of the encroaching dark when the wagons are formed into a circle for the night. She is terrified of the man Snake. Her fear of him creeps over her skin, crawls up her legs, spiderwalks up her back to her neck and nestles under her armpits. Alowa slips away when no one is looking. She takes a blanket. She is determined to hide until Snake has gone to bed. She enters a grove of trees. The elk teeth rattling around her ankle. She sits down against the trunk of a tree. Soon she is cold. She climbs the tree to keep warm. From her perch she can see the fires of the camp. She can see huge grotesque shadows shifting over the canvas of the wagons. When a search party is sent out to find her she hides in the crook of branches. She can make out the faint gleam of buttons on coats. She can make out moving shadows, flecked with a faint glint of light showing where eyes are. *Who I am. Hiding in my blood, flowing through my veins, pumping in my heart. Never entering my head. Who I am. Hiding in my blood.*

When they leave she climbs down from the tree and then climbs back up again. Again and again. To keep her body warm. The moon ghosts an elusive glimmer among the thick shadows. Shadows swell and gather around her. They seem alive, pulsating and breathing, rhythmic and graceful, like a circle of dancers. Later she sees the eyes of animals, like a broken ring of burning red lights in the dark. She climbs back up into the tree and stays there, shivering.

# 16

The open-topped gunmetal grey vehicle with Her Holy Eminence the Observer inside turns slowly into the plaza. There's a flurry of enthusiasm from the small crowd lining the road. The observer, visually, is both known and unknown to Solstice. He has never seen her in the flesh and yet her face is as familiar to him from UniCorp streaming messages as his own knuckles. Solstice is mesmerised by the glow and glamour of her celebrity. She makes the world around her seem as though it is freshly minted.

Then an echoing explosion breaks the spell. Birds flock to the air. The flapping of wings is a cymbal crash in his ears. This is followed by two more resonant explosions in quick succession, one of which seems to originate somewhere above him. He sees the observer has brought both hands up to her neck. The car slows down almost to a halt. Solstice is aghast the vehicle has slowed down. All his protective instincts swarm towards the hurt woman. He wants to shout at the driver. Yell him into decisive action. But the driver waits. Then there is another jarring crack and the observer's head is rocked back. A spatter of red brain matter explodes from the back of her head. It's an image that stays on his retina, that won't disappear. There is lots of shouting. Finally, now that it is too late, the driver accelerates. The gunmetal grey vehicle is gone. People are running up the grassy slope, towards a picket fence.

Solstice still stands by the window. And then the revelation arrives. It's like someone is tugging at him from behind. Solstice understands what he has just witnessed is the recreation of a history moment. He has been scripted into one of the UniCorp's history moments. The severed line to the past is mistily restored to him. For a moment he is as if shrouded in fog, sliding and slipping on ice. He knows this has all happened before. What's more, he can recall fragments, even though, like all cash neutrals, he has supposedly been denied access to each and every historical newsfeed.

Eyria-O is down there on the grassy knoll. An unfriendly gleam in her eyes. *You know what to do if anything goes wrong.* Who is he in this unfolding story? What happened to his historical predecessor who went to the picture house? He can't remember. It's like there's an enormous force pressing down on his chest when he tries to remember.

Down on the street his heart beats too fast. He looks down at his shadow. Almost expecting it to leap free of him. He expects to be arrested. But no one takes much notice of him. So he walks away. Keeping close to the walls. Concealing his face from the scanners. Slowly the hubbub recedes. The air becomes quiet again. He is not going to the picture house. He soon finds himself in a disused railway yard. There is one ruined old goods train. Solstice slides open the door and slides it shut behind him. Peeps through a crack. He sees three shifty men. They have an air of pretence about them, like inebriated men pretending to be sober, guilty men pretending to be innocent. But they are walking away.

Solstice takes the games console from his backpack. Opens the thimble. His avatar Zima Scribes appears on the floor at his feet. He is hugely relieved to see her. As if she is the best friend he has in the world. Zima stands on the summit of a ridge and down below in the valley, in a thick swirl of snow, is the large village of tepees. There is snow underfoot but Solstice sees Zima has left no footprints. She stands on a tract of deep virgin snow. There is a bird of prey. Circling. As soon as he becomes aware of the bird of prey it disappears. He scans the grey sky for the bird. Then he sees the detailed silvery black wings flapping close to

Zima's head. The bird of prey strikes Zima between the shoulder blades. Solstice staggers back in alarm as he feels the contact between his own shoulders. He looks around, expecting to see the bird of prey in the railway carriage with him. When he turns back to the graphics of the game the old grey-haired avatar is standing in the snow on the summit of the ridge. She is smiling at him.

"It's now or never," she says. A fresh fall of snow begins swirling around her and Zima.

Solstice shivers. Cold streams up through his plimsolls. He hugs himself against this burgeoning blast of icy air. His teeth begin chattering.

"Take Alowa's memories from your rucksack and hold them in your left hand," she says.

He does as he's told. Grips the mysterious red bundle in his left hand. For a moment it's as if Solstice floats through darkness. As if there are no weights in his body. There is one searing globe of brightness in all this darkness. He can see nothing else. This bewildering sense of levitating outside the moment, of being a stranger to himself is reinforced by the alien material jostling strangeness over his skin. When he looks down he sees he is dressed in his avatar Zima's huntress outfit. A skimpy skirt of synthetic hide strips, a virtually transparent top of off-white calico, synthetic fur-lined boots and an enormous synthetic fur coat. He holds a bow and has a sheaf of feathered arrows slung over his shoulder. He also holds Alowa's memories. A hunting knife in his belt together with a coil of rope and a painted buckskin bag.

The artificial world of snow begins moving towards him, sucking at him. It takes on three dimensions. He has a sense of it taking form behind him. He begins to hear the sound of drums. The cold sets his whole body shaking. He blacks out for a moment. Then he is no longer sitting cross-legged in the disused railway carriage. He is standing in the snow on the ridge above the circle of tepees down in the valley. The village has a fictitious quality to his eyes. As if it might suddenly dissolve in the smoke of the fires. The old grey-haired woman is within touching distance. He can see her breath on the air. Snowflakes settle on her face and hands. He looks down at himself. The swell of breasts beneath the thin calico shirt. He thrusts his hand down between his legs, groping for the organ that makes him a male. Then he screams before passing out.

# 17

Solstice wakes up covered in buffalo hides. A twisting rope of smoke leads his eye up to the scattering of stars beyond the point where the poles of the tepee cross. The walls are covered in brightly painted hides, shields, beaded painted bags and strange bundles from which feathers and animal tails hang. Beaded and quilled clothes hang from the lodge poles. A small wood fire surrounded by a circle of stones smoking at the centre of the circular floor. Solstice wakes up in a sick body that doesn't feel like it belongs to him. He edges his hands down between his legs again and what he discovers there makes him pass out again.

The next time he wakes up a fierce bare-chested old man wearing buffalo horns is leaning over him. He also sees Mitakuye Oyasin through the whorls and arabesques of the sweet smelling smoke.

"Now tell me if I'm the dream you are dreaming or you are the dream I am dreaming," she says.

Solstice feels he is being starved of oxygen. He has to fight to keep his thoughts from being sucked into the encroaching black void in his head. His overriding idea is that he has fallen asleep inside the disused railway carriage. He channels all his strength into trying to wake himself up.

"What are you doing to me?" he says, his voice high and cracked with fear. Except it is not his voice. It is a female sing-song voice. The voice of his avatar Zima. There is nothing but panic in his body now. He jumps up with the intention of running. Running until the panic is behind him. But the man in the buffalo mask holds him down.

"Lie with your body shaped like this and take deep breaths." Mitakuye Oyasin lies back with one leg tucked under her and the other stretched out. "For the time being think of this as a dream. Relax into it as if nothing that happens will have any consequence. Even though I have to tell you the consequences might be deadly."

His throat is so constricted he can barely breathe. His hand instinctively goes to the thimble around his neck. It is a relief to find it there, the only thing about himself he recognises. He holds onto it and his breathing slows down.

The man wearing the buffalo horns takes something from a little pot and puts it between Solstice's lips.

"What is it?"

"Peyote dreaming medicine. It's almost time for you to meet the Ancestor. But if the Ancestor doesn't come when you call your game is up. If the Ancestor does come you will be honoured because the Ancestor has been dead for eight hundred years and you will see the Ancestor in the flesh. If you want to survive the ordeal you have to be disciplined, steadfast and focused. The Ancestor will make a warrior of you. The Ancestor will restore to you your power of memory."

Solstice has trouble swallowing the bitter pellets and the taste makes him retch. The man in the buffalo horns puts his mouth to Solstice's lips and breathes air into his mouth. Then he picks up a small yellow drum and begins pounding it while performing birdlike movements in a circle around Solstice. He is singing. A high impassioned wailing. Shifting his weight gracefully from one foot to the other and moving forward in little jumps.

"Everything sacred begins with a circle of motion," says Mitakuye Oyasin.

Solstice begins perspiring and trembling. Every time he closes his eyes he is subject to an inrush of dark in which tiny red circles, flitting from right to left, threaten to carry him away. The smoke begins to distort his vision of the dancing old man banging his drum. The smoke removes him into an apparition.

He becomes mesmerised by the dainty movements of the man's feet. The song too becomes hauntingly beautiful, like a plea for understanding or enlightenment. Solstice feels himself rolled into a weightless ball hurtling through eternity.

When he comes to there is a circle of people around him. The faces shift in and out of focus. Solstice feels he has a high fever. The muscles in his shoulders and thighs aching, his mouth parched. Incapable of formulating a thought. And the terrifying rupture, the feeling that he is no longer able to pick things up where he has left them.

A huge bare-chested man with elaborate jewellery around his neck and two feathers in his long braided hair gets to his feet. "I am Wahkan." He shouts in a deep strident voice that has no soft smudged notes. He also signs with his hands as he shouts. "I will call you Afraid of Little Dogs because this is what my eyes see when they look at you. Mitakuye Oyasin tells us you may walk in the sacred manner and bring honour to the Sa'i Tor Shyela so I welcome you. This is my wife, Looks To Both Sides. And this is my daughter, Fights With Her Fists. You will stay with us in our lodge until your feet can walk and your voice can sing again. Tomorrow I will teach you to build a sweat lodge. After you have cleansed yourself Mitakuye Oyasin will take you to meet the Ancestor. That is all I have to say."


Again Solstice wakes up alone in the tepee. The alienating smell of his new body in his nostrils. He feels as though he is examining the contents of his mind from a distance. But the terror has gone from his body. He even manages to elicit a moment of wonder from the sensation of sliding his hands over his breasts. Even manages to smile at the thought of squatting to relieve his full bladder. He crawls outside into the daylight and bristling activity of the Sa'i Tor Shyela village. The snow has melted away. The high tepees, as firmly anchored to the ground as trees, have crow and eagle feathers fastened to the ear poles and tiny bells that jingle when the wind blows. He studies the paintings on the hide covers. Enjoys the bold virgin colours. He tries smiling at two old women bent over hides pegged to the ground but they don't return his greeting. Neither does a man painting a white horse on a shield. One or two dogs inspect him but otherwise he might be invisible. Until he sees a warrior looking at him. The warrior is sitting outside a tepee on which strange yellow and green birds are painted together with lots of bright red dashes and blue circles and black triangles. When Solstice catches his eye the warrior looks away but not before Solstice has seen the shy intensity of wanting in his eyes.

"So you already have an admirer," says Mitakuye Oyasin who appears as if from nowhere.

Overhead there are two drone cameras circling like birds of prey.

"This is a dream, isn't it? I'm dreaming I've become a woman."

"You haven't even begun to experience yourself as a woman yet. So how does it feel to have a pussy? Has it begun pining yet?" Mitakuye Oyasin winks at him. "Think yourself lucky you've woken up inside a very attractive woman's body. Certainly that's what Wicasa thinks. He keeps ogling you. I think he's going to ask you to step under his blanket tonight."

Solstice sees the warrior is still looking at him with wanting in his fierce dark eyes.

"This isn't real, is it?"

"You are learning to speak awake while dreaming. The peyote spirits are protecting you. You might dream yourself back into being a man. That all depends on the Ancestor. Now let's go to the willow grove."

Solstice smiles at an old man with long grey hair tied into two braids wrapped in otter skin. The man doesn't smile back. Never has Solstice seen such a glum and surly face.

"Why does no one greet me? It's as if I'm invisible."

He looks down at the ground. A tuft of grass springs back up after he flattens it with his foot. Relief that at least the earth registers his presence.

"You're certainly not invisible to Wicasa. In fact to Wicasa you're larger than life."

"Why is that old man so crestfallen?"

"Whatever you do, don't make him laugh," says Mitakuye Oyasin nodding over at the glum old man.

"Why?"

"Because that's No Laughter No Pain and it hurts him to laugh. He is a great medicine man. His power comes from the rocks."

"Why does it hurt him to laugh?"

"When he was a young boy lightning struck his horse. The horse threw him to the ground. Before it died the horse told him he would be a great medicine man but his ribs would hurt and his gums bleed every time he laughed. Therefore he avoids laughter."

Mitakuye Oyasin leads him to the willow grove where he has to collect branches for his sweat lodge. There are shy young girls picking berries or collecting firewood. They meet Fights With Her Fists, carrying a painted water skin bag. She is wearing a deerskin dress with beaded red and green strips. Solstice guesses she is about five years his junior.

"Wicasa was asking me about you," she says, surly.

"Wicasa is the warrior of Fights With Her Fists big wanting," Mitakuye Oyasin tells Solstice after she has left. "You've made your first enemy."

"Why is she called Fights With Her Fists?"

"You'll probably find that out soon if Wicasa carries on ogling you. Look," she says, pointing over to the riverbank. Solstice sees Wicasa watering three ponies in the river.

After collecting twelve white willow branches Solstice sets about building the skeleton of his sweat lodge. He grows frustrated with his new female body. The diminishment of strength in his upper arms. He is dismayed to see the glum old man No Laughter No Pain is closely watching him. He is puffing on a pipe beneath a sun shelter. The camera drones are still circling overhead.

First Solstice has to draw a perfect circle on the ground. Fights With Her Fists' father is overseeing the task. His voice is stern, as if his mouth is full of stones. He signs with his expressive hands as he talks. Solstice likes the effect of this sign language and wants to learn it himself. He ties a strip of rawhide to two sticks and draws out the circumference of the circle. He has to apologise to the earth for cutting open its skin. Offering it a handful of tobacco that he sprinkles over the ground. He digs a small hole for the rocks. Before staking the branches he has to recite an ancient prayer formula to the Elephant Mother. Has to plead his humility and weakness and ask the Elephant Mother to take pity on him. He is dubious about the credibility of his prayer. He casts a covert glance at No Laughter No Pain while he is reciting his prayer. The old man is fighting off a smirk that twitches at the corner of his mouth. Solstice then has to peel the bark from the willow branches and sharpen the ends to a point with a knife so as to drive them into the ground. Having driven them in he has to bend all the sticks together so as to tie them. One escapes his grasp and springs back and strikes him in the face. The blow knocks him to the ground. He hears a strange stifled noise. No Laughter No Pain, he sees, is doubled up with laughter. He is holding his ribs in pain. He is trying not to look at Solstice. Quickly No Laughter No Pain takes to his heels. Wahkan laughs now as well.

Later Mitakuye Oyasin helps him lace the buffalo hides that form the canopy. The front entrance faces east as do all the openings of the tepees, to honour the rising sun, even though the sun rarely appears in the world anymore. He now has to collect stones for the sacred fire pit inside the sweat lodge.

He walks with Mitakuye Oyasin through the village. Bare-chested feathered warriors are racing ponies across the valley. Women sitting in groups, tanning and sowing hides. A tiny girl riding bareback an old pack horse that a woman holds by the girdle.

When they are out on the prairie Mitakuye Oyasin says,

"You need to choose your stones carefully. Stones have memories. And there are different kinds of power in those memories. You have to choose stones you feel an affinity with. The stones we need are called bird stones because if you study these stones closely you will see drawings on them. Birds leave these drawings. But only for a few days. Then the drawings vanish."

Solstice looks hard at her to see if she is making fun of him.

## 18

Mitakuye Oyasin is boiling the roots of a plant in a kettle over an outside fire. Solstice watches some young girls chase each other in and out of a tepee. Then he looks up at the drone camera circling the camp. Mitakuye Oyasin told him earlier that there are cameras everywhere. Tiny things the size of buttons. She also told him there is presently a manhunt underway in search of him.

"Why?"

"Because you assassinated the observer."

"No I didn't."

"That's just your word against theirs. Just as well even your own family wouldn't recognise you now."

"Do I have a family?"

"If you pay attention to me one day soon you will find your family."


Later Solstice asks Mitakuye Oyasin what happened to him in the sweat lodge.

He was inside the sweat lodge for twelve hours but has little memory of what took place within the honeycomb structure he built with his own hands. He remembers crawling in naked. Aware the warrior Wicasa was slyly watching. He doesn't feel any shame or vulnerability naked because of the sense he has of his female body shape as a second skin he is wearing. So, frightened as he is by the warrior's attention, he couldn't resist also provoking him a bit. Turning his entry into a piece of seduction theatre. Mitakuye Oyasin immediately scolded him. Told him to go back outside and enter the sweat lodge with the due humility and sobriety. The rocks he had chosen placed in the hole in the centre and wood stacked over them in a circular fashion. The ground was covered in sage. He remembers Mitakuye Oyasin telling him she was the sacred fire keeper. While the wood burnt down and began heating up the rocks she held a torch of plaited grass and sang songs in groups of four accompanied by Wahkan. The braided harmony of the two voices was spellbinding. Then she made him smoke a pipe and usher the smoke over his body. The green branches fizzled and popped as flames licked at the sap. Mitakuye Oyasin threw water over the rocks and great clouds of steam rose and made his vision waver. He remembers it becoming unbearably hot inside. Mitakuye Oyasin and Wahkan's songs intensifying the atmosphere. His hair soaked through. At one point he thought a bird had come inside. He could hear wings flapping and then brushing his naked female body. He felt himself become smaller and smaller until something seemed to lift him in the air. Down below he saw a figure in a long black robe with its back to him. He was terrified of this figure turning round to face him. Then he remembers nothing else.

"Your body remembers what happened. That's all that matters. Your mind is still an obsolete piece of software. What matters is that you're now better prepared for your vision quest. And if you are lucky, or if you are very unlucky, you will meet the Ancestor. I should warn you, the Ancestor is quite capable of frightening you to death. You will now have to learn your dreaming song, your warrior song, your love song and your death song."

"Are you going to teach me them?"

"No. Your songs are as much a mystery to me as they are to you. Your dream ally will teach you your dreaming song; your shadow foe will teach you your warrior song; your death will teach you your death song and the Ancestor will teach you your love song. Only when you have been restored to the sacred path will you remember the ghost dance."

"What's the ghost dance?"

"It's our salvation and the salvation of the elephant nation. You were taught it by the Ancestor when you were small. Somewhere amongst all the trash in your circuitry it's there waiting for you to remember it. You and Alowa are the custodians of the ghost dance. When she arrives you have to be ready."

"Alowa's coming here?"

"The Ancestor is dreaming her here. I have seen it in my own dream. You return her memories to her. Together you sing the ghost dance within the sacred circle. Together you teach it to our people."

Solstice and Mitakuye Oyasin have been out on the plains all day. She carries a knapsack. He saw her place an eagle wing fan and the cowhide drum inside. When Mitakuye Oyasin finds the plant she is looking for she begins digging a circular hole around it. She says it is leaning towards the south so that's where his dream ally will come from.

When it is dark she plants six poles in the ground in a circle around a tree. She collects leaves and twigs. Builds a fire inside the circle. Tells him to sit inside the circle with his back to the tree. Facing south. "I'm going to dust your wrists with the pollen of the plant and then smear the ashes of the burned leaves over your belly, your genitals, the inner thigh of your left leg and the sole of your left foot."

Solstice frowns. He has the feeling the ashes and pollen is nothing but a ruse. A tactic to introduce into his mind the bizarre and thus make him more susceptible to it. Mitakuye Oyasin begins fanning the smoke of the fire towards his body with her eagle wing fan. Then she starts spreading the ashes over his naval. He has the feeling she is deliberately trying to arouse him. Her hands dwelling tenderly on the inside of his thigh. She looks him in the eye with a lewd provocative expression. Mimics an impassioned tenderness as she smears the ashes over his naval. He is astonished to see she looks about twenty years younger.

She tells him to stare into the flames. That his dream ally will take form in the smoke.

Mitakuye Oyasin begins beating out a hypnotic rhythm on the drum and dancing in circles around him.

He is engulfed in the scented smoke of the willow bark.

"If anything frightens you, curl up into a ball, close your eyes and yell as loud as you can. Seeing as you haven't yet won a war song you'll have to improvise. The fact you haven't yet got any songs will render you extremely vulnerable but as long as you don't move from the sacred fire nothing can hurt you. I want you to bring back something from your dream."

"Bring back what?"

"Anything that takes your fancy. You can bring back Wicasa if you see him. But you have to learn to move from one body to another otherwise all your dreaming is nothing but water colour."

For a while his senses are at fever pitch and the possibility of something taking form out of the smoke seems imminent. Then he finds himself thinking exactly as he has always thought. He thinks of Alowa. Misses her. She is a voice in his head, a feeling in his blood that makes him feel rooted but also swishes around inside him like a fluid. He pictures Alowa in a painted buckskin dress. For a moment she is so vivid it's as if she is standing next to him. His eyes become heavy. He fights to keep them open. The smoke seems to separate from the darkness. Curling around him like tendrils. Then he sees a figure. About six feet away. Not moving. Wearing a hooded black robe. The figure has its back to him. The figure lifts up its right arm. Solstice suddenly realises how terrified he is of seeing the figure's face. When the figure takes a step towards him he begins shaking. He curls himself up in a ball like Mitakuye Oyasin told him. He closes his eyes and yells like Mitakuye Oyasin told him. When he closes his eyes the figure becomes more vivid still. It's as if it is inside a globe of light. He sees it is enmeshed in a web of silver filaments. He knows if it turns round and shows its face he will die of fear. He has no doubt of this. His heart hammers; his stomach heaves. The figure glides to the left. He now sees it is standing within a circle of stones. And at the centre of the circle is a dark shape. He understands it is going to lean down towards the dark shape. And then it is going to turn round and reveal its face. There is a flash and a displacement of air. It's suddenly much colder and there is a strong unfamiliar smell in his nostrils. The ground, he notices, is different, soft and shifting like a cross between sand and snow. It's now he realises he is much closer to the terrifying figure in the black robe. It no longer possesses the shapeshifting blur of a mirage. He watches it bend down elegantly from the waist. The figure is male. He is singing as he bends down. His singing is throaty, otherworldly and quietly impassioned. His song empties Solstice's mind and sends a jolt of electricity through his body. He follows his gaze. The figure is looking down at another figure wrapped in hides. He realises with a start that the bundle on the ground is Zima. Or that it is him in the form of his avatar Zima. He looks down at his own chest. It is the chest of a man. He is back inside the body he was born into. He remembers Mitakuye Oyasin's admonition to bring back something from the dream. But he cannot move his hands or feet. He is rooted to the spot. A rolling tide of green fog moves towards him. Every so often forming into hoops that he has a sense of drifting through. Then he knows the figure in black is about to show his face.

# 19

In the light of the new day Solstice looks ridiculous to himself, his naked female body smeared in ashes and the pollen dust that has hardened into a cracked brown crust. However he feels better than he has for ages. There is a tingling in the soles of his feet. He feels refreshed and invigorated. Except he cannot remember anything about last night. Mitakuye Oyasin is disappointed he has seen nothing during the night. She shows him the prints of an elephant that form a circle around the spot where he sat. She tells him the elephant is his dream ally and has tried to teach him the songs he would need to dream awake.

He pictures the elephant circling him while he slept. Sees it vividly, can even feel the warmth of its pulse and smell its animal smell. Out of the corner of his eye, instead of the old native woman, he sees Alowa. Or rather, he catches a flash of Alowa's most quintessential expression pass over Mitakuye Oyasin's face. He is even aware of Alowa's smell. A wave of excitement breaks over him. Mitakuye Oyasin looks up at him and, almost imperceptibly, winks.

"It's in our dreams that we pull people towards us," she says.

It's only now he remembers the figure in black. He tells Mitakuye Oyasin about him as they walk.

"That was the Ancestor," she says.

"He terrified me."

"You must honour the Ancestor by addressing him. The Ancestor will come again tonight."

They walk together across the plains. The rolling hills in the near distance covered with sage and prairie grass. The shimmering shades of colour make Solstice want to sing out his wonder. He begins humming.

"Finally you've remembered the dreaming song your dream ally taught you. You must sing that tonight."


All day she makes him chew the roots of plants. Whenever she finds a plant she is looking for she begins tenderly digging a circular hole around it with her long slender fingers while apologising to it. "This is a female plant. The female plant is distinguishable from the male by the more delicate nature of its stems and more vigorous and flexible nature of its roots. Female plants are notoriously more possessive and violent. They also have a greater thirst. Caress her."

He does as he's told, running his fingers lightly over the plant's spikes of red flowers. He notices the underside of the sticky lips conceal a delicate design of white rings which has a strangely hypnotic effect on him.

"I told you how possessive the female plant is. She'll devour you if you're not on your guard."

They climb up into the foothills. The ground is soft with moss and trailing vines. Larks and thrushes are singing. There is a clearing in a wood where four different coloured flowers are growing. A single white flower. Tall and erect with tiny lips and gold-tipped stamens; a cluster of purple flowers whose petals, Mitakuye Oyasin tells him, close in the rain; a cluster of prickly many-stemmed yellow flowers whose buds all seem on the verge of bursting and contain green seed heads; and a solitary red flower which seems to him the most beautiful and intriguing of all. Its tightly packed petals are a deep wine-red colour. Mitakuye Oyasin tells him the flowers represent the four attributes of the successful lover.

"Why didn't the snow kill the flowers?"

She pulls a stupid face. "*Why didn't the snow kill the flowers?* Stop asking dumb questions and take a petal from each of the flowers and chew on it. Apologise to the flower. Explain to it your motives."

While he is reluctantly chewing the petals Mitakuye Oyasin is down on her knees carving shapes in the earth with a knife. She then collects stones and places them in a circle around the figure she has etched in the dirt. The etching is of a rudimentary life-size naked woman. Solstice sees the vagina has been drawn with more attention to detail than any other part of her anatomy.

Mitakuye Oyasin tells him to sit by the figure inside the circle of stones. She tells him to sit facing east. That she is going to call down the spirit of the place. He watches her chop up some nettles and dried leaves she takes from her knapsack. She passes them to him and tells him to slowly chew on them after he has undressed.

"The less bravely we live the more stifling becomes our fear of death," she says as she begins making a fire. She tells him to stay still until the smoke envelops him. "The smoke will cleanse you of your physical smell which is distasteful to the spirits. Focus your attention on the smoke." She sprinkles some kind of powder onto the fire and the flames grow brighter and higher.

"If at any time you're scared out of your wits stretch yourself like a cat. Like this." He watches her entire body slowly unfurl in a series of youthful rippling arcs as if an undulating force passes through her. "And then lie down and press your mouth to the vagina of the shadow woman. If you want to return to your male body do as I say."

It is dark now. Beyond the fire he can only make out the vague outline of things. He calls out to Mitakuye Oyasin but there is no reply. He feels he has announced his presence to lurking enemies in the dark. Feels himself a tiny isolated figure in a vast simmering landscape of shadows. He finds he no longer has any trouble believing that the world around him is ordered and animated by unseen powers. Or even that everything that happens on one level is preceded by an omen, or a related event, on another level. He is feeling pleased with himself and his acquisition of new wisdom when Mitakuye Oyasin suddenly appears by the fire. He watches her lift up her skirt, thrust her hands between her legs, as if enticing something out, and then clap her hands above her head. A shower of silver sparks rain down from her hands.

Solstice wonders if the shower of silver sparks is a hallucination on his part, brought on by the flowers and plants Mitakuye Oyasin has made him chew.

"What are doing?"

"I'm making you sad. Sad for all the wonders you have never known. All your sadness will well up in you. You have to use your sadness to make a gash appear in the world of appearances."

Mitakuye Oyasin dances and sings. Beating the cowskin drum. She dances back and forth in a straight line. Every so often she turns a circle and goes back on her tracks in strange birdlike hops. Her head rocking from side to side. She wears a long tasselled painted buckskin dress. The flow of the fabric over her body like the seamless choreography of windswept patterns on water. She bobs delicately up and down, tassels swaying. Like a bird leaving a message on the ground. Like a bird that at any moment might take flight. She looks solemn and beautiful in the light of the fire and the moon. Then, having circled the fire four times, she stands saluting the four directions in turn and begins fanning the smoke with her eagle wing fan. Suddenly the wind changes direction and the smoke slowly drifts towards him. Moving in a solid mass. It takes on a green hue. He is instantly terrified. His jaw clenches, all the muscles in his stomach contract and he draws blood by inadvertently biting his lip. His legs shake violently. He has to change position. As he moves the smoke stops. It seems to tower over him like an arching wave. He freezes and again the smoke eases its way towards him. He can smell its sweet smell. It shows no sign of thinning as it drifts over him. He feels drawn into it. It clings to him like a second skin. His body is soaked in sweat. The smoke seems to exert a physical hold over his body. The more he gives in to his fear the more the smoke suffocates him. Tightening its hold according to the level of his resistance. He feels something breathe close to his left ear. A chill creeps down his spine. He is scared out of his wits. He can clearly make out the outline of the woman Mitakuye Oyasin has etched in the earth. It's as if he possesses the night vision of an animal. He lies down on the ground and presses his mouth to the vagina. He has the sensation of being sucked into the earth against which his mouth is pressed. Rolled through an infinity of black space. He is flooded by a sadness whose source seems to be outside of himself. Then he sees Alowa. All his fear leaves him. She is looking at him with disbelief. Except he doesn't really feel seen by her. He tries to walk over to her but he cannot move his body. He tries to speak but his voice is muted. He watches her walk away a little. There is a small elephant next to her with a little red bundle tied around its neck. The sight of the elephant, its vulnerability and innocence, floods him with the sadness again. He seems to glide through the air. Only then does he realise he is humming the song. He hums it consciously and is suddenly within touching distance of the elephant. The ground, he notices, is again shifting and powdery, like a cross between wet sand and snow. He is curious about the bundle. It looks like the container of Alowa's memories. Then he discovers he is holding the red bundle. A spider crawls out. He feels seen by the spider as he didn't feel seen by Alowa. He feels infinitely smaller than the spider. The spider releases a single thread that it curls around his finger. He watches mesmerised as the spider produces a second and third thread. Solstice has a vivid image of its serrated claws and the tiny hairs on the end of its spindly legs, as if the creature is under a magnifying glass. The spider circles his wedding finger, lightning fast. His hand burns. He can see the spider is threading its silver filament around his finger. Before long he is looking down at a beautiful filigree ring on his finger. His deep longing to bring this ring out of the dream strikes him as futile and in that moment he knows he is dreaming and that he will now wake up.

When he wakes up he sees the figure in black again. The web of quivering gossamer threads and the man in black with his back to him. He holds something aloft in his left hand. A flowering branch, painted red. He is five paces away. Solstice senses he is about to turn round.

# 20

Solstice can't stop touching the ring on his finger. He swivels it round and round, moves it up and down. It seems to connect him to the pulse of his heart, the flow of his blood. He expected Mitakuye Oyasin to congratulate him when he showed her the ring but she simply blew out her cheeks and puffed up at the hair on her forehead. Told him to stop feeling so pleased with himself.

Solstice is still inside a female body. He did not see the face of the figure holding up the flowering branch. He did not wrestle his shadow foe to the ground. He passed out. Mitakuye Oyasin made no secret of her exasperation with him and brought him back naked to the village. A new humiliation.

He is lying beneath his robes with his head propped on the fox skin pillow watching the clouds pass overhead through the smoke hole when the flap of the lodge opens. A warrior wearing a red breechcloth and his chest and arms covered in neat tiny scars. Solstice with alarm recognises Wicasa.

"Come! You must learn to ride," he says. Shyness makes his voice severe. He tries a higher octave when he says, "Do not be frightened."

Outside the tepee Fights With Her Fists glares at him. Fights With Her Fists with her long thin legs and the faint swell of her breasts beneath her painted deerskin shirt. When she turns her back Solstice looks down the length of her spine. Trying to find something of Alowa in her shape. Wicasa points to a spotted mare with a smooth glossy coat and slender legs. He tells Solstice the horse is a gift from him because she is poor and without ponies.

"I'm not a she," Solstice says. "I might look like a she but I'm not," he says.

Wicasa looks at him as though he's speaking a foreign language.

Wicasa encourages Solstice to mount the mare. Fights With Her Fists looks on, willing misfortune. Solstice and the horse look each other in the eye. She has enormously expressive eyes, liquid with mischief. She lifts her head and shows her teeth. Then rubs her nose against his hand. Solstice feels she is teasing him. The tail of a beaver hangs from her bridle and a pair of coloured blankets serve as a saddle. The stirrups are made of rawhide and appear fragile. He notices No Laughter No Pain outside his tepee, half hiding his face behind an eagle wing fan. The mare's crafty eyes tell him she will not make this easy for him. Wicasa mounts the horse himself, leaping up and perform-ing the gesture in one easy flowing gesture. He climbs down and motions to Solstice to try. Solstice tries to settle his foot in the stirrup but as soon as he is about to swing his right leg over the horse she moves and he falls to the ground. A group of women painting hides staked to the ground smile and No Laughter No Pain's gums are bleeding again. Even Wicasa is smiling. Wicasa lifts him up, his hands hot on Solstice's waist. Solstice man-ages to straddle the horse. He is immediately unnerved by her withheld power. Wicasa gives her a pat and she begins trotting off. When he trots past No Laughter No Pain, Solstice calls out "Hoka hey" – his voice charged with irony. He knows his words will double up No Laughter No Pain and hurt his ribs and this is what happens except the mare thinks his voice is a signal to break into a light canter. Solstice clings fast to her mane as she skips through the camp towards the pony herd. Eventually she stops to nibble at the bark of a willow. She refuses to budge. And he doesn't want to dig his heels into her flanks in case she bolts.

Later Mitakuye Oyasin arrives to collect him. The entire

village is outside watching Blue Feather and his clan leave. Blue Feather is the warrior who wants to take his clan to the reservation. To submit to the rule of the yellowstripes. To relinquish protection of the elephant nation. At a council last night his voice had been loud and scornful. He was accused of cowardice and one of the young warriors stepped forward, unhitched his breechcloth and wriggled his rump in Blue Feather's face, the worst insult a Sa'i Tor Shyela warrior can offer another. Several other young warriors dashed forward and counted coup, touching Blue Feather on the head and shoulders with their bows.

"Behold someone even more stupid than you," says Mitakuye Oyasin.

"What will happen to them?"

"They will become statistics."

Mitakuye Oyasin walks with her fingers curled. She tells him to keep singing the dreaming song he has been taught.

"Tonight you will either earn your warrior song or die of fright," she says. "Remember everything has to be beheld twice before it acquires reality. It has to be seen and it has to be registered as a memory. What you don't remember is carried off by the smoke. Now you have to climb trees," she says. "Every tree we come across you must first apologise to and then climb."

"Why?"

"Because to outwit your shadow foe you have to pretend to be something you're not. You pretend to be something you're not until you become what you're pretending to be. A squirrel for example. Shadow foes have no power over squirrels."

He looks at her with the beginning of a disbelieving smile.

"Do you think you can become a squirrel?"

"No."

"How about an otter then? Instead of climbing trees you can nose your way through water and build a dam all afternoon."

Eventually he does as he's told. After she has told him he wastes most of his energy brooding on perceived affronts to his vanity. He apologises to every tree before climbing it. He begins to enjoy the vigour and agility of his body. Memory is awakened in his muscles of similar physical exertions long ago. Except he can't remember ever being smaller than he is now.

"Why do I have no memory of myself as a child?"

"You are a child."

At sunset they sit down by a lake on the outskirts of a dark forest of spruce and pines. There are some fallen trees. The raucous cry of night creatures.

Mitakuye Oyasin begins dancing and singing around him. A feverish look in her eyes. Shifting her weight from one foot to the other, moving forward in little jumps. She puts her hands together and moves them like flapping wings. Circles him four times repeating the same throaty chant.

"Tonight you must centre yourself between the two female powers – the moonlight and the water."

"Where's my real body, Mitakuye Oyasin?"

"The Ancestor has it. You could say it's trapped between two dreams. This is why you're in great danger. Tonight you have a chance to make the two dreams coalesce."

"What do I have to do tonight?"

"You will encounter a shadow being and you have to wrestle it to the ground and force it to sing you your warrior song. Once you have it on the ground it will be only too pleased to help you but first it will test your courage. Everyone has a shadow foe. The shadow foe is the entity that is determined to lead you astray. It preys on our tendency to put things off or out of mind. It takes hold of this tendency and moulds it into despicable forms, pits it against us. You could say the shadow foe preys on wilful ignorance."

"What will it look like?"

"Horrendous. It will try to frighten you to death by assuming the appearance of what you most fear."

"Supposing I fail?"

"I will have no one to annoy me when I return to the village. But it is a grave mistake to prepare yourself for disappointment.

This is the gash in our intent through which the shadow foe steals our fire. A warrior, like a child, is always on tenterhooks. He doesn't plan ahead with disappointment in mind. When a warrior goes into battle he has to withstand the war cry of his opponent. The object of the war cry is to intimidate the opponent into dwelling on his own feelings. If you dwell on your feelings tonight you will be eaten alive. Now, take off your clothes."

Solstice does as he's told.

She begins chopping up some nettles and herbs she takes from her knapsack. Tells him to slowly chew them. She builds a fire. She adds angelica roots and the smoke takes on a pleasing scent. He sees with alarm that she is burning his clothes. Or rather the clothes of his female avatar. The skimpy skirt of synthetic hide strips, the virtually transparent off-white calico blouse, the synthetic fur-lined boots and the synthetic fur coat.

"Why are you burning my clothes?"

She throws more sticks on the fire and the flames leap up, spitting out embers. Her shadow is suddenly enormous and doesn't at all resemble anything human.

"Because if you are successful tonight you won't need these clothes anymore. And if you're unsuccessful you won't need them either."

She picks up two handfuls of ashes. She lets them trickle through her fingers while walking slowly in a straight line. As usual he has the suspicion that what she is doing is just theatre to heighten his wonder.

"Your shadow foe will use this pathway of ashes to reach you," she says.

She tells him to focus all his attention on an archway of thicker blackness among the trees. He is sitting close to the water. He hears the call of night creatures. The creaking of boughs and rustling of reeds. He thinks he begins to discern an order in the night's noises. He feels implied in everything going on around him.

Mitakuye Oyasin places twelve stones in a circle around him.

"If you think you're in mortal danger return to this circle as quickly as possible, assume the battle position and begin hissing through your teeth," she says.

"What battle position?"

She perches on tiptoes with her back arched and her hands curled on her thighs. "Poise yourself for a giant leap forward."

A piercing cry from within the darkness of the forest makes him leap to his feet.

"What was that?"

"That is the war cry of your shadow foe. It is waiting for you. Every time it shouts out its war cry like that clap your hands four times."

"Why?"

"To show you won't be shaken in your resolve."

Mitakuye Oyasin takes a scarlet bundle from her sack. "Lie down on the ground," she says. She kneels down over his prostrate body.

"What's that?"

It is the hollow bone of an eagle wing. She places it on his naval and begins sucking at his flesh. She sucks so hard he squirms to free himself. Except he is as if clamped to the ground. Finally she pulls away. Her hair is dripping wet and only the whites of her eyes show. Her whole body is shaking. He then realises she has something in her mouth. She spits it out and holds it in her hand for him to see. It is an insect with a black shell and razor teeth and two pronged feelers, the likes of which he has never seen. It seems to be cleaning itself. He retches and then vomits.

"That is your self-pity. Now lick up your vomit," she says.

He has no intention of licking up his vomit, like a dog. Mitakuye Oyasin prods him with the stick. He jumps to his feet, seething with rage.

"Now, while you are still boiling with rage, is the moment to go and meet your shadow foe. If you don't go to meet it, it will come to meet you which is infinitely worse."

Mitakuye Oyasin pushes him towards the trees. As he walks

a trail of leaves follow him on either side as if scuttled along by a wind. When he stops the leaves stop moving too. He takes a few steps more and then the piercing cry stops him in his tracks. It is like the darkness, ubiquitous. He is reluctant to clap his hands. He is reluctant to do anything Mitakuye Oyasin tells him. He is full of loathing for her. He marches forward, determined to show the old woman he is not frightened. Sticky filaments cling to his face. Seeming to exert more resistance than is rationally feasible. This time the piercing cry goes right through him. He claps without thinking. He claps four times. There is a booming echo as if he clapped his hands inside a tiny confined space. He hears a rustling. And has the feeling he is being stalked. He freezes. An icy chill runs down his spine. He hears the same rustling but this time behind him. He thinks he feels something brush against the back of his head. He yells in fright. His yell is answered by the piercing resounding cry that seems to fill the entire night. His chest tightens with fear. His legs sag. Then he feels the breath of something on his face. A foul stench. As of rotting onions. He thinks he is going to be sick again. Braces himself for it. Then he sees a flurry of blue light ahead. Gone almost as quickly as it appeared. But in that faint light he catches a glimpse of the familiar figure. As always, with his back turned to him. He looks down at his feet. He is standing above the line of ashes. They glow in the dark. There is another high-pitched scream. Followed by a deep vibrating growl. A dark form flits across his field of vision. He is beside himself with fear. Again the dark form flits across his field of vision. Then he feels as if something is coiling itself around his chest and his thighs. There is a buzzing in his ear. He is face to face with a black creature. It resembles a panther except it has wings, a carapace and the flickering tongue of a snake. It is looking him in the eye. His bowels loosen. His bladder opens. His stomach contracts and heaves and his legs give way. He hears Mitakuye Oyasin's voice in his head. *If you feel yourself in danger adopt the battle position and begin hissing through your teeth. Poise yourself for a giant leap forward.* Solstice perches on tiptoes with his back arched and his hands curled on his thighs. Without quite knowing why, he begins singing his song. He sings even though his mouth is bone dry. His lips gummed to his teeth. He sings loud and resonant in a voice cracked by fear. Then, without any sense of physical effort on his part, Solstice is grappling with the beast which has a slimy feel to it like wet seaweed. He rolls on the ground with it. It forces its tongue inside his mouth. Smelling of rotting onions. Its long rough tongue moves over Solstice's tongue, flicking at it, caressing it. The beast stops struggling. With its tongue in Solstice's mouth, touching his tongue, it begins singing a song. The song is a whisper. A whisper that ripples wellbeing through him from head to toe. He feels a moment of elation as he realises he is back inside his male body for the first time since clambering into the disused railway carriage.

A greenish mist arises around him, dampening his skin. The smoke moves around him with a soft rhythmic sound. It enters into his mind and parts, revealing pictures. He and Alowa are standing on a plot of overgrown land. Watching a wizened old man blackened with dirt in loose scarecrow clothes. The sleeves of his coat so large they look like black wings when he lifts his arms. Together he and Alowa watch the wizened old man make a fire. Burning a heap of leaves. The old man makes mesmerising moments of dance among the smoke. He abandons himself in the smoke. He dances and sings. The dance steps return to Solstice. The ground beneath his feet seems to vibrate with the dance steps. He enacts the dance steps but he doesn't know the song. It makes him sad he doesn't know the song. He can no longer see Alowa. He senses the black grass sway. He hears the unmistakable rustle of agitated foliage. He continues the dance. Then a black shadow appears out of the smoke. He can see the figure now, a shifting outline. It is defined by liquid silver lights, a stitching of interwoven silver threads. It has its back to him. She turns to face him and it is Alowa. For a moment her familiar face and figure take on a luminous glow as if she is lit from within by a thousand candles. He is teaching Alowa the dance; he waits for her to teach him the song. Her figure seems to float very slowly over the path of ashes.

"Alowa," he says. His voice has an echo, just as his feeling for Alowa always contains an echo, an echo that connects him to a deeper part of his being.

But it is no longer Alowa he sees. It is the living corpse of a man with rotting skin. There are maggots feeding on his flesh. He opens his mouth to reveal animal teeth.

# 21

Alowa does not return to the wagons. She is too frightened of the animals in the dark. The circle of eyes burning red holes in the darkness. She is too frightened of Snake. She remains perched in the tree. Whenever she gets too cold she climbs down and climbs back up. Over and over again. To quicken the circulation of her blood. When the sky lightens she notices a tree where a canopy made of wooden poles has been constructed up among the branches. There is a deerskin bundle on the canopy. All her instincts tell her there is a dead body inside the deerskin bundle. A black bird of prey is circling overhead.

Then there is a loud flapping of wings and the bird is perched thirty feet from her. It is looking at her. Hard staring implacable eyes. Ruthless eyes. She thinks of Esawa, the bird that alighted on the janitor's arm. She jumps down from the tree. When she walks towards the bird, it hops away and then stops. It is still looking her in the eye. She walks towards it. It hops away. She decides it wants to lead her somewhere. She follows it until the sun rises.

When she emerges from the grove into an expanse of flat-lands, a buffalo appears. The buffalo is an ugly scruffy beast. The wretched remnants of its winter coat are caked in dirt. Its matted beard almost touches the ground and is soaked by the white foam drooling from its mouth. Alowa sees it has a feathered arrow buried in its shoulder.

A gust of wind makes her skirt flap. She moves her hand to push it down. The movement of her hand triggers some instinct in the buffalo. It throws up its head and slowly trots towards her. When it is about ten paces away the buffalo stops. It is staring at Alowa. Sizing her up. Its stink becomes like a sack over her head.

At that moment Alowa notices a flicker of movement behind a nearby wild sage bush. Then the rattlesnake appears. Slithering with queenly nonchalance towards her. Alowa can't believe her bad luck. First a wounded buffalo, then a rattlesnake. She recognises both animals from the brochure given to her to study by the girl in the costume department. She knows both creatures can kill her.

"Please snake, don't come any closer," she says. It is the first time in her life she has spoken to a snake. The first time in her life she has seen a snake. The creature tattooed on the hateful man's neck. She is relieved to see the snake stops slithering. However it is looking at her. Its forked tongue flicking out. The primeval rattling noise in its throat. The buffalo too is looking at her. Alowa is running out of courage. It's oozing out of her with her perspiration.

Then she becomes aware of a tiny black dot on the horizon. She sees it out of the corner of her eye. A small black dot flickering on the sheets of early misted sunlight. It is only a dot, no bigger than a full stop in a printout, but it brings with it more menace. That is Alowa's feeling. For a moment she has the chilling conviction that the tiny black dot is her death. And she sees now that the black dot is heading towards her.

The dot suddenly vanishes. But far from reassuring Alowa the vanishing trickery of the dot further agitates her. She hears a barrage of noise in the distance. A relentless muffled volley of noises which she thinks are gunshots.

The black dot then reappears as mysteriously as it vanished. Except now it is no longer a black dot but a figure on a horse. And it is galloping towards her. The snake slithers off. The buffalo turns its head. The black dot reveals itself to be a painted warrior riding a pony at full gallop. When he is close enough for her to see his face she notices the black paint around his eyes, the blue zigzags on his cheeks. Alowa likes the effect of the paint at the same time as feeling frightened by its implications. *The hosts told me they tie up prisoners with their own entrails while they're still alive. They know no mercy.* The warrior brandishes a bow and lets out a full-blooded yell. The buffalo begins to trot away. The warrior ignores Alowa and takes up the chase. The buffalo is brought down by three arrows. It settles back on its haunches. It lays panting heavily on the ground. Blood oozing out of its nostrils and mouth. Alowa watches the warrior jump down from his painted pony. She sees now he is little more than a child. About thirteen years old. She watches him hold his hands up to the sky. He is saying something but she cannot understand the words. He then cuts open the black beast and thrusts his hand inside and yanks out from the bloody viscera what she supposes to be either the heart or liver of the animal. The young boy walks towards her. Dressed in blue leggings and a tasselled yellow and green shirt painted with symbols. Silky black hair reaching almost to his waist. Still holding the knife he hasn't cleaned. The organ in his hand is dripping blood through his fingers. He holds out the bloody pulp to Alowa and smiles. Alowa recoils. The painted boy takes hold of Alowa's hand and tries to force her to take the liver or heart. His hand smears blood over Alowa's hand.

"No," she says. "I not want," she says, unsure what language this boy speaks.

The boy, who is astonishingly beautiful she now realises, shrugs and devours the bloodied flesh with savage relish.

"Now you come with me," he says. There is blood smeared around his mouth and over his hands and wrists.

She looks down momentarily at their two thin shadows lying side by side on the bloodstained dust.

"Then Wahkan will decide what to do," he says.

The boy helps her up onto the pony. Soon they are galloping across the plains. Her groin crushed against the small of the boy's back, her hands pressed to his hips, the blood warmth of the horse in her loins, the wind a dance in her hair. Galloping over these plains with the sun warming the back of her neck is the most exciting thing that has ever happened to Alowa. She feels a moment of compassion for all her former co-dispensers inside the monitored control grid of the dome.

He has taken a circuitous route back to the circle of wagons. For a moment her heart is heavy with the prospect of encountering Snake again. Then she sees there are many warriors inside the circle of wagons. Alowa notices Snake sprawled out on his back. A film of red froth between his chapped lips. There are about eight feathered arrows in his chest. Slate's lifeless body nearby only has two arrows embedded in it.

"He was my friend," Alowa says.

"They are ivory seekers. They deserve to die," says the boy.

The horse snorts and bucks her head away from the smell of the dead bodies. Every single member of the wagon train is lying in a pool of wet blood. Every single member of the wagon train has a fixed bewildered expression on his face. Digger and Wilf and Bolt and Niles and all the other men. Eyria-O looks even more astonished in death than any of the other dead bodies. Only now does Alowa realise she didn't really trust Eyria-O, or even like her very much. That something about her bearing, her offhand poise of entitlement, reminded her of the executives in the dome.

One warrior is hunched over the dead body of another warrior. He is making mournful noises. When he sees Alowa he draws a knife and runs over to her. He pulls her by the leg off the pony. He holds the knife to her throat.

"Wait! She is wearing a Sa'i Tor Shyela sacred memory amulet. Who are you?"

*Who I am. Hiding in my blood, flowing through my veins, pumping in my heart. Never entering my head. Who I am. Hiding in my blood.*

## 22

Alowa sits astride the pony behind the boy. His name is Mnihala. They arrive on the ridge of another hill. Down in a valley, beside a river, is a circle of about sixty tepees. The rays of the setting sun dust the bleached painted hides red and gold. In the near distance the river forks in two before vanishing behind the slope of another hill. On the hillside and on the banks of the river a great herd of ponies is grazing. There are young girls knocking berries from the bushes by the river. Young boys flicking mud at each other from willow branches. Bare-chested warriors, some with a single feather in their hair, racing ponies across the valley. Alowa has never seen so much galvanising colour.

The boy leads her on foot into the inner circle of the village. Women sitting in groups, tanning and sowing hides. Old men sitting beneath shelters made by throwing a buffalo hide over a tripod of long branches. Dogs everywhere. Her presence is greeted with little curiosity.

The village is permeated by a scent of burning sweet grass. The brown-skinned tepees are decorated with elementary pictures of animals and abstract symbols. Everything painted in enhanced chalky blues, yellows, reds and greens. The boy leads her to a tepee on which is painted a bright red snake with lots of bright green dashes and yellow circles and black triangles. Horsetails hang either side of the opening. Inside, facing the entrance, sits a lone old man shrouded in smoke. He is bare-chested with two feathers in his long white hair. He wears a necklace of beads and feathers and holds a very long pipe also adorned with feathers and streamers. The old man points to one of the backrests made of willow wood arranged around the walls. Alowa sits down. A small wood fire surrounded by a circle of stones smoking at the centre of the circular floor. Robes and blankets lay strewn over the ground.

"Welcome, child," says the old man. He has two missing teeth. The effect is to make him look like a trickster. He is wearing quilled yellow leggings. His bare chest is crosshatched with old scars. He looks down at her ankle bracelet. His eyes widen with interest. "Already you make me think of things that are dead to me now. The path to the past was intact then. Now it is severed. Now I sit with my back to the world. Which is how you feel too, isn't it? That you sit with your back to the world."

Alowa wonders if she should be offended. But there is only playful kindness in the old man's eyes. Then she remembers the janitor once said the same thing to her. He keeps looking at her ankle bracelet.

"Do you know the janitor?" she asks.

He ignores her question. "I have seen you in a dream walking the pollen path. And so you must wear clothes the colour of pollen. I will call you Bearer of Pollen." His narrow wrinkled eyes glint with mischief in the firelight.

"My name is Alowa," she says.

He winks at her. He fills the space around him with a kind of liveliness. "Bearer of Pollen," he says. He takes another puff of the pipe.

Alowa stares at the painting of birds on a piece of hide above the old man's head.

"The returning of the snow geese to their mating ground," he says.

Outside Alowa hears the laughter of girls, the neighing of horses and the slow pounding of a medicine drum.

"What will happen to me?"

"I have studied the medicine power of plants, and roots and herbs. I can cure the spirit with songs and I can cure the body with dance. You too know these things but you have forgotten where you come from. The elders will decide if you can walk the sacred path. I think though your presence here brings peril to our people."

"I'd like to stay here."

He gets to his feet and begins chanting in a language she doesn't understand. He shakes a rattling gourd over her head and shoulders. Then he kneels down by the fire inside a circle of stones and ushers the sweet smelling smoke up into his face.

"I have looked into the smoke," he says, "and the smoke shows me you dancing. In my dream your thighs were bare. In my dream I held your ankle in the palm of my hand," he says and winks at her again.

*The Sa'i Tor Shyela are all immigrants, you know. Every single one.*

"Are you an immigrant?"

"I am Mahkah," he shouts. His voice suddenly huge and gruff. His face is so close that his nose makes contact with Alowa's mouth. He spills out ash from his pipe on Alowa's feet.


Alowa has been given new clothes to wear. A beautiful blue and golden yellow fringed dress, with white painted stars and adorned with a few red feathers. She is naked beneath her dress. Which makes her feel light-headed, as if a blast of wind could lift her in the air or knock her down. Mahkah leads Alowa out into the inner circle of all the lodges. In the firelight and the moonlight the drums start up and the rattles and male voices begin chanting, in and out of which weave impassioned female voices. Alowa is jealous of the girls dancing. The buckskin dresses they wear are dyed beautiful shades of red and pale blue with tassels that swing like wings as they dance. They all wear a single upright feather in their braided hair. They look like elegant creatures from another world. Alowa is mesmerised by how secret they make themselves. Lightly pawing the earth with dainty feet as if the earth is a responding living thing, as if the earth is a lover. Alowa wants to be one of the dancing girls. She feels the dance is happening inside her. The choreography pulses in her feet and hips like an imperative. She asks the old man if this is some kind of mating dance. The old man's shoulders shake with laughter. Then he winks at her again.

The women make a trilling noise and seven warriors begin dancing. They all have black and red stripes painted across their eyes. They carry red shields and feathered lances. They have bonnets of feathers strapped to their backs. Painted ribbons of cloth hang from their waists. They move in circles, stamping the ground with quick agile steps. They look up, they look down, they look from side to side, with quick birdlike flicks of the head. The drum pounds. Becomes the rhythm of Alowa's heartbeat as she watches. The women provide harmonies to the song the men sing. Alowa is mesmerised by one warrior in particular.

A gust of wind blows a wave of smoke towards Alowa's face. *Come closer, Alowa. Let the smoke envelop you. The sleeper in you must awaken.*

The women provide harmonies to the song the men sing. Alowa becomes still more mesmerised by the warrior wearing seashell earrings and a red feather in his long loose black hair.

Again the wind changes direction and the smell of smoke drifts towards her. *Look at the smoke. I'm dancing in the smoke, Alowa.*

The warrior moves in circles, stamping the ground with quick fluent steps. He looks up, he looks down, he looks from side to side, with quick birdlike flicks of his head.

"What's his name," she asks when the dance is finished.

"This is the dance of the brave hearts and black faces. He is Enapay. Tomorrow you can stand outside the tepee. Maybe Enapay will come."

"What do you mean?"

"If you are ready for love you can stand outside your tepee. Let's say a warrior approaches who you like, you give him a sign that you are willing to be wrapped in his blanket. Then you can talk. If you tire of him you slip free of the blanket. Then he will go away."

When the dance is over and she is lying beneath animal furs in the dark inside Mahkah's family tepee she hears the sad lilting melody of a flute. The dying embers of the fire throw strange shadows over the canopy and the music of the flute seems somehow connected to these changing shapes.

"Who's playing the flute?"

"Again that is Enapay. You seem bewitched by a love potion, Bearer of Pollen. He is playing his love song for the girl of his long waiting. Enapay will be a great warrior when the yellow-stripes come. It has been told him in a dream."

"And who is the woman of his long waiting?"

"He does not know yet."

Alowa stretches out her toes beneath the furs. She cannot keep the smile from her face.

It has long been an involuntary habit of Alowa's to perceive herself under the scrutiny of a fantasy male. This fantasy male sometimes applauds her, sometimes spins her around and lifts her in the air. More often, though, he finds fault with her, censures her, pulls her up short. He is like the keeper of all her passwords. She now has a name for this male. She will call him Enapay.

# 23

When Solstice wakes up his body is performing a magic trick. He lifts the blankets and peers down at the yearning shaft of flesh and blood and muscle between his legs. When he touches it, desire swirls around inside him like a deeper heartbeat. Then he remembers the living corpse with the animal teeth and his erection becomes soft and collapses back into its old self. So he tries to picture Alowa naked and eventually his blood tingles and swarms down into his loins again. He keeps goading it to perform its magic trick. He makes it disappear by picturing something horrific; he makes it return by picturing something beautiful.

"I'm back in my body," he says when Mitakuye Oyasin enters the tepee.

"I wouldn't want to be in your shoes when Wicasa sees your new body. He will feel you have been making fun of him."

"Wicasa will have to get a new song."

Mitakuye Oyasin smiles. It is the first time Solstice can remember her smiling at one of his jokes.

"You are back on the sacred path."

"What happens now?"

"Alowa has arrived."

"She's here?"

Solstice begins to see pictures in his head. It's as if the accelerated beat of his heart is producing the pictures. He wills the pictures to acquire texture and depth and animation. He remembers how snugly they fitted together. He and Alowa. That being together was like a mystery they had been given to solve. He knows he would know himself better, believe in himself more if he had her by his side. He pictures putting his hands underneath her clothes. He pictures her removing her panties. He pictures her handing him her panties. She is smiling. His sex organ fills with blood.

"Yes. The smoke finally brought her here."

"I saw Alowa while on my song quest but she turned into a living corpse. Why did Alowa turn into a living corpse?"

"Alowa has a history of rejecting you. The survival of our people now depends on her not rejecting you. The Ancestor taught you and Alowa the ghost dance. Only when you join hands will you both remember it in its entirety. Later she will be outside her tepee. You will take to her your blanket and her memories and hope she agrees to enter your blanket with you. First of all, you will make the peace with Wicasa. You will tell him you are Iktomi."

"Who is Iktomi?"

"Iktomi is the trickster. Iktomi means spider."

Solstice remembers again the spider on the old man's dead body, the man who danced for him and Alowa in the smoke. The dance is a vivid memory in his body. His body wants to perform the dance.

Wicasa is outside his tepee. He is painting stick figures on the neck of his pony. Solstice has been given blue leggings to wear, a pair of moccasins tied up around his ankles. He has a long painted robe thrown over his shoulders. He still wears his thimble. He still wears the ring given to him by the red spider. Given to him by Iktomi.

"Wicasa, I am Iktomi," he says uncertainly.

Wicasa looks him up and down. Wicasa's eyes harden. Wicasa scowls at him. Wicasa walks up to him and touches his bow to Solstice's forehead. "I count coup," he says. Then he turns his back on Solstice, unhitches his breechcloth and bares his buttocks at Solstice. No Laughter No Pain is watching and when he splutters into laughter his gums begin bleeding and he holds his ribs with a grimace.

Solstice can't remember ever being so nervous. He holds the bundle of Alowa's memories. He has long been curious to know what Alowa's memories are. He knows the shirt is inside but not what else. Her memories are wrapped and tied in red cloth. On numerous occasions he has been tempted to open the bundle. But he knows memories are private and require consent to be shared. Also he has always feared that if he opened them it would mean accepting he would never see her again, consigning her to oblivion.

He sets out for the far side of the village. He misses Mitakuye Oyasin. He can't believe she has vanished. If it's so important Alowa doesn't reject him why isn't she on hand to help? All his attention is directed inwards. He notices little of the activity in the village. He has decided he needs to prepare his opening speech to Alowa. He has so much to tell her his mind is a muddle. *Your kiss was already inside my mouth the first time I laid eyes on you.* He wonders if this would be a good thing to say to her. He rehearses it in his mind. "Your kiss was already inside my mouth the first time I laid eyes on you," he says to her and he imagines a wide smile lighting up her eyes. "You're always the last thing I think of before I go to sleep," he says to her and again he sees the wide smile, the brightening of the eyes. He decides all the topical stuff about the janitor and the observer and Eyria-O and Mitakuye Oyasin can wait. He will begin with a declaration of love.

There is a smell of roasted meat from the battered blackened kettles suspended over fires. Dogs troop back and forth between the fires. Shields and lances hanging on poles in front of the lodges. Old women sitting in groups, tanning and sowing hides. The large camp is permeated by the scent of burning sweet grass which, along with red willow bark, the Sa'i Tor Shyela use as incense.

Then he sees her. Sees Alowa. Never has she appeared so

beautiful. The sight of her is a still point around which every-thing else swirls. He worries the heat of his blood can be seen on his face. He screws his hands into fists to counter the trembling of his fingers. She is standing close to a fire with a warrior inside a blanket. Her face is very close to his face. They are whispering. Almost touching noses. She is so enthralled with the warrior that she doesn't even notice him walk past. Three old women are in attendance. They look at Solstice with barely concealed mirth.

He decides to walk around the village and then return. Even though the mirth of the three old women intimidates him. Eventually he musters the courage to return. Outside every tepee a trained war horse is picketed. Horses, he knows, that have been trained for years to obey the rider's prompts of weight shift, leg pressure and voice. One solitary warrior is composing a song to honour his horse. And outside every tepee is the willow tripod containing a warrior's weapons. Solstice wishes he was a warrior. He fears Alowa will reject him again because he is not a warrior. He begins to feel sorry for himself. There are fires now and dances.

Alowa is still whispering with the warrior inside the red blanket. At least he presumes it is the same warrior. This time Alowa and the warrior are hidden beneath the blanket. The three old women look at him. Now there is a hint of sympathy mixed in with the mirth in their eyes.

# 24

Alowa has a sense of having been startled awake. It's a sensation like reaching out for something in the dark and it not being there. She remembers the boy in the red coat; he has spoken to her in a dream. *Look how beautiful the flames are, Alowa. Look how beautiful my naked body is, Alowa.* Never before has he seemed so close. Then she remembers the happiness of last night. The glow, the delicious warmth of last night returns to her body. When Enapay wrapped her in his blanket. The image of Enapay feeds wellbeing through her arteries.

She crawls out of the tepee. It is her favourite time of day. Everything seems to quiver with the expectation of light. A ghost mist suspended over the frosted earth. Webs sparkling with beads of dew. The smell of the earth absorbing the early morning moisture. Every memory of yesterday as if erased. Everything about to begin again.

It is cold and she can't stop shivering. She wraps her arms around the neck of a tethered horse. To steal some of its pungent warmth. But as she stands on the hoarfrosted grass she has a feeling something is wrong. She looks across the frozen plain to the surrounding slopes where the ground is covered in moss and fragrant ferns and dead leaves and the wind rushes through the tops of the trees. It is then she notices many men appearing out of the morning mist. Someone else in the village notices them at the same moment and lets out a loud warning cry. Before long, men, women and children are emerging from their tepees. There is a flash of light and a loud explosion. Clouds of grey smoke appear. Whistling metal tears up chunks of earth on the outer circle of the camp. Flocks of birds take to the air, a great swirling black cloud of them.

Alowa returns to the tepee to warn Mahkah. She is surprised to see him applying paint to his face with his fingers.

"What are you doing? The yellowstripes are attacking the village."

"My time has arrived. I am preparing myself to meet my ancestors and the thunder beings," he says. He picks up his lance and his painted shield. Alowa can hear the thunder of hooves and the rattling of packs and jingling of harnesses behind all the shouting now. The sound of bugles rises above the explosion of the guns and the cries and shouts and the barking of dogs. She follows Mahkah out of the tepee. He ignores her pleas and begins walking towards the soldiers. He is singing. He is singing his death song.

*With visible breath I am walking.*

Alowa spots Enapay on his war pony. His face too is painted. But he has no eyes for her. She notices his black pony has a white star shape on its flank. The pony snorts and slings its head.

*The world has lost its centre.*

There are many warriors now on horseback. They are riding off to meet the enemy. Alowa watches. Her fists clenched. Her fists opening and closing.

*In a sacred manner I am walking.*

The women and children are running towards the river and the belt of timber beyond. Alowa watches. Her fists clenched. Her fists opening and closing.

*May it be beautiful before me.*

Bullets whistle all around, cutting up clods of earth, tearing fiery holes in tepees. Darkening smoke hangs over the village. Alowa looks down at a blackened circle of ground where a fire had burned last night.

*The world has lost its centre.*

Alowa cannot move. She cannot tear her eyes from the walk of Mahkah.

*In beauty I walk.*

A few of the mounted soldiers have entered the village now. Alowa watches as they shoot at running women and children. Watches them shoot at the elders who do not run. A bullet rips into Mahkah. He keeps walking.

*In beauty it is finished.*

Another bullet spins Mahkah round. The soldiers trample down everything in their path. Alowa is about to run when a familiar face appears. *Look how beautiful the flames are, Alowa. Look how beautiful my naked body is, Alowa. Are you looking at my naked body? I'm dancing towards you.*

# Part Two

## 2010

### 1

It's the third time the boy has kissed the dead man's forehead.

"Come on, Felix. Time to go."

"Mum! You'll never see him ever ever *ever* again."

"Yes I will," says Zinnia. "We still have our memories of him."

"Memories don't go forwards," he says, unwilling to take his eyes off the body on the bed that has ceased to talk or move or breathe.

"I'm not sure that's true, dear," she says, watching her son lean over the open-mouthed effigy of her father and daub on it another kiss, this time on the cheek. She wonders if it is natural for a child to be so excited by the presence of death.

Everything seems inappropriate to Zinnia – her dress with its hint of transparency, the flowers gloating with vitality on the bedside table, the television on its wall brackets whose blank screen reflects the dead man with the impartiality it reflects the carpet and the empty chair beside the bed.

Zinnia recalls a succession of expressions by which she knew her father's face – tenderness, laughter, disapproval, anger. All of them more easily borne and assimilated than this final one sculpted on his sallow face. She can barely look at him because of the overwhelming sense she has of him no longer being there.

"Okay, let's say goodbye now," she says. She looks at the watch on her wrist that bewilderingly, cruelly, reassuringly is still counting off seconds. Her need to reassert her pulse, restore a connection with the ticking continuity of her existence, compels her to check the contents of her bag, dust down the sleeve of her dress and then place her hand on Felix's shoulder.

"Aren't you going to kiss him goodbye, Mum?"

"I've said goodbye in my own way, Felix," she says.


Later, Zinnia is down on her knees in front of her father's wardrobe. She presses one of his shirts to her face. It's a shirt she has never liked. A shirt that caused her embarrassment whenever he wore it in her company.

"What's wrong with it?" he once asked when she made fun of it.

"It makes you look like you're on a package holiday," she said.

She is curled up inside his smell. He always made her feel both safer and smaller – the latter the price of the former. She wants to see her father again as a vivid living force, even as an obstacle, before her mother removes his memory from the room. This is his bedroom. The house's most private and sacrosanct chamber. Even to enter is to feel a chill of heresy followed by the sludge of guilt. There is a masculine order here, as calculated and forbiddingly esoteric as the electronic components etched into a piece of silicon.

Zinnia invariably becomes a little girl when she thinks of her father. She wears the same floral dress, damp with grass stains, she made into a fan by twirling round in circles. It was while spinning thus that she felt she found the centre of her being. She remembers once handing her father a flower she picked and how in the act of giving she experienced herself as that flower - the sticky stalk resin, the hard green shoots, the sheltered stamens and raw red anthers. She needed him to understand her no less than she needed to remain a mystery.

There is a large cardboard box at the back of the wardrobe. She tugs at one of its flaps and slides it out into the light. Battered cardboard boxes remind her of Christmas decorations.

She was, is, looking up at her father. He is half way up a ladder he has instructed her to hold steady. Her grip is not as firm as she might wish. Her father is clambering up into the dark attic to reclaim the large cardboard box full of Christmas decorations. He holds a torch. She watches him hoist himself up into the dark void, his legs dangling comically in mid-air. Zinnia feels in her own body the surge of effort with which he heaves himself up through the gash of blackness. She hears floorboards creak overhead and imagines the feel of the splintered wooden planks beneath her own feet. Without authorisation she too decides to climb the ladder. If she rises on tiptoes on the unsteady top rung she can just see the wandering beam of the torch as it tears things out of the darkness - the sloping wooden beams, the rusted watertank, mysterious boxes and trunks.

"Can't we bring *everything* down?" she says. She loves sharing conspiracies with her father, loves saying 'we' in a secretive intimate way.

Her father's head appears above her. He lights his face from beneath with the torch and makes a ghoulish noise.

"Stop it!" she commands. She does not like it when her father makes himself look ugly. He reaches out and grasps Zinnia by the wrists and heaves her up into the high air. For a moment she swings in space and feels the blood rush into all the secret corners of her body. She screams with delight and fear. There are, were, red marks on her wrists when her feet were back on the ground.

Zinnia sorts through the contents of the old box. She is looking for something that will make her cry. There are magazines, old newspaper cuttings, some official documents and certificates, a few photographs of people she does not recognise. Nothing that makes any emotional claim on her until she finds an old envelope with spots of mould on it. Inside are three old creased photographs. She recognises her father's mother in one of them. Sheathed in a thin summer dress and an expression of amused disbelief on her young face. Zinnia has never before taken stock of how exotic this young woman's face is. Her slanted eyes, her high cheekbones. When she looks at the photograph through a magnifying glass the girl take on a mirage quality, as if she is about to leave the frame of the photo. Yet her inner life is as mysterious to Zinnia as the underwear she is wearing under her summer dress. Another photo is of a dark-haired handsome young man astride a bicycle with a white marble statue behind him. On the back is written in blanched ink, Max, Lerici, 1942. An older photo is of a different man and woman. Why, Zinnia wonders, has she taken so little interest in her bloodline?

She hands the photos to her mother. Mrs St Aubyn takes the photos without any of the reverence Zinnia feels for them. Zinnia winces at her mother's absence of awe, her lack of tenderness. The lonely once-upon-a-time musty smell reawakened from the curling yellowing paper.

"This one is your grandmother. Ada. I don't know who the young man is. I've never heard of anyone called Max. And this is your great grandmother and great grandfather. Ada's parents. I remember your father once showing it to me. Her name was Marisa. I forget his name. They were both gassed at Auschwitz."

"Why did I never know that? Did I even know I have Jewish blood?"

"You tell me. You've never shown much interest in your heritage. For example, you don't have a clue what I was like before I became your mother."

Zinnia accepts the truth of this. "Why do we ask so little about each other? I never talked to Dad about his life either."

"Your grandmother died long before you were born. I suppose that meant no one felt any need to explain her to you. She got out of Italy during the war. Her parents didn't. Apparently she never recovered from the heartbreak and sense of guilt. I think there was a dramatic story. At least that's my understanding.

Your father didn't open up much about these things. If you want to learn more you ought to speak to your Aunt Phoebe. She kept many of your grandmother's things. You know what a hoarder she is. Your father and she fell out over something to do with this story. I believe there was a rumour his mother was illegitimate."

"If that's true it explains why Dad was so angry when I had Felix out of wedlock. He barely talked to me for a whole year."

"You were repeating the past. Perhaps confirming something he didn't want to believe. I could never get him to open up about it. Remember he didn't speak to Phoebe for virtually the rest of his life."

## 2

Zinnia opens the front door. Felix in his green school uniform shuffles past her into the hall, hiding his face. She looks at her watch, registers that he is home twenty minutes later than usual. She also notices his hair is wet.

"It hasn't been raining, has it?"

When she touches his hair the smell of urine reaches her.

"Felix? What happened?"

"Some boy threw a cup of wee at me."

"You've got a mark on your face as well."

"Then another boy hit me."

"What boy?"

"I don't know. Just a boy."

"A boy at school?"

It is new this instinct on his part to sulkily detach himself from what he says to her. To wedge a barrier of wanted misunderstanding between them. She has watched it gather impetus in the last month or so. His voice has sounded smaller too; his reluctance to speak increased.

"It was after school."

"But it was boys in your class?"

"No."

Zinnia begins shouting out her anger. She curses the school she has sent her son to. Curses the headmistress. Curses London. Curses the whole of England. Then she sees her anger is making Felix uncomfortable. He is waiting for it to end, as if it is a constant stream of traffic on a road he needs to cross.

"Let's get those clothes in the washing machine and run a bath for you," she says.

Bath-time is one of the bonding rituals they share. Chatting and laughing together in the purging swirls of steam with the scent of the frankincense or pink grapefruit bath oil rising up from the jostled water. The cabinets and shelves are a bright busy choreography of oils, shampoos, conditioners, scrubs, lotions, salts, unguents. Zinnia loves buying pots and bottles and tubes of alchemised essences that smell like yearning or intimacy on the skin.

"Come on, or the water will get cold!"

"Why do things get cold?"

"What do you mean?"

"Like hot water. Or cocoa."

"I don't know. It's something to do with room temperature, I suppose."

"But water still gets cold even when there's central heating."

"The Earth's temperature then. It cools everything down."

"So the Earth is the same temperature as cold cocoa?"

Zinnia grins.

"Well why do we get hot when we're not well then?"

"Don't you feel well?" She places her palm on his forehead.

"Do you think Dad knows why?"

"He might do."

Felix takes off his clothes, casts them aside as if they have no relation to him. He stands by the tub in his shorts. They look at each other through the condensation. He is refusing to participate in the rite today. There is a skip of new knowledge in Zinnia. He has begun to understand that she is telling him a lie by treating nakedness as something ordinary, as something not worthy of attention. She places the banana shampoo on the edge of the tub and leaves the bathroom.

While Felix is in the bath a text message arrives to her from his phone. It says: **CUNT FROM FELIX**. Three minutes later her mother calls. She too has had a text message from Felix. She is unable to say the word. She calls it the C word. Then her husband's sister calls and finally Josh's father. They have all received the same text message from Felix. Behind what they say Zinnia picks up a reproach levelled at her: there's an implied suggestion that she is not bringing up her son very well.

Then a link to a YouTube video arrives. The camera is fixed on Felix. Zinnia's legs begin trembling. Felix's susceptibility to harm has been a constant worry to her throughout his life but never before has she been so starkly confronted with his vulnerability. He looks shy rather than frightened. He is holding his phone. He is alone in the shot. Then a boy appears, with a loosened tie, greasy hair, a pimpled narrow face. He looks a lot older than Felix. He grabs the phone from Felix and throws what Zinnia knows to be a plastic cup of urine in his face. Three other boys move close to him. No one speaks. Felix wipes his face with his hand. Then the pimpled boy suddenly appears again. He hits Felix in the face. A full-blooded punch that catches Felix by surprise. The blow knocks Felix to the ground. Zinnia can feel the electric shock and pain of the blow in her own body. Bewildered, Felix looks now, heaped on the floor. And much more helpless and frightened. "Get up," says one of the boys. Felix does as he's told. Warily, he gets to his feet, his eyes expecting more violence. He stares into a void between the ground and the eyes of the boys. Zinnia's entire being goes out protectively to her son. Zinnia's entire being is flooded with a rage such as she has never known. Then the boy hits Felix in the face again. The blow knocks him to the ground. The video ends. If she had the little shit who hit Felix before her she would be capable of tearing out his fucking eyes, of bludgeoning his fucking skull to a pulp.

Later Felix is sitting at his computer when she enters his bedroom. A song she recognises but cannot name is playing through the speakers. He is absorbed and doesn't hear her enter and looks round guiltily when she asks him what he's doing.

"Just playing a game," he says. On the screen lots of scantily clad avatars are dancing in what appears to be a nightclub. Text scrolls down at the bottom of the screen. She catches the word *wankstain* before Felix leaves the site.

"You and your computer games," she says. "What's this one called?"

"It's not really a game."

"What is it then?"

"A virtual world."

Zinnia knows he is doing something she would forbid if she knew about it. At the same time she knows he wants to share his excitement and some mysterious sense of achievement he feels. He likes doing things that make him feel grown up. It's often how he likes to show his worth to her. And this is one of those things. She worries about this. It's as if he doesn't enjoy being a child.

"And what's this virtual world called?"

"AfterLife," he mumbles.

She makes a note to google it later.

"You're very clever with computers. Do you want to tell me what happened today?"

He mumbles something she can't make any sense of.

"I've just had a text message from you. So has your grandma, your Aunt Sophie and Grandpa Castle." She has decided not to tell him about the video. The video has been deleted. When she tried to send it to Josh it was no longer there.

"They stole my phone too," he says sheepishly.

"They've stolen more than that. They've stolen your identity. Everyone they send this message to thinks you wrote it. Who else's number have you got on your phone?"

"I dunno. Lots."

"Poor Mrs Giles next door?"

He nods.

"She's just been told she's got cancer. Imagine her face when she gets that message."

Felix seems to shrink inside his body. He stares down at his bare feet.

"Why are these boys picking on you, Felix?"

"I don't know."

"You must have some idea why."

"Today because I understood algorithms and they didn't."

"But you do have some friends at school?"

"Harriet."

"That fat girl who's so shy she's turns bright red even if you look at her?"

"Mum!"

"What?"

"That's not very nice. She can't help being fat."

"I don't imagine she's very popular either."

"She isn't. She gets called names all the time."

"What do you do at lunchtime?"

"Eat my lunch," he says with a smirk.

"You know what I mean. In the playground."

He tugs at his sleeves so they cover his hands. "I don't know. Hang out with Harriet."

"And what do the other boys do?"

"Stuff. Play football. Muck around. Make jokes. Have fights."

"Don't you like playing football?"

"I don't mind it. But I'm rubbish at it."

"I don't understand. You charm the pants off all my friends. Why is it you get on so well with adults but can't get on with children your own age?"

He puffs up at his long fringe. "What are genes, Mum?"

Zinnia runs her hands back and forth over her thighs. She feels her heartbeat travel back and forth along the length of her arm.

"Genes? Why?"

"Today in Biology, Mrs Holmes said genes are what make us who we are."

"That's a bit of an exaggeration. Lots of things make us what we are. Not just genes."

"What are they though?"

"I'm not sure I can explain, Felix. Let's google them."

"Okay."

"Here we go. Genes are inherited from our parents and carry the information that contributes to what we look like and how we act," she reads out. "For example, if both your parents have green eyes, you might inherit the trait of green eyes too."

Felix looks at her eyes.

"You've got blue eyes," he says.

"Yep."

"What colour eyes do I have?"

"You've got beautiful green eyes."

"What about Dad?"

"Brown. But I think sometimes genes skip a generation."

"What do you mean?"

"Let's stop talking about genes. Look at all this stuff written here – chromosomes and proteins and DNA. You're only ten, Felix."

"So?"

"Well. Perhaps you're too young to understand what genes are. Harriet is probably fat and shy because her mother or father is fat and shy. Because fat and shy are in her genes."

"Stop calling Harriet fat, Mum."

"I'm just trying to explain."

She pulls him down onto her lap and presses her mouth to his ear and strokes the back of his head. "You're not asking about genes because you don't like yourself, are you?"

"No."

"No meaning what?"

"Mum…"

"Yes?"

"I'm not going back to school anymore. I hate it. It makes me not want to be alive anymore."

"Please never say that again."

"How can I stop saying it when it's true?"

"What about me? How do you think I'd feel if you weren't alive anymore?"

"You didn't cry once when Grandfather died."

"That's not true. I did cry."

"I didn't see you."

"When we're older we usually cry when we're alone. That's just the way it is."

# 3

"What's going on? I got an obscene text from our son last night."

Nowadays the sound of her husband's voice is like a needle poised to enter a vein. "And it's taken you twelve hours to react," she says into the handset. "So did your father and my mother and god knows how many other people we know. He's had his phone stolen."

"Felix called your mother a cunt?"

His delighted grin is so palpable over the airwaves it is like a physical presence in the room, an animal with eager eyes and a wagging tail.

"It wasn't Felix. He had his phone stolen. Do you listen to anything I say?"

"I do my best."

"Felix is being bullied at school."

"You spoil him. I've always said that."

"Is it any wonder?"

"Hang on. Parking the car."

Inadvertently, he is always compelling her to imagine his existence when they are apart. Soon he will stand for a while admiring the job he has done parking his car. It's an achievement, like closing a business deal, for which he expects recognition. He invariably finds fault with the way she aligns her car to the kerb. He delivers up a critical running commentary while she reverses into the space that puts her on edge. Once upon a time he silently measured her progress in a similar way when they made love. Or that was her feeling.

"I can't really talk right now," he says. "How about I call you back in an hour?"

Zinnia removes the phone from her ear and frowns at it.

"Zinnia?"

"What?"

"You are still there then? Actually, I've got some bad news…"

"Has it ever occurred to you that perhaps you *are* bad news?"

"Hey! That's a bit below the belt."

"What's the bad news? Why must you always leave everything in suspense? You're not a crime novel, Josh."

"Bad investment bad news. We're going to have to make some serious adjustments to our budget."

"Go on."

"Well, Stowe for Felix is probably now a no-go. I can't afford to send him to public school, Zinnia. But we'll discuss it more at length. I'll call you later. Okay?"

Josh is both sensitive and stubborn – quick to take exception, slow to make amends. She sees one of his gestures with starkly nuanced clarity, a hand with nails trimmed fastidiously down to the cuticle moving through the air, and she flinches at the overexposure of the image. They are like direct sunlight to each other now – each washes all colour, all shadow out of the other.

Zinnia is suspicious her husband is having an affair. She has no watertight evidence; only an instinct. But she is losing confidence in so many aspects of herself that she feels she can ill afford to lose trust in her instincts as well. She was convinced she wasn't the kind of woman who would ever go through her husband's pockets for evidence of a betrayal and then she had gone through his pockets. There's something new in the way Josh carries his body. A lightness she doesn't recognise. He takes stairs two at a time. He spends more time in front of the mirror. He works late three nights a week. In the past month he has spent at least seven nights in hotels due to an unprecedented number of out-of-town business meetings. At the same time she wonders if her suspicions aren't simply a sign of a new insecurity in her, a further failing of her self-esteem. Once or twice she has come close to asking him point blank. But to do so would be to confess to a lack of trust in him and there would be no going back after such a damning confession. She also knows he will deny all charges no matter whether he is guilty or innocent. He always begins proceedings from a defensive position.

Once she went onto his computer. Her skin beneath her clothes prickling with guilt. His recent searches led her to footage of an unseen man being masturbated by two women. She watched the ten minute clip in its entirety. Her heart racing at the expectation of being discovered. She wondered if this was Josh's ideal scenario. To receive pleasure without lifting a finger. She recognised a truth in the notion. Under review, even if her current appraisals are short of generosity, Josh does emerge as a taker rather than a giver. He is well-suited to his work as an investment banker. He expects more back than he invests.

She calls her best friend Evie.

Evie asks: "Are you sure this isn't wishful thinking on your part?"

"You mean, I want him to have an affair?"

"With hindsight, I enjoyed my moral indignation when Chris cheated on me. That's what we all read newspapers for, isn't it. A daily hit of moral indignation. It makes us feel better about ourselves."

"I wouldn't call what I feel moral indignation. And this certainly isn't making me feel better about myself. Just the opposite. I've become much more dependent on Felix for feelings of self-worth."

"Forgive me for saying this, Zinnia but I've never been convinced by Josh. By you as a couple I mean. You were in a burning building when he came along. He was the fireman. He had strong shoulders and a muscular will. He's given you Felix. Perhaps that's all he really has to contribute to your life."

Zinnia laughs because she can see the smile on her friend's face as she speaks.

"Actually, he didn't give me Felix. That was someone else. It's a ruse we've maintained to protect his dignity."

"Hang on. I need a cigarette. Zinnia! What a dark horse you are. But I thought we were friends? I can't believe you've never told me this."

"It's a secret. Only a very few people know."

"So who is the father?"

"His name is Milo."

"And does Milo know he's fathered a child?"

"No, he doesn't know."

"Tell me more. I want to hear about Milo. He's Italian?"

"Half Italian. He lived in Florence. We were very close friends for about three years. With Milo, I was myself without my biology. I never wanted to have sex with him. I didn't want to ruin what we shared. Then we got drunk one night towards the end of my stay there and had sex. Florence until then had been like a fairy story. I had never been so happy. I suspect something in me needed to ruin it all now that it was ending so it didn't hurt so much leaving it all behind. I was frightened the next morning. I discovered I didn't trust him. Or rather, that he didn't make me feel safe. Josh had been courting me on and off without success for ages. His family are acquaintances of my family. He did make me feel safe. I flew back to London and we became lovers."

"So how do you know for sure Felix isn't Josh's?"

"I knew I was pregnant the next morning after sleeping with Milo. I can't explain it. I could feel it in my body like a kind of clairvoyance. And Felix doesn't look anything like Josh. In fact he looks like Milo."

"No. I've noticed that. That he doesn't look like Josh."

"And we've since discovered that Josh can't have children."

"So where's Milo now? Do you ever hear from him?"

"No. For all I know he might be dead. He has no online presence."

Zinnia can see the big grin on Evie's face when she says, "So you've looked?"

"It's not like that."

"Of course not. Just idle curiosity."

"Exactly."

"Unless we marry them, we never quite fall out of love with our first loves."

"He wasn't my first love. We were friends."

"But he worshipped you and that's something we never want spoiled. I understand why you got rid of him. So you could protect what he made you feel."

# 4

Zinnia's heart is thumping wildly. Her skin beneath her clothes prickles with fire and ice flushes. She is in the throes of sinking down beneath the security of everything recognisable and sustaining. What she outwardly sees bears no correspondence to what she is experiencing. There should be a circling fin, the swell of a vast body of black water implacably sucking at her body's resistance.

It is an effort to control the expression on her face. No one must see how mad she has become. She pretends to look inside her bag. The act of pretence acquires some sincerity during its performance. She takes out the photograph of her grandmother. Only realising when it sits in her lap that it is an eccentric thing to parade on a packed tube train. She stares down unseeingly at the image, presses her thumbs firmly against it as if seeking a current there that might slow down her intake of oxygen.

"Why do you keep looking at that photo?" Felix asks.

Her panic has obliterated him to a painted transparency, a crackle of static, just as it obliterates everything she depends on for solace, for hope, for the orderly meshing together of one moment to another.

The train makes its grinding clanking metal noise inside the tunnel. It hammers its way through the darkness under the city. A row of strangers sit opposite her. Although they don't look at her she is convinced they are aware of something strange about her, some whip of distortion in the way she is experiencing the moment. She cannot bear anyone to see her struggle, to witness this inexplicable insurrection of her body's chemicals. There is no air to breathe. That is her sensation. She is asphyxiating, hyperventilating.

She stuffs the photograph back into her bag and rises abruptly to her feet. The momentum of the train throws her forward. She is giddy with her own lightness of being.

"This isn't our stop."

She has forgotten about Felix. He has left his seat but is half poised to return to it. He knows what he says is indisputably correct and he speaks with unusual authority. He expects her to realise her mistake and perhaps congratulate him.

"Felix, just do as you're told," she says in a contemptible harsh tone.

"But this isn't our stop, Mum." He raises his voice and the nearby passengers discreetly look their way. "This is Earls Court. Look!"

"Stay on the train then if you don't want to get off." There is a hiss in her voice that she has kept as low as possible. It will appal her three minutes later when her breathing is back to normal, will make her unrecognisable to herself that she was prepared to leave her son behind on the train.

The doors open and she stumbles out onto the platform as if someone has shoved her from behind.

Felix is sullen with muted righteous indignation. He sulkily follows her out of the train.

When they are back outside in the open air, on the busy high street with its jostle of comforting smells and directed animation, she is shakily repentant. She moistens her fingers and rubs them over his mouth.

The panic attacks have been a part of Zinnia's life for almost six months. They allow no pathway back to the innocent complacency with which she once made sense of the world around her. With every new attack more of her identity crumbles. Every day the panic rubs something else out that has been achieved with application, sometimes with inspiration.

"I just had to get out of that carriage, Felix. There was no air."

"If there was no air we would be dead," he says.

"I bet you almost wish you were back at school."

"No."

Zinnia met with the headmistress of Felix's school earlier. The woman, with dry frizzy doll's hair, made Zinnia feel that she herself was partly to blame if Felix was being bullied. Mrs Speedie told her that Felix didn't apply himself. That he hid behind a nervous laugh and wasn't able or willing to concentrate on anything said to him. That he retained little of what he was taught in his memory. That he was very young for his age. Mrs Speedie implied he might be a touch autistic. She smiled and nodded when Zinnia spoke. Zinnia was angry with herself afterwards for not standing up to the woman.

She and Felix walk side by side. She has taken his hand and is relieved he offers it with no apparent resentment. As she looks for a taxi she sees a familiar face. For an instant she can't place the woman. She is like a five second sample of a song she recognises but cannot for the life of her name. There are too many doors in her memory that won't open. The woman though recognises her.

"Who was that?" Felix asks after they have parted company.

"A girl I knew a long time ago. I met her in Italy. One day soon I want to take you to Italy."

"Why?"

"Because it's my favourite place in the world."

"I don't have a favourite place in the world."

"Perhaps it will be Italy. Your great grandmother was Italian."

"What was great about her?"

"That's what I hope to find out from Aunt Phoebe."

Her mind is working quickly. There is the money her father bequeathed to her in his will. She has already rejected the idea of flying. She knows the prospect of being trapped in an aluminium canister will body forth the panic in her mind every day until the day itself. She thinks of the ferry. She has a memory of herself and her father on the deck of a ferry. The painted white rail, the slippery slanting boards and the taste of salt on her lips and spray cascading up into their faces. Watching him thrown from side to side by the heave of the boat and how he enjoyed this, how he laughed out loud and made a game of it with her. That was the only time she saw him unsteady on his feet until the cancer arrived.

There is no panic when she imagines herself on the deck of a boat.

"Let's see what Aunt Phoebe says," she tells Felix.

"Why do you keep saying that?"

# 5

Zinnia is still fascinated by the two photographs her aunt has given her. She can't stop looking at them. One is a luridly coloured postcard of a group of Indians in feathered headdresses on horseback. They all have painted faces and hold feathered lances. In bold black type are the words, **Seymour Villiers presents The Gateway to the Wild West**. The other is a sepia photograph of a solitary man standing by the sea with a castle on a rock in the background. His long black hair is wind-flustered, the bone structure of his face elegantly severe, the look in his slanted eyes fiercely impenetrable. He looks to Zinnia like a holy man. He also looks like the loneliest man in the world.

"Obviously he came to Europe as part of some kind of wild west circus. And ended up staying," says Aunt Phoebe. There is little expression or emotion in her aunt's eyes. She is like a bird in her hard dispassionate way of meeting Zinnia's gaze, a temporary visitor, who at any moment might fly away. Her home is like a nest, enveloping, intimate, like something hidden behind the surface of things. "Perhaps because he fell in love with your great grandmother. One thing you need to realise is that your father was very defensive about the subject. I think he felt ashamed. He simply didn't want to countenance the idea that our mother was illegitimate. Personally, I found the possibility rather thrilling."

This is new knowledge for Zinnia. That there was a deep and possibly inhibiting source of shame in her father. She remembers now how dismissive he was when she chose to study Italian at school. Remembers also that not once did they go to Italy as a family on holiday.

"But what exactly is the evidence that he was Ada's father?"

"You have to remember I was only five when my mother died. Obviously she never spoke to me or your father about her past. But it was something my father said at the end of his life. He had dementia so no one took much notice of the things he said. But he kept saying, the ghost dance dress was a gift from her true father. When he died we found this." She hands Zinnia a brown paper package.

"What is it?"

"Open it."

Inside is a very old buckskin dress or shirt. It is elaborately decorated with tassels and animal hair and four painted hand-prints, two green and two red. The material is so ethereally soft Zinnia can't stop caressing it.

"Beautiful, isn't it?"

"It's one of the most beautiful things I've ever seen but it also gives me the creeps a bit. This looks like a bullet hole and a bloodstain."

Felix, who has been restless, reaches across to touch the dress. It has a broken line of black animal hair sown across the shoulders which he fondles.

"Do you know anything about the ghost dance?"

Zinnia hates showing ignorance, especially in front of Felix. Hates every hole in her education. Should she know what the ghost dance is?

"The ghost dance was the last desperate stand of the Lakota nation against the genocide they faced at the hands of American settlers. It was a holy dance they believed would make them invincible to bullets and lead to the restoration of their land. Everyone was required to wear a specially designed shirt or dress. The ghost dancers were massacred at a place called Wounded Knee."

"I can't believe I might have Indian blood. We might have Indian blood, Felix. What do you think of that?"

Felix blows up his fringe.

"Lakota blood actually. Indians come from India, Zinnia. Your father too always called them Indians. It still makes me smile just how appalled he was by the idea that he might be a Red Indian."

Zinnia can't help mirroring her aunt's smile.

"The weird thing is, I always used to tease my dad about his dark skin. I assumed he had spent a long time in the sun when he was young. I thought of it as a permanent tan. I feel so stupid now. And I've always thought what beautiful exotic features you have."

"One thing I will say in your father's defence is that it takes a long time to work out who one is. To feel comfortable in one's own skin. What if your father's grandfather turned out to be a scoundrel or something worse? New knowledge can bring chaos rather than clarity. Your father would have had to start putting himself back together."

"Why would he turn out to be a scoundrel? Is there something you know you're not telling me?"

"No. Not at all. I'm telling you everything I know."

"What about after the war? Did Ada go back to Italy? Did she try to find her father?"

"Apparently not. But sometimes the heart of a woman comes close to bursting point. She has to take a step back. Who knows what her relationship with her stepfather was like? And who knows at what age she found out he wasn't her real father? And then she finds out he was gassed. Can you imagine the hurt? And the guilt too. Would she want to disown him after finding out he died and how he died?"

"How did she escape?"

"I don't know. But I'm happy you're taking an interest. I want you to find out, Zinnia. Isn't it much easier nowadays to get information? What with the internet. And you speak Italian. Go to Lerici. See what you can dig up. Why not? And I want you to have that dress."

Zinnia leaves her aunt's home with the deerskin dress and a

letter addressed from Italy to Ada, her grandmother. The ancient postmarked stamp on the envelope as silently talkative as a gravestone in its way. She is excited at the thought of reading the letter. Excited too at discovering how well she has remembered Italian which she hasn't spoken for almost ten years.

"Why are you so interested in all this old stuff?"

"If it wasn't for the woman who once owned this dress you wouldn't be here, you wouldn't have got born. The Nazis tried to stop you from being born."

Felix shows he finds this idea preposterous. Another footnote in the long book of irrelevant information she passes onto him.

"It's true."

"The Nazis?"

"They belonged to the dark side. Like Darth Vader."

Felix frowns, as if she is making fun of him, of the fact he is a child.

# 6

"I had no idea you were Jewish let alone Native American."

"Just shows how little interest you've taken in me," says Zinnia, smiling. She doesn't tell her husband she had no idea either until a few days ago. "Anyway, I'm not Jewish. I've got Jewish blood."

"You told me you had Italian blood."

"I do have Italian blood. Italian Jewish blood."

"So what are you saying?" He smiles before taking another sip of red wine. There is the faint sickening aftersmell of the Thai takeout they ordered for dinner in the sitting room. "You want to have Felix circumcised? We have to stop eating pork and clams? I could give up pork. Not so sure about the clams though."

There is a kind of avuncular kindness in Josh tonight. It throws her a little. Another small mystery connected to the larger mystery she feels she has to solve.

"Haven't we been here?" he says, referring to the castle in the photo.

"No. We went to Vernazza. This is Lerici."

"I still remember that seafood spaghetti I had there. On the terrace of that restaurant overlooking the sea. Remember? One of my all-time top ten meals. No doubt."

"I remember we had an argument."

"No way. How could anyone argue in a place that beautiful?"

"I remember that's what I thought."

"But back to your question, your father was a very good-looking man. He looked wise. So, no, I have no problem believing this might have been his grandfather," he says handing her back the photo. "I've always said you have something exotic about you."

"Have you? I've never heard you say that."

"Yeah, you take after your Aunt Phoebe. She looks like she's got Indonesian or Thai blood. Always thought that. The jet black hair, the high cheekbones, the wide-set shapely eyes. All things you share. Anyway, I've got some emails to write."

"Are you happy here, Josh? I mean, it seems to me we only tell each other what we think when we argue."

"Hey, look, I know your father's death has upset you but there's no need to turn it into an identity crisis. I understand you're curious about your grandmother. But it won't change who you are. You want to find out her story. I can understand that. Sounds exciting. You want some high adventure in your family history. Who doesn't want that?"

She returns his smile but wonders if he's implying she's turning to an ancestral past to fill an emptiness in her own life. And in turn realises how defensive she's become. As if everything said to her is encrypted criticism.

"Actually, I've always wondered how I would cope in a war. How brave I'd be. Would my nerve hold up? So, your grandmother was hunted by the Gestapo. Go for it. That's what I say. Try to find out what happened to her. How she escaped."

"I've googled her."

"And?"

"Nothing. I've also ordered three books about Italy during the second world war." It surprises her how much she is looking forward to their arrival, like a love letter. "I was thinking, maybe we could go to Italy for a holiday. I'd like Felix to see Italy."

"Absolutely. How's he doing? I tried to have a chat with him earlier. He's like you. He says no to everything."

"I don't say no to everything."

"No? Only what I ask you then." He smiles and gets jauntily to his feet. "Those emails," he says.

She listens to him climb the stairs, two at a time and shut the door of his small study behind him.

*Dear Ada,*

*I'm sad you left but happy too that you might now be in a safer place. Your parents are in a camp near Modena. That's all I have been able to find out. I heard "the janitor" helped you in your troubles. I remember the night you told me about him. He was always kind to me at school. I hope one day we will see each other again.*

*Max*

# 7

Zinnia knocks on Felix's door before turning the handle. The door doesn't yield when she pushes at it.

"Felix? Why can't I open the door?" she asks.

"Because I've pushed my bed against it."

This brings a wide smile to her lips.

"I know you were just pretending to be sick this morning. Because you didn't want to go to school."

No reply.

"How are you going to eat if you don't come out?"

"I've brought up some supplies from the cupboard."

"I wondered where all the biscuits had gone. What about when you want to go to the loo?"

"Washing up bowl. I brought that up too."

"You've thought all this out with some precision, haven't you?"

"What does precision mean?"

"Felix?"

"It's not your fault, Mum."

"It is a bit, Felix."

"No, it isn't. I'm not going back to school, though."

"Are those kids still bullying you?"

"No one likes me much."

"I like you."

"You don't count, Mum."

"Thanks."

"Are you still looking at those old photos all the time?"

"Wouldn't you like to know who your great great grandfather was and what happened to him?"

"What did happen to him?"

"I don't know yet but I'd like to find out."

"Why?"

"Well, for one thing, it might give us a better idea of who we are. You and me. Hang on, I'm going to get something and then I'm going to quiz you."

"I'm not coming out."

"You don't have to come out."

"Okay."

She returns with the postcard. She sits down outside her son's door, pushing her long cadmium red skirt between her raised knees. Bangles slide down her wrist as she slips the postcard under the crack at the foot of the door.

"Which of the men in the photos do you like the best?"

"I don't know."

"Yes you do. If you had to go to the zoo with one of them which one would you choose?"

"If I went to the zoo with one of those men everyone would be laughing at us. Why are they all wearing those feathers on their head?"

"I think they're like symbols of their achievements. Every time you do something well you get awarded a new feather." She slips the photograph of the loneliest man in the world under the door. "The man in this photo is also in the other photo. Can you spot which one he is? I can't. I think it's either the one second to the right or the one on the extreme left."

"I don't know what second to the right means."

"If you'd open the door I'd point him out."

"I'm not coming out."

"Felix, what if I said to you, you don't have to go to school for the rest of this week? Would you open the door?"

"Promise you're not just tricking me?"

"I promise."

When she enters the room she pushes the bed back to its original place beneath the window that overlooks a small garden and the backs of a row of identical houses. She and Felix have been talking for about half an hour when they hear the front door downstairs open.

"That must be your father. Quick, hide! Under the bed. He'll be angry if he knows I allowed you to skip school."

Zinnia isn't quite sure why but she too scrambles under the bed, why she too feels compelled to hide from her husband. In the intimate darkness beneath the bed her heartbeat increases its take of blood. She can sense Felix is both excited by the conspiracy they share and perplexed by its unprecedented nature. The noises Josh makes downstairs ring out crystal clear. Twice he calls out her name. She listens to a succession of kitchen sounds - the fridge door being opened and shut, a tap being turned on and a forceful jet of water splashing into the sink. Then he makes his way up the stairs. She recognises the creak of the floorboard two steps from the landing. The one she avoids when she can't sleep and goes down to the kitchen in the middle of the night. He is checking the bedroom and then the bathroom. Finally the footsteps approach Felix's door. She takes Felix's hand, to steady her own wild heartbeat. The door opens.

"Where the fuck is she now?"

It shocks her how much impatient dislike there is in his voice. Worse that Felix has heard with how much disparagement he refers to her. She pictures the expression on his face, as if he is looking down at a dead bird. Then his phone rings.

"Hiya, babe."

"Been thinking of you too."

"At home. Forgot some papers this morning."

"Yep. I'll meet you outside the British Museum at five. I'll have to be home by about nine."

"What colour underwear are you wearing?"

"Sweet."

The spirit of complicity and guilty adventure that she and Felix shared when they scrambled under the bed is replaced by mutual discomfort when Josh leaves. Zinnia has difficulty looking Felix in the eye. He too is obviously embarrassed and a little bit frightened. He has withdrawn into his shadow. When he is troubled he doesn't edge towards her but always edges away from her. She can't help taking it as a criticism. *What colour underwear are you wearing?* She can't begin to imagine how Felix's young mind has processed Josh's words. But it's not the words, which possibly would be meaningless to him, it's her own horror that has been transmitted to him. She rings for a babysitter. She has made up her mind to go to the British Museum.

# 8

The Kings Road has an elegiac quality to Zinnia as she sits in the black cab. As if it is no longer part of her active life. As if she is a ghost of herself revisiting one of the memories she takes with her into sleep. The same is true when she passes Green Park and The Royal Academy. She feels alienated from her old life. The sleek fretful traffic is aggressive and menacing, like a dirty syringe poised to enter a vein. She feels everything is moving away from her. Everything except danger.

The museum is closing when she arrives. A leisurely exodus of tourists flooding out onto the streets of Bloomsbury. She enters a café opposite the front gate. When she's ordered a coffee and sat down at a table with a view of the gate she realises she has no intention of confronting him. It is her nature to shy away from open conflict. She wants to see the woman. Her curiosity about this woman has already developed into a personal rivalry. As if the appearance of this woman will show her what it is she herself lacks. The subterfuge involved makes her think of the anxious vigilance to which Ada and her family must have been relentlessly exposed in wartime Italy. Except, she realises, she is playing the role of the secret police.

A rush of air fills her lungs when she sees Josh. Her head is whirling, like wheel spokes disappearing in the speed of the rotation. She feels conspicuous in her agitation. She watches his face light up. The girl is very young and her extravagant high heels give a kind of precarious drama to her movements. She has a mane of blonde hair with a ribbon and a rose in it. She is like the update, the new improved model of female beauty. She and Josh kiss on the mouth. Exchange wide smiles. When they walk away they are so close that their hips brush. Zinnia remembers that physical compulsion for contact with the lover in her own body. Then she feels an unexpected tide of triumphant dislike for Josh sweep through her. And realises she can't remember the last time he made her feel better about herself.

# 9

When Josh enters the living room after his date it is an effort for her to keep the distaste from her face. Made all the more difficult that she knows the light in his eyes, the smile with which he greets her have their inspiration elsewhere.

"Productive day?" she asks, not rising from the sofa.

"Not bad. Knackered though." He takes off his shoes before leaning over to kiss her on the cheek, both acts part of an automated ritual. His big toe pokes through a hole in his yellow and green school socks. This man whose pants and socks she has washed for nine years.

She imagines she can smell the other woman's secretions on his skin, in his hair. She is avid for irritation and deems him smug with his secret. But she also enjoys the power of her clairvoyance. It makes him seem small and a bit pathetic which is how she needs to see him at the moment. She finds herself staring at his hands, hands that have cavorted inside the clothes of another woman and all her dislike of him centres on his fingers. She tells him about Felix. That she has given him a week off from school.

"This is the problem. You spoil him. You always let him get his way. How will he ever man up if you're mollycoddling him all the time? He goes to school and that's the end of it. Even if I have to drive him there myself. I know you think I've got no right to overrule you because he isn't mine but I've been a good father to him and I think of him now as my own blood."

It takes her aback, his anger. Anger, currently, is surely her prerogative. What right does he have to be angry? Guilt should be his lot. And anyway, the way he talks to Felix, the depth of his engagement with his son often of little more input than a dog whistle. But she remains silent. Recently they watched a film together about Ted Hughes and Sylvia Plath. "Thank heavens you're not like her," he had said at one point. It had irritated her, his complacency, the implication he could take her for granted. As if he was saying she was incapable of explosive emotion. But perhaps she is. Perhaps she is so well-defended that her true emotions no longer breach her fortifications?

Tonight, it's as though she has come out of a coma. And this man who she ought to recognise as her husband has become a stranger, like someone who has pushed in front of her in a queue or stolen her taxi. She wonders if it's more her vanity than her heart that has been wounded. Sometimes of late the opening refrain of a song has buffeted her into reclaiming for an instant a former emotional incarnation of herself. Always she is aware of a diminishment having taken place from then to now, a waning of resources. And then she always realises that it is emotion rather than time that charts the continuity of a life. She remembers once reading about protons and how they leap about without ever occupying intervening space. She saw a wisdom in that. When there is no emotion time stops happening and leaves in its wake little more than an intervening space. She herself has been living in a kind of intervening space for too long. Time has begun running backwards as much as forwards.

She expects Josh to announce his intention of showering before going to bed but he doesn't. He is quite happy to bring the smell of his transgression into her bed, rub it into her sheets.

Josh is gently snoring when she enters the bedroom. She closes the door noisily behind her and turns on the light. When Josh blinks open his eyes she says, "I know you're having an affair."

# 10

"I know you're having an affair."

She watches alarm sweep up into his eyes and then watches his efforts to hide it.

"What are you talking about? What's the time anyway?"

"You're having an affair."

He picks up his phone on the bedside table. "It's three o'clock in the morning, Zinnia."

"Did you hear what I said?"

"You're not making any sense." He performs his third theatrical yawn. She can sense how quickly, how urgently his brain is processing possibilities. Straining to satisfy himself she could not possibly possess any foolproof evidence of his transgression. "Are you seriously asking me if I'm having an affair?"

"Are you?"

"Of course I'm not. How on earth have you got that crazy idea into your head?"

"You tell me."

"Tell you what? You wake me up at three in the morning… I don't get it. All right, we haven't been getting on great lately but that's not all my fault. You've been pretty distant. I know your dad died and that's upset you. And I admit I've been a bit distracted by the stresses of work lately…"

"So you're not having an affair?"

"No. Of course I'm not having an affair. I wouldn't dream of having an affair."

Dashes of rain patter on and streak the window pane, as if to commemorate and fix the present moment. It doesn't surprise her how brazenly he can lie. Solution, to him, is always something expedient and of the moment. She catches a glimpse of him in the mirror. It's as if he already exists in a different medium. As if she has already removed him into a realm behind glass.

"Okay, let's leave it at that," she says.

"Can you stop looking at me like that?"

"I can't help how I look at you."

"Come to bed, Zinnia. I'm sorry about your father. I really am."

She feels her throat contract and the tears well up.

# 11

The taxi pulls up outside Gare de Bercy. Felix asks questions throughout its stop-start passage along the wide congested boulevards of Paris. It is a long time since he has been so alert, so curious. His excitement makes Zinnia feel like a good mother again.

He is quick to retrieve his bag from the taxi's trunk. There has been a thoughtfulness about his instincts all day. Zinnia announces her need for coffee and he goes charging off ahead into the station to locate a place where it can be procured.

Felix waits for her at the kiosk. The woman behind the counter is smiling at him, waiting for him to explain himself. She strings together more mysterious words. He grins back at her, as if she is an animal in a zoo.

"What do you want?" Zinnia asks.

"What are you having?"

"Coffee. And I'll get a couple of baguettes for the journey. Want some crisps too?"

"Can I have coffee?"

"No. Have some of that orange muck."

"I don't want that orange muck."

"How about the red muck then?"

"I want what you're having."

"Right. But if you keep me awake all night chattering and bouncing about I'll move to another compartment."

"Another couchette you mean."

Zinnia takes her disposable cup of café au lait outside the station. She wants to smoke.

"I've never seen you sit on the pavement before, Mum."

"You've never seen me in Paris before. Does it embarrass you?"

"No."

"You going to join me?"

Felix sits down beside her. He watches her carefully so he can copy everything she does – shake the little packet of sugar while holding it at a corner between forefinger and thumb, stir in the sugar with the plastic stick, place the discarded items neatly down on the pavement by her side.

"Will we have other people sleeping in our couchette?"

"Yes. Probably."

The train is three hours late. Even Felix's excitement begins to wilt and sour during the delay. There is the sense of being expelled from any active part in the unfurling of life while the wait prolongs itself. The passengers waiting for the Paris-Florence-Rome night train are now easily distinguishable: a theft of assurance, of orientation, of identity even has taken place in their demeanour; they shuffle closer together, exchanging recriminations and tired glances; they begin to resemble a disenfranchised straggle of refugees.

Zinnia thinks about the war. Finds she is able to envisage a similar scenario to the one she is now a part of at some railway station in 1941 and feels, with a rasp of fortifying tenderness, how protective she would be towards her son. The ghost dance shirt is in her bag; it has become one of her most precious possessions. The thing she most fears losing. Its power over her is irrefutable. It is making her think back. Something she has avoided doing for a long time. Now it is taking her back too, back to Italy.

Zinnia is nervous about boarding the train. Not to know how the mind is going to react is a terrifying thing. But the panic seems contained. Not preparing to rise up like steam in a kettle coming to the boil. It is a sleeping presence locked inside a vault at the back of her mind. She and Felix share the compartment with a Brazilian hairdresser and a French chessmaster on his circuitous way to Macedonia for a tournament. Felix keeps shaking her arm, asking irrelevant questions while she speaks Italian to the Brazilian boy. It is the first time she has spoken Italian for years. There is a delight when she finds words coming easily back to her, like a collection of precious things discovered at the bottom of an old box.

When the train gathers speed and a guard has collected passports, the men help her pull out the ladder and then begin making their makeshift beds. They take off their shoes and a faint boyish odour of sweating feet overlays the smell of humid upholstery. Zinnia and Felix are on the top bunks. She has to tell Felix off for continually finding an excuse to climb up and down the metal rungs.

The rhythm of the train vibrates up through her feet, along the insides of her thighs, rocking her this way and that. She staggers past the long line of compartments with drawn blinds. Landscapes of fields and small clusters of buildings hurtle past outside like fragments of songs never sung in their entirety. She feels somehow more a part of God's plan. Then she inwardly smiles to herself because she doesn't know what she means by that. She locks herself inside the rocking bathroom. It smells of urine – disarmingly pleasant in its power to evoke a quick blur of old pictures, youthful memories. She lights a cigarette and watches herself smoke it in the mirror.

When she returns to her bunk and stretches out with her hands behind her head the train seems to tilt to one side as it climbs a bank. Suddenly the moon appears directly in her line of vision from behind a scrum of black clouds. For a moment it shines down at her. Then it vanishes inexplicably out of sight. She props herself up on one elbow, looking up in the sky for it. It isn't there anymore. It is as if the train is rocketing through space and has already left it light years behind.

She wraps herself in the provided sheet and blanket. The vision of Felix asleep on the bunk opposite takes her back to when he was the swell of her belly which she held as she walked; to when she felt the awakening of his life against the bones and fat of her body. She recalls the moments of self-doubt, the stirrings of fear he caused her before she knew his face. And how all those doubts had been swept away the first moment she and Felix had looked at each other; how she felt she would never now have the desire to look at anything else ever again in her life.

Zinnia drifts back into sleep.

A wash of light enters the carriage as the train pulls into a station. She can see herself on the dark glass. Her face super-imposed on a background of oleander shrubs and a palm tree. Translucently pearl pale, bloodless, she looks, as someone might distantly remember her. The train moves forward then comes to an abrupt halt. There is a crunching jolt as of thick ice cracking underfoot. The night's wide silence is broken by the sound of running feet on the marble platform and excitable male Italian voices calling to each other. She moves her head to get a better view, a view of a secret world inhabited by a few men in uniform. She watches a solitary man take a bite of a sandwich and feels in her body how good everything tastes at this time of the night.

Footsteps trample past in the corridor; an excited dialogue accompanies them.

The train begins moving again. The air coming through the partially open window has a fecund quality as of the earthy part of roots. She shivers and feels herself glow into an exhilarating fullness of feeling, a broader sympathy.

She falls asleep again and then awakes to the sun coming up over cornfields and she feels slightly sick and dizzy because her body has assimilated the rhythm of the train and the iron engine noise. The glass, no longer dark, no longer throws her own reflection back at her. There are olive trees outside and the imagined smell of their bark and silvered leaves brings with it the first unfurling of some new imperative she feels coiled up within her. Her whole body with a joyful shout knows it is back in Italy.

# 12

The gracious choreography of Piazza della Signoria. For a moment it is like standing transfixed at the centre of the world. Then a note of sadness arrives, a moment when the back of her neck feels suddenly vulnerable and she has to press her hand there. Because of all the years that have gone by since she was last here, all the hurtling elapsed time, the loneliness it has left in its wake.

Felix stands in the spray from the Neptune fountain. He shuffles about finding the spot where he will get most wet. Zinnia takes a photo of him. In the photo Felix is hugging his llama. She hadn't noticed how much support he seeks from his toy animal until she looks at the digital image. Is it normal for a ten year old boy to hug a cuddly toy? As a mother, she is constantly questioning what is normal and wanting it for her son; constantly trying to be more normal herself as a mother. Sometimes it is this censorious monitoring of her natural inclinations that makes her resent motherhood.

They wander around the piazza together, intruding into the snapshots of other tourists. She is anxious that Felix should feel on his skin how beautiful everything is. She can't feel it for herself unless she feels he does too. In front of the bronze Perseus she says, "Look at that, Felix!"

"Why has he cut her head off?"

"That's Medusa. She could turn men to stone just by looking at them."

She is trying to help him make memories. Perhaps he will

one day recall this moment and it will be a stepping-stone of sorts. She perceives no sign though that he is registering what he looks at. It makes her feel momentarily lonely that she has no idea what details of a day, what pieces of information he retains.

She notices memorials of the war. There are lots of them, marble plaques that are too prosaic and curt to convey the sadness of their stories. There is a plaque in Piazza Santa Maria Novella commemorating the Jews transported from the prison there to the death camps. She has never liked this piazza. The church and the loggia at either end should lend to it a bracing enchantment. But the wide square with its trampled down grass has an oppressive unclean fume about it, an atmosphere that rasps over her skin like the lick of a cat's tongue.

She stops half way across Ponte Vecchio and points out to Felix the vista of the river and the fairytale arches of Ponte Santa Trinita.

"That bridge was blown up during the war. Can you imagine anyone wanting to destroy something so beautiful?"

"Who blew it up?" he asks with a flicker of interest.

"The Nazis," she says, lowering the volume of her voice and glancing around for potential Germans among the knots of tourists.

The word still means nothing to him. He has forgotten what she told him about his great grandmother. Zinnia tries not to become disheartened. If nothing else surely it is a relief to change the pattern of his days? Children are able to leave behind what isn't part of the present moment. Perhaps that's why they love to cut pictures out of magazines, isolate them from context. He has already forgotten how unhappy he was at school.

"Where are we going now?" he asks.

They are climbing the steep narrow road of Costa San Giorgio. The incline of the stones of different shapes, the green paint and pink stucco of the tilting houses. Reflected in a car window she sees a campanile, a medieval wall frescoed with blossoming vines. For a moment it's as if she is her younger self experiencing Italy for the first time.

"I'm going to show you my house when I lived in Florence all those years ago."

"How many years ago?" says Felix. He is walking backwards in front of her. She remembers, with a start, that Milo often walked backwards in front of her when he wanted to tease her about something.

"Hundreds and hundreds," she says, ruffling his hair.

It occurs to Zinnia that she has no idea where she herself was conceived. Is it a significant piece of information? She decides it probably is. She gives a moment's thought to Felix's father. She can't quite think him into being but she remembers how easily she became what he thought of her. The excitement and fearful resistance she knew as she took shape as herself in those years. Is he still here in Florence? It's a question she has not let herself ask as yet. But it's there, somewhere in her neural corridors, creating mysterious chemicals. For a moment she feels as if her naked body is pressed against the glass of a full-length mirror.

At the fork in the road where Costa Scarpuccia begins its twisting descent down towards the river, the dome of the Duomo, the tower of Palazzo Vecchio and the hills that cradle Florence appear like a postcard of themselves. Zinnia takes Felix's hand and runs with him down the slope until they reach the gravelled forecourt of a church. Next to the church, covered in jasmine and wisteria, is the high outer wall of the palazzo where she once rented an apartment.

The church is now some kind of pristine business centre. It has an automatic sliding glass door. Her shoulders stiffen as she walks past it. She suspects a ten-year-old boy would prefer an automatic glass door to a heavy wooden one. Is the world becoming more childish?

She remembers now what she told Milo she couldn't remember.

*"I'd like to be this rain, falling on you, darkening your hair," he said, clasping her around the waist from behind. They were crossing Ponte Santa Trinita at four in the morning.*

"*I've got to take these shoes off. They're killing my feet.*"

*Holding onto him for support, she removed her shoes.*

"*Be careful you don't step on any glass,*" *he said.*

"*I'm always careful,*" *she said, fanning out her skirt by clasping it at either side and treading on the tips of her toes like a ballerina.*

"*When we get home I'm going to wash your feet.*"

Extraordinary really that these words brought Felix into existence. *When we get home I'm going to wash your feet.*

He was angry the next day when she faked amnesia. "*I don't remember what happened. I was so drunk that it's all a blur in my head.*"

"*So everything is to be swept under the carpet,*" *he said.*

"*I don't even know what everything is...but no, I don't want to sweep under the carpet. I just want to get things straight in my head.*"

"*Perhaps this is something which cannot be got straight in the head? Why not try feeling for once? Your mind always refuses the events of your body.*"

"*What do you mean?*"

"*How about if you actually started living inside yourself a little more? If you're not going to feel how are you going to know what to think? Isn't it in the nature of feeling to evolve thought?*"

He was angry the next day when she faked amnesia but also perhaps secretly relieved. As if some of his anger was directed at himself, at the discovery of a disinclination within himself to continue what they had started. His company for three years had the effect of restoring everything to the liveliness of its original colour. She guessed her presence had the same effect on him. But she needed to think of him as bodiless. She was frightened of his hands. Frightened of what the touch of them threatened to bring into being. Maybe he needed to think of her as bodiless too. Maybe he was as frightened of the touch of her hands as she was of his.

Zinnia points up to a green shuttered window.

"That is where you were made, Felix. In that room."

Felix frowns.

She grins at his discomfort.

"One day you might be glad I told you," she says. For a moment she is tempted to reveal to him who his real father is.

Back in the hotel Felix joins his friends in one of the virtual realms he spends much of his time in at home. His best friend in the world is someone he has never laid eyes on. She is called Wagtail 77. They build things together in AfterLife or fly virtual planes together and crash them. Felix shows Zinnia clips of his crashing planes on YouTube and is impatient with her for not complimenting him on having received 74 views.

"Why do you have to always crash the planes?"

"I dunno. It's more fun."

"But you made these films?"

"Yes, Mum."

He tells Zinnia more about Wagtail 77 and their virtual adventures together than he has ever told her about school or his classmates. He shows her his AfterLife avatar.

"Why did you choose a female avatar?"

"Dunno. Just did. I made all her clothes."

Zinnia has difficulty following his language. What are widgets, what is rezzing, what are UV maps, what is scripting language? Childhood for her was tactile contact, holding hands and running and skipping and dancing on solid ground.

"Some say this is where we'll predominantly live in the future," she muses. "Online. And that already our online existence is a kind of afterlife."

Felix blows up his fringe.

Zinnia has not suffered a panic attack since being in Florence; has not known the shame of swallowing one of her little blue pills. But neither has she yet been brave enough to cross one of the open bridges. She wonders idly if Felix has noticed her aversion to crossing the river by any other bridge than Ponte Vecchio. How much do children notice, how many dots do they join up? Ponte Santa Trinita was once a moment in her life that made her feel blessed and lucid and part of the world's beauty. It is denied her now by a quirk in her chemistry. She imagines telling her younger self that she is frightened of walking over bridges above water. Younger Zinnia looks back at her with an awkward perplexity that makes her feel she is a bit mad.

# 13

Their home for the next three weeks is a self-contained out-building in the landscaped garden of an 18th century villa on the Ligurian coast. A green door in the garden wall opens onto the rocks by the sea. It was at night, when Felix was asleep, that Zinnia first adventured through the green door. On the other side was the great black sweep of the sea. She clambered over rocks and sat against the trunk of a pine tree. She could smell the salt of the sea behind the earthy fragrance of the pine resin and licked her wrist, enjoying the taste of brine on her skin. The high moon resembled her childhood moons when she felt the future coiled up inside her like a sleeping spider. She watched the changing forms of the waves and flashes of suddenly height-ened light. She could hear the tide sucking at the fossilised rocks beneath her, swirling in and out of hidden crevices and secret underground channels.

Tonight they are to meet their landlady for the first time. Lady Lydia Wentworth lives in the villa. Zinnia walks with Felix through the garden. Fireflies perforate the darkness with their elusive watery lights. Lady Lydia is holding a chewed chicken wing when she holds open the back door for Zinnia and Felix to enter.

"*Buonasera*," says Zinnia.

"I'm most awfully sorry but we don't speak Italian here," says Lady Lydia, grease glistening on her chin.

She leads Zinnia and Felix into a musty drawing room where the lighting is dim and one lamp keeps flickering on and off, repeatedly snatching away the shadows it throws on the walls.

"This is my son and heir, Hugh."

Hugh is obese. About thirty-five years old. Two buttons have come undone on his shirt and a tract of his swollen stomach is visible through the gash. The blue transparency of his flesh looks like the skin of a drowned corpse.

"So why have you come to Italy, Zinnia? It's not, I hope, the myth of the Latin Lover that has lured you here. If I were you I'd be beware of good-looking men. Good-looking men are dangerous. They're more likely to understand a woman, which is the last thing a woman wants. What do you think, Hugh? Do you think Zinnia is here to sow some wild oats?" Lady Lydia perches forward on a thin-legged chair adorned with capricious arabesques and whorls. Her green staring eyes, abetted in their devilry by an arching eyebrow, bore into Zinnia with disarming divination. Over the disused fireplace a portrait of her as a sultry wild-eyed siren brutally makes plain how much damage the years have done to her face: there is no trace in the painting of the furrows of cynical asperity around her mouth; only her finely chiselled high cheekbones have retained their hieratic grace. "Or has that expression gone out of coinage? You see, we are very much a world unto ourselves here."

"A world unto ourselves," grins her son Hugh, slumping down further on the sofa. Every time he moves a drift of dust rises from the stained gold cushions. By his side is a plate smeared with a red and yellow haemorrhage of sauces which Lady Lydia sometimes uses as an ashtray.

"Tell me the truth," she says, "don't you find England simply ghastly nowadays. It's the worst."

"The worst," repeats Hugh.

"I've always loved Italy," says Zinnia, watching ash topple from the cigarette Lady Lydia holds in her trembling hand into her lap.

"But I expect you enjoy London. The drugs and nightclubs. If I were young again I would not have children. One receives little gratitude for the sacrifices one makes. Of course Hugh here is a good boy but my daughters are just waiting for me to die. Between you and me, I've cut them out of my will. But tell me about your own predicament. You're a friend of my sister's daughter, I hear. Don't you find her husband to be a preposterous man?"

"Preposterous man," says Hugh.

"I did warn my sister not to marry him. There was something of the stray dog about him. Always sniffing about under tables so to speak. But my sister always did have a weak spot for maimed animals. She once brought a wounded sparrow home and then cried all night and told tales when I gave it to the cat. She still brings that up, even now. Do you have any sisters?"

"No. I'm an only child."

"Lucky you. Sisters are the worst. But before you go, I would like to ask you something. What did you think of Filiberto, the gardener? You met him when you arrived, didn't you? Did you find him rather sinister? You see it's Hugh's contention that he's probably an axe murderer. I haven't told you, have I, Hugh? Filiberto was doing his disco dancing in front of the mirror again. I went to ask him about the parsley."

"About the parsley," echoes Hugh knowingly as if his mother is speaking in a private code.

"He had the music up so loud he didn't hear me enter. He was gyrating in front of the mirror wearing nothing but pink underpants. This is what he was doing – " Lady Lydia staggers drunkenly to her feet and thrusting out her pelvis makes erratic mating gestures with her arms. "Oh, he was absolutely eating himself up in the mirror – "I am irresistible," he was telling himself, "I am the gold at the end of the rainbow." Of course when I was young, men probably weren't quite so narcissistic. Things though have to change, I suppose. One just wishes it wasn't always for the worse."

Hugh is now playing a game on his mobile phone. His greasy fat fingers with bitten down nails surprisingly agile on the keys.

The acoustics of the eighteenth-century drawing room echo the retching of staccato bleeps and bips. The concentration on his face is admirable in a way. It was probably with a similar level of concentration that the theory of relativity was formulated.

"Perhaps he had known I was there all the time?" After stubbing out her cigarette in the carnage of ketchup and mustard and lighting another one she says: "Wouldn't that rather confirm my suspicions? Are you winning, Hugh?" she asks with unconcealed disdain.

"You can't win, Mother, not really," says Hugh, still frantically punching keys. "You can only score points. I suppose I could win if someone else will play."

"Don't ask me to play. The cynicism of such games appals me. When I was a child we invented our own worlds - worlds where high endeavour ensured glory and triumph. Children ought to feel on top of things when they're playing. Just think of the damage you might be doing to your character, Hugh. Games like that might lead you to believe that nothing's worth the effort."

"Like you, you mean, Mother."

"Why don't you play with him, Fred? I'm sure Hugh would like that even though he's too shy to say."

"Actually, I rather fear Fred is called Felix," says Hugh, censoriously.

"I think Joan, my secretary will be arriving soon. Oh well, it can't be helped. I hope she settled you in. I expect you noticed what a sly woman she is. Always trying to get her money's worth. I don't mind so much that she's cheating me; it's her conversation I can't stand. Aren't you dead yet, Hugh?"

"You get three lives."

"Thank heavens that is not the case in nature," she says pouring herself another glass of gin. "So what will you do, Zinnia?"

"I'm actually looking for someone who knew my great grandfather. His name is Max. Massimo, I would imagine. That's all I know."

"So it isn't Shelley? We thought you'd be looking for Shelley. Didn't we, Hugh?"

"Shelley the poet?"

"Percy Bysshe," says Hugh, facetiously.

"This, I imagine, is a wonderful place for a young person wishing to play at being Shelley. I sometimes wish Hugh would play more at being Shelley. Hugh collects butterflies. Don't ask me why. Why *do* you collect butterflies, Hugh? Why don't you write poetry like Zinnia here?"

"I think you've got the wrong end of the stick," says Zinnia, struggling to repress a broad grin.

"Wrong end of the stick," repeats Hugh, getting to his feet. There is a stink of singed hair as Lady Lydia lights another cigarette with her flame thrower lighter.

"How I do wish my daughters were more like you. You're so sensible. One of them has a faddish eating disorder and the other stabs herself with syringes and screwdrivers. I think they're both lesbians. Do you think that's my fault? Or do you think it's all a question of genes? I have my doubts. Virginia Houghton's son Quentin is gay and I think Virginia was responsible. She couldn't abide her husband and shared a bed with poor Quentin until he was eight. That is surely not healthy. The idea of sleeping with Hugh is, well, simply repulsive. I was just saying, dear, that the idea of sleeping with you is repulsive."

Hugh, re-entering the room with a huge plate of microwaved oven chips and a red stain around his puckered mouth, smiles as if he has received a compliment.

Out in the garden the night air is thick with hoarded scent.

"Are they for real?"

"For real," says Felix, imitating Hugh.

Zinnia bursts into laughter, tickles Felix and picks him up. They are happy conspirators together, mother and son. In the mornings she throws open all the windows onto the water-coloured light and heightening scents of the garden. Sleepily, smelling of toothpaste and their own body heat, they get in each other's way in the kitchen and in the hallway leading down to the small bathroom. She and Felix share such a silently eloquent map of understandings that talk is often mere decoration. They walk out onto the gravel path under the trees, wait while the huge electronic wooden doors creak slowly open and go to a local bar where, on a terrace overlooking the sea, he has a hot chocolate and a chocolate brioche and an elderly woman with crooked teeth and eyes bright with memories makes an expansive fuss of him. Felix needs ritual, repetition; needs evidence that things remain in place. She herself has never realised how much happiness there is in habit.

# 14

The crescent of beach is half sand and half shingle, with folded sun umbrellas, their bright colours soiled with age. Zinnia watches Felix play with three Italian children. Sometimes they all charge off together into the water and become smudges of bright colour against the outcrop of rocks. The top notes of their voices ring out with a zest of cleanliness. Italian as a language, she thinks, suits children with its singsong cadences and rising lingering inflections, its quick swinging gait and easy adaptability to argument, to passionate outbursts.

Initially Felix was not able to join in the games without continually calling out to her –

*Look, Mum!*

*Did you see that, Mum?*

*I beat him, Mum.*

*Mum? Mum! She thought she was going to catch me but she didn't!*

It worries her how eager he is to prove to her his worth. His smile always jeopardised by uncertainty. He insatiably seeks her attention. She is his point of convergence. As if nothing is settled until she is connected to it. Has she made him too dependent on her point of view? Zinnia's own mother gave off an embalmed fussiness like flowers wrapped in cellophane. She didn't allow any feeling that had a swell and a momentum to it. Zinnia was determined to break the pattern. Her aim has always been simply to make Felix feel loved.

The Italian children have now made him forget her presence.

He no longer keeps exiting from the moment. The children are managing to communicate through sign language and patience. Two dogs join in with the games on the beach and Felix doesn't even seem to mind them.

Later they walk through the maze of narrow sloping alleys where the houses are the colours of ripe fruit. A lizard, the same colour as the blistered green shutters, shoots off into invisibility. Now and again there is a vista of the sea, motionless with a glittering silver bloom over it. There are cats and potted geraniums everywhere. The doorways of the houses have pebbled mosaics. Zinnia is looking for a bar. The woman who serves them breakfast told her about it when Zinnia asked if she knew a man called Massimo who was alive during the war. She sees no bar. Every set of steps, every sloping alley leads up to the pink stucco church on the precipice or down to the small harbour and its creaking fishing boats. She stops to ask a grim heavy-set woman dressed in charity shop clothes who is leaning out of a window. The woman looks down at her with a grimace of mistrust. The dusty peach coloured façade of her house is like the otherworldly pigment of an early Renaissance fresco. Zinnia has already sensed Lady Lydia isn't popular in the village and, by association, neither is she. Or wouldn't be were it not for Felix. The people here love children. At siesta the children all play in the main piazza while the largely elderly population bring out chairs from their houses and sit watching and petting them. This woman too softens when she sees Felix.

"*Cerco un bar che si chiama Giorgio,*" she says. Nervousness starches her accent into a caricature of an English woman speaking Italian. She has difficulty understanding what the woman says. She's talking in a local dialect.

Eventually she finds the bar. It is squeezed between two houses in a back alley. A large shadowy glass-fronted room that probably hasn't been decorated since the war. Lots of old men are playing cards at a table. They are all smoking and drinking grappa. They are engaged in a good-natured argument. There is the vigour of the sea tides in the way they develop the logic of their arguments. Zinnia, intimidated, takes Felix's hand for support and enters. It is moments like this that make her realise how little progress she has made in overcoming her girlhood shyness.

"*Cerco un uomo che si chiama Max che viveva qui durante la guerra,*" she says.

Her mention of the war immediately gets everyone's interest. They look at her with heightened interest but also added hostility. Zinnia is reminded the Italians were allied with the Nazis for most of the war.

"*Non c'è oggi. Forse domani,*" says one of the men.

She is relieved to leave.

That evening she and Felix are sitting beneath a canopy of bougainvillea, jasmine and myrtle on the terrace of a restaurant in the hills between Tellaro and Fiascherino. The three tall waiters, deftly juggling the hand-painted plates and carafes of wine, waltz in figures of eight around the ten or so tables. Now and again they stand sharing a joke by the entrance. In a moment of boredom Zinnia checks her phone. There is a Facebook message from Milo Cristellotti. Her heart leaps and begins thumping much as it does before a panic attack. Her Milo though was called Wilson. She is fearful of opening the message.

"Is that from Dad?" asks Felix.

For a moment she is taken aback by her son's divination but she quickly composes herself. "Do you miss him? Do you miss your dad?"

"Sometimes."

The shadows of bats circling in the glow of a lamp flit across the paving stones of the terrace.

She doesn't open the message until Felix is in bed. She doesn't open the message until she has changed into her white nightdress. Sand falls from her clothes when she takes them off; sand crunches beneath her on the sheets when she gets into bed. *I never stop wondering how you are.* That's all he writes. She writes back guardedly. He replies, almost immediately. She learns he is in Sri Lanka. Making a film about an elephant orphanage. She had forgotten he went to film school in Rome before she met him. She learns he fell out with his father after he betrayed his mother for a younger woman. "That's why I now use my mother's maiden name." She doesn't ask if he is married. She learns he will be back in Italy soon. "Give me your number and I'll call when I arrive," he writes.

Then Josh calls.

# 15

Zinnia doesn't bother to change her clothes or reapply her makeup before going to meet Josh at La Spezia station. She is finished with flattering him. Even her attire has now been dragged into the argument she is having with him.

"I've booked you a hotel," she tells him after he kisses her and ruffles Felix's hair.

He is hurt, she sees, but he also smells of alcohol. She doesn't want him staying with her and Felix. Italy, like areas of her childhood, is a part of her world she has always kept secret from her husband. These are places she goes to renew her virginity.

There is an argument of subdued rancour, repressed bitterness in the taxi. "We don't talk anymore; we interrogate each other," she says. The tension in the white car makes her shoulder muscles ache. She has the detachment to feel embarrassed on behalf of the driver. For a while the sea is at their side, black glass with sliding discs of lustre. Then they are up in the hairpin twists of the hills. The lemon trees, the oleander shrubs, the terraced olive groves, the grey stone walls, shrouded in darkness. The headlights tunnel into blackness, stirring into life ghostly visions of what lies ahead, like phantasmagoria in a crystal ball.

Now they are having dinner, in a trattoria in the main piazza at Tellaro.

He looks around for a waiter. He wants more wine. Josh likes to project himself as a man used to getting his own way. He is vain about his ability to flag down life and make it obey his commands. His steady hand, his facility of creating order and security, was what had attracted her to him once upon a time. He could fold life into an easy manageable shape. His confidence though has a crack in it now: another snub and she feels the crack will widen. She thus finds herself willing the waiter to respond every time he lifts his hand - the closest she has got to a tender protective feeling for him tonight.

"Well, Felix. Perhaps it's time you knew that I'm not your father."

Felix is twirling spaghetti round his fork. He gives little sign of registering the words, no apparent thought to their meaning. His thoughts, if he has any, are on not drawing attention to himself.

"Felix is learning Italian," she says.

"*Buono*," says Josh and empties his wine glass. "Say something to me in Italian, Felix," he says.

"Ciao," says Felix, after catching his mother's eye uneasily.

"Any idiot can say that, Felix."

Felix looks suitably contrite, for form's sake, as if automatically following a grown-up order. It isn't the manifestation of a real hurt. She sees Josh doesn't have the power to hurt him, not really. It surprises her.

A waiter finally arrives. Josh flashes his gold signet ring at him as he gives his order. Through the serving hatch Zinnia catches sight of someone scouring a pan in the kitchen. An Asiatic man with a scar on his cheek wearing an apron smeared with grease. Above the sink is a mother and child image. There are mother and child images everywhere you look in Italy. Mother and child with no trace of a father, a husband.

Josh leans forward, resting both elbows on the chequered tablecloth bearing fresh wine stains.

"Why don't we talk about the father?"

Zinnia wipes her mouth with her napkin.

"Shall I tell you both the first significant memory I have of my father?" he says, screwing his napkin up into a nugget, a missile that might now be thrown. "Are you interested? It's of him missing a six-inch putt on a golf course. The ball, I remember, followed the curve of the hole but tantalisingly refused to disappear from sight. Something in my father at that moment snapped. He looked up at the sky and then began wreaking his vengeance on the putting green, hacking up the pristine turf with his club. Everyone just stared at him, doing their best to hide their secret guilty pleasure. That's the first real memory I have of my father. Out of interest, Felix, what's your first memory of me?"

"I remember you making me a toboggan," he says.

"Did I?"

"Yes."

"Why did you take him away from school for three weeks?"

"You know why."

"Where's the loo, Mum?"

She looks around, disregarding the candlelit faces intent on private conversation, then points to a wooden door in a far corner.

"Do you want me to come with you?"

"Oh, for god's sake. Can't the boy even take a piss on his own?"

Her body arches with an inward ache as she watches Felix get to his feet and wander off towards the bathroom. With how much anxiety she follows his forays out into the world, how little confidence she has in his safe return.

"Why are you being so obnoxious?"

"Me? I come out to see you and you pack me off to some vulgar hotel."

"I saw you with your new girlfriend. Outside the British Museum."

"Outside the British Museum? What are you talking about? I haven't been to the bloody British Museum since I was a child." His stupefaction is badly acted; so too his dramatisation of revelation when it arrives: "Oh, you saw me with my secretary. Ellie. We had to meet a client in Russell Square."

"You asked her what colour underwear she was wearing, Josh."

"What are you talking about?"

"Felix and I were hiding underneath his bed when you came home that day. You had a phone call."

His guilty bewilderment will, she knows, make a humorous anecdote one day.

"How many women have you slept with during our marriage, Josh?"

He doesn't have to answer this question. Felix returns to the table. She is glad of the shield he provides. She wonders how often she has used her son for this purpose. And what effect it has on Felix. He keeps his eyes lowered. His body is tense, eager for flight. She is aware of his feet fidgeting under the table.

Zinnia notices a pubic hair on the tablecloth, a little token of menace curled like a spider before it stings. She feels her body go clammy. Then the spinning void sucks at her thoughts, overthrows her mind's familiar parameters, its laws of organisation. Her heart begins beating too fast. The world around her recedes as though someone has turned the volume down. She is left floundering in what seems a stark black place of origin. She gets hurriedly to her feet and locks herself in the bathroom. When the panic passes she again doubts her ability to care for her son, to bring him up without help. How can she when she can no longer even trust her own mind?

# 16

"Let's go back in time," says Josh.

"What do you mean?"

Not much more than an hour has passed since he and Zinnia and Felix left the restaurant. Felix is in bed, under the pale blue duvet in the split-level loft above the sitting room. She and Josh have to go into her bedroom so as to not keep him awake with their talking. All the aggression has gone from Josh's voice. He is standing by the window which is glazed with his own reflection and the silhouette of the night outside. It has been ten years since Zinnia has had a bed that wasn't his too and she can sense that he is made shy by its independence of him.

"When you agreed to marry me…"

"I don't blame you for disliking me."

"I don't dislike you, Zee. And I'm sorry I was so obnoxious in the restaurant. The old demon took hold. Sometimes I can't help trying to live up to your worst idea of me."

"I thought everything would be easier if I didn't like you but I realise now that the opposite might be true."

"Be nice. Is that what you're saying?"

"You are nice, Josh. Most of the time."

"But you wouldn't have married me had you not been pregnant with someone else's child?"

"That's like saying you wouldn't have married me had I had a different figure or different memories."

"Is it?"

"I think so."

"We were always better at being friends than lovers."

"It hurt when you stopped being my friend."

"I wanted to be your lover. I didn't want to be your friend. The male ego and all that. I knew you weren't in love with me. I suppose I quite liked that to begin with. It was a challenge. You know how competitive I am. I need targets; I thrive on deadlines."

"You can make fun of that *now*," she says, smiling up at him.

"I also needed to think you were better than me."

"And now you've found out I'm not."

He looks unsure of himself, physically ill at ease. The cadence of his voice is checked in its usual easy clarity of tone by a thicket of hesitation. The only chair in the room is piled with books – books about Italy during the war and Felix's homework. There is nowhere else to sit except the bed, beside Zinnia. He has the look of someone who has lost his place in the world, the dumbfounded self-consciousness of the child left standing in a game of musical chairs. Zinnia realises how rarely he ever gave her an opportunity to feel sorry for him. Realises too that he was probably following some silent command of hers, as if she forbade him any outward displays of vulnerability, insisted on him always striding with confidence in advance of her, as solid and impermeable as armoured plating.

Josh walks over to her dressing table. She watches him cast his gaze over the bottles and tubes and tiny caskets, the strewed jewellery, the smudges of coloured dust on the wooden surface, the one or two fingerprints and misted patches on the glass.

"You're wrong about Felix," he says, addressing her image in the glass. "It's not true that I never loved him. I would have sacrificed my life for his. It's just that I always felt awkward around him. I could never work out if it was him or me. With hindsight it's almost as if he knew. Knew I wasn't his real father. He isn't at all like me. He's like you."

"He's much happier here."

"Who wouldn't be? This isn't the real world though, is it? It's a holiday place. It's all once-upon-a-time."

"The world doesn't have to be aggressive and bullying and frantic to be real. He's made friends here."

"Good. Have you told him I'm not his real father?"

"No. Not yet. The last thing he needs is another roof collapsing."

"I don't think he understood what I meant tonight when I said I was no longer his father. He probably thought I was referring to the fact that I'm no longer around. So is that why you've come to Italy? To find his real father?"

"No. I came here because Felix was unhappy where we were. And because I want to find out more about my grandmother."

"Are you really going to send me back to that squalid hotel?"

When they are in bed together he reaches out and touches her in the dark with an unaccustomed infusion of shyness. She registers in this touch all his youth of once upon a time, the early days of their marriage when he was avid for reassurance and compliments, when he brought her surprises and was happy to send himself up in exchange for the gift of her laughter. That period of bounty though was short-lived. She recalls how often she lied awake in the dark while he slept placidly beside her, his back to her, one hand screwed up into a fist and pressed against his cheek.

She nestles into his embrace but pretends to be asleep.

# 17

It both surprises and annoys Zinnia how nervous she is. She studies herself in a long green dress. She twists and contorts herself in front of the mirror. She reminds herself she never found Milo physically attractive. She studies herself in a long cadmium red dress. She gathers her long black hair up into a roguish beehive. She remembers how Milo used to tease her for making him feel so physically unattractive. "Like a slimy repulsive toad. But you know how that story turns out."

Milo steps off the bus. She sees herself diminished to fingernail size in the black glass of his sunglasses. Ten years and he's barely changed. She wants him to tell her the same thing. He doesn't. He says her name. She is surprised by how alien her name sounds on his lips, how vulnerable it makes her feel. He kisses her on either cheek. His lips leave a faint dew on her cheeks. Her own lips, she is sure, are more nervously dry. His eyes ask their first question of her face. She feels their probing for knowledge. Her body remembers how much bracing emotion she once took from his approval of her.

"Different shampoo but the strawberry lip gloss is still the same," he says.

They are finding it difficult to look at each other, to bring any sustained focus into their eyes. They slept in each other's arms; she told him she didn't want to repeat the experience and this, ten years later, is the next moment in their story. There is no sense whatsoever of continuity. The bridge back has been swept away. She pushes at her wedding ring with her thumb.

Realises what she is doing only when she sees him watching this reflex movement of her hand. He turns his attention to Felix. He shakes Felix's hand. She senses Felix likes this. Usually men ruffle his hair.

"So how old are you, Felix?" he asks.

"Ten."

Zinnia watches this first ever communion between father and son. The secret she possesses seems suddenly like a sorcerer's wand.

"Have you learned yet that everything meaningful in life is gravitational?" He gives Felix a big broad smile with some self-mockery in it and Felix smiles back. "You're very handsome, by the way."

"Shall we have a drink?"

"You didn't waste much time then," he says.

"What about you?" she says, fighting down an emotion she doesn't want him to see.

"Barren," he says. "No woman, no children. Haven't even managed a dog. Just me and my camera equipment."

Heat from the asphalt thieves up through her espadrilles. The scent of the hanging arabesques of flowering blossoms is enveloping. She sees Lady Lydia and Hugh enter the piazza. Hugh is in a wheelchair. Lady Lydia totters over on high heels.

"Poor Hugh has been raped by mosquitoes," she explains. "His ankle has swollen up like a bloated corpse. Mosquitoes don't seem to care much for my blood. Hugh blames it on the nicotine."

Hugh is performing stop start manoeuvres in the wheelchair.

"Mosquitoes have that clever trick of vanishing," Milo says. "It's like they can time travel. You're about to strike and then they simply aren't there in space and time any more. Their sudden disappearance makes you think you blinked or blacked out for a second. They create black holes."

"Oh, nature's constantly making fun of us. Mockery seems to be its raison d'être."

Milo is trying and even succeeding to some extent to charm Lady Lydia. He could always draw a charmed circle, a lively intimacy around himself and any women. It was a trick or a trait of his nature that contributed to her distrust of him.

At dinner, after he has booked into a *pensione*, Milo talks about conspiracy theories. Again Zinnia is reminded of why she distrusted him. He isn't grounded in the practicalities of life. Then he shows Felix footage of the elephant orphanage. Zinnia is pleased Felix has forgotten to bring his toy llama to the restaurant. Felix is clearly enchanted by the footage of the small elephants. "All of these elephants lost their parents to ivory hunters," he tells Felix. "If hunters continue to kill elephants at the current rate there will be no elephants left by the time you're sixty, Felix. This tiny chap here is called Faruk. Poor little thing is blind. And this one is Namar. She's limping because her foot was caught in a trap. She was my other favourite. She swallowed my phone. I thought it was a goner. And I was worried about her digestive system. But guess what happened? It came out her other end twenty-four hours later. In perfect working order! I left it by her to see if she'd do it again. She did. It felt intimately personal, not to mention mischievous, this game she was playing with me. I can't tell you how much I missed those elephants when we left. Almost as much as I missed your mum when she left."

Zinnia feels the sand furring the hairs on her arms.

"I've never grown up very much, Felix. When out in the world, I'm always a bit uncomfortable, always impatient to return to my own solitary world. Do you feel like that?"

Felix gives a slight shrug of his shoulders.

"Is that how you feel now?" Zinnia asks with a smile.

"The wonder of you was that I was never bored, never uncomfortable. I never wanted to be anywhere else when I was with you. Every night ended too soon. It's not often you can say that. I've found boredom is the killer in life. Find people and something to do that doesn't bore you. That's my advice, Felix."

"And you've found a job that doesn't bore you," says Zinnia. Her lips shine with the spiced oil in which the clams have been cooked.

"Next month I'm filming in America. I'm making a documentary about Pine Ridge. The Lakota reservation. The Lakota land has been polluted by uranium mines. There are 380 uranium leases on Native American land as opposed to only four on public land. Why are you looking so breathlessly surprised?"

"Oh my god! That's so unreal. You won't believe this! I've recently discovered Felix and I have Lakota blood," she says. "Or that's how it would appear. I've come here to find out." She tells him the story of her grandmother and about the ghost dance dress she now has in her possession.

"Do you have it with you? I'd love to see it."

"I'll let you see it in exchange for a favour."

"What's the favour?"

"The only way of meeting the man I need to speak to is to go into this bar full of old men and I know this is pathetic of me but they intimidate me. So if you come to the bar with me tomorrow I'll let you see the dress."

"Deal," he says.

"Do you know anything about this ghost dance?"

His phone rings in the middle of her question. She watches him emotionally leave her as he checks his phone. He gets up to answer and walks off beyond hearing range. She finds she is jealous of this other life he has. It's not a passionate emotion. More a sadness at the realisation of how fragile is intimacy.

"You like him, don't you?" she says to Felix.

"He's kinda cool."

"Kinda cool?" she mocks.

"It was cool of him to look after the baby elephants."

"I'm not sure he was looking after them."

"Does he know Dad?"

"No. I don't think so. I knew him before I met your dad. Why did you ask that?"

"Dunno. What's the ghost dance?"

At that moment the ghost dance seems to Zinnia like the relationship of two people who never quite consummate the love they feel for each other.

# Part Three

## 1935-1945

My father worked as an insurance salesman. He offered people protection from the perils of the future.

You can tell a lot about a person by how much noise they make. Some people seem to think the world isn't paying them enough attention, so they increase the volume of their presence, they turn up the dials. My father never for one moment allowed you to forget he was nearby. Every sound he made was a loudspeaker announcement. He blew his nose or cleared his throat raucously, he groaned and grunted and yawned as if performing for an auditorium. He slammed cupboards and doors and stamped heavily on his heels from one room to another and clattered pans down on surfaces in the kitchen.

We're in England. Leeds. 1935. My father kept a framed photograph of Mussolini on the mantelpiece. More than once this caused an argument between my mother and father. Usually after guests had been to dinner. Visitors to the house always seemed to leave something behind when they left that made my parents critical of each other.

My father prided himself as a strict disciplinarian. Whenever I slouched at the dinner table he inserted a chessboard inside the back of my shirt. Every evening he made me read aloud thirty words from an Italian dictionary. And if, as I always did, I mispronounced any of them the chessboard was inserted inside the back of my shirt. My father was a short man but always stood with his shoulders thrown back as if he was being measured for a new suit. Everything about him was carefully measured. It was as if what he most prided himself on in his conversation was the precision of his punctuation. I have a memory of my father taking me to the zoo and clipping me around the ear because I felt sorry for the caged animals. He also disapproved of my new passion for drawing birds. There was another argument between my mother and father when I requested *The Illustrated Book of British Birds* for my birthday. My father forbade it on the grounds that it was cissy of me. "He's not a bloody girl," he said as if I wasn't in the room, listening.

My mother came to dislike the conspicuous long wire antennae in our small fenced garden. She maintained it looked suspicious. But my father prized his radio set above all other possessions and sat in his armchair listening to long wave Italian broadcasts every evening. My father was jubilant at the news that Mussolini had invaded a country I had never heard of. But at school afterwards and more and more frequently I was called an eyetie and a dago and shoved about in the playground. I began to blame my diminishing popularity not only on Mussolini but also on my father for his treacherous hero worshipping of a man who was making Italians disliked. This was to get much worse.

One day two designated captains were picking boys for their football team. One by one they selected boys from the nervous huddle. Usually I was among the first to be picked. Each captain had now picked five boys each and I began to feel troubled. An order I took for granted had been overturned. I felt alone and shrunken. When two more boys were picked ahead of me strength drained from my legs and I didn't know where to look. One of the captains was Billy, my best friend. Billy was purpose-fully avoiding eye contact with me. Then Cyril, a fat boy with glasses, was chosen ahead of me and I looked around expecting some sign that a practical joke was underway, that I was the victim of a collective prank. I justified the scant confidence shown in my footballing skills by playing badly. After school Billy offered up no explanation. He acted as though today was just a continuation of yesterday. But from now on I would always be one of the last to be chosen. I threw away all my cigarette cards of footballers, one of my most cherished possessions.


Initially the war was a source of excitement. Gas mask drill at school induced lots of muffled illicit sniggering. The sandbags outside the town hall and the barrage balloons hovering overhead invited flights of imagination. I felt an affectionate bond with my father while the two of us dug up an enormous hole in the back garden for the air-raid shelter. The black-out was exciting too. The world became more mysteriously pressing and intimate, both more exciting and more frightening. Best of all, the searchlights crisscrossing the night sky, lighting up the clouds like a screen, as if a thrilling film was about to take place up there.

The day after Mussolini declared war on Great Britain I was cornered in the playground by a gang of boys from the year above. It wasn't the first time I discovered how little physical courage I had. I tried to charm my way out of the ordeal, offering apologetic smiles when I was insulted for my racial origins. I told the boys I hated Mussolini as much they seemed to. My voice squeezed as thin as a filament. I barely recognised it as my own. The boys took it in turns to punch me in the stomach and the groin. I was still trying to charm them with my apologetic smile. My shame at putting up no resistance plagued me. I replayed the ordeal countless times with a different outcome.

Of those days I remember the shrill whistle of the paint factory further up the street, barely registered before, which implanted itself in my mind. Setting the anxious tone of all my thoughts. I was only happy when I took Nera, our dog, to the park. I was almost relieved when, one evening, two men in plainclothes arrived at our house and marched my father off.

When he returned three days later, looking like a shrunken version of himself, he told us we were being repatriated.

"What does that mean?"

"It means, my boy," my father said, removing his flat cap, "we have to go to Italy. We're allowed one suitcase each. Everything we can't take they're going to steal, including the dog."

Like all the Italians on the train, we were under armed guard. I stared out of the greasy window at the departing landscape. I couldn't get the image of Nera out of my head. The way she looked up at me when we left. Beseeching is the word I would choose for the expression in her eyes. As if I was betraying her. I had never felt so shrivelled and misunderstood, nor so guilty. Not even when my mother found the postcard of the bare-breasted woman I swapped all my favourite marbles for and we stood looking at each other and neither of us quite knew what to say to each other.

My heart was thumping when we stood in line at customs on the dock at Glasgow. It was forbidden to take British currency out of the country so my father had made me hide a wad of banknotes in my underpants. I was expecting to be caught. To be exposed and humiliated in front of everyone. The customs and immigration officers all had fixed stern expressions on their faces. There wasn't a kind face among them. Like everyone else I was made to empty out the contents of my suitcase on one of the line of trestle tables between the towering ocean liner, painted battleship grey, and the railway tracks. The officer confiscated the bag of sherbet lemons I had stashed in the bag. "No food allowed," he said. He also confiscated all three of the books I had brought, including *Murder on the Orient Express* which I was half way through and looking forward to finishing on the boat. Worst of all though he confiscated my Rose album, disguised as a stamp album, which contained all the things Rose had either given me or I had stolen. Rose lived at the back of our garden. On the other side of a creosoted fence. I used to climb a tree and jump down into her garden. Mostly the album contained things she had touched that I could afterwards pick up and take home, like a chocolate bar wrapper or a button that popped off her cardigan that I slyly pocketed. The source of all the beauty and wonder of my life was secreted in that album. I stole a shy glance at the officer, a plea for sympathy. The man looked back at me as if I was an annoying insect. A sense of injustice and resentment replaced fear as my overriding emotion.

"Good riddance to this bloody country if you ask me," said my father. "Still, we got one over on them, didn't we, my boy?" He flustered my hair, before picking up his suitcase.

I had heard stories of passenger ships being sunk at sea by the Germans. But we were told the boat would not be attacked as the German and Italian authorities had been notified of its route and purpose.

Soon we discovered we were not allowed on deck. We were quartered in a large storeroom in the depths of the ship with three other families. The boat didn't move all day and all night. I thought of all the things I had left behind – my Hornby train set, my threadbare teddy bear who was still a comfort when I felt unfairly treated, my bow and arrow, my leather football, my fishing rod, my scout uniform and most of all, Nera, our dog. When the liner finally set sail I was soon sick. I vomited until there was nothing left inside me. Until I was utterly hollowed out.

All the men talked excitedly about the war and the likelihood of being enlisted when they arrived in Italy. I saw this prospect frightened my father. I still looked to my father as a beacon in adult situations. I had never before seen my father at such close intimate quarters in adult company. I began to see he was an annoyance and a figure of fun to the other men. They sensed how reluctant my father was to fight and advised him to register himself and his family as Jewish when we arrived in Italy.

"That way you and Max will be exempt from military service. Jews aren't allowed to join the military. Otherwise they're pretty much left in peace. I know that's what I'm going to do."

We went to Lerici, in Liguria, where my father's brother lived with his family. I couldn't believe how beautiful the small fishing village was compared to Leeds. I was sleeping on the floor in the laundry room. I liked sleeping on the floor. I liked how moonlight crept through the slats of the green shutters in thin smoky shafts. There's something liberating about the absence of home comforts which appeals to the child in us. It's perhaps the first time in our lives we get a hint of how exciting it can be to be naked. But, of course, I didn't know then that in four years I would be sharing a straw pallet with two men in a German concentration camp.

The pink house was tilted half way up a steep slope where washing hung overhead from one house to the other opposite. At the summit of the slope were the remains of a Moorish castle on the promontory overlooking the bay. There were also alleys like caves. There were many things I liked about my new home - the green shutters, the scent, growing stronger at sunset, of flowering vines, the smell of the sea ingrained in the stones, the green lizards, the smell of pine resin, the exotic lemon and orange trees.

My father was talked out of registering the family as Jewish. What this meant was that he was almost immediately called up. He was pale and irritable with apprehension before leaving. Secretly I was relieved my father was no longer around.

But I wasn't allowed to bask in the beauty of the fishing village for long. There was a group of boys who always stared with hostility at me when I walked towards them. I had done everything possible to make myself look like all the other Italian boys but something always gave me away as an outcast - the cut of my trousers, the lapels of my shirt, the style of my shoes. Teenagers notice the tiny details that single anyone out as an outcast, a foreigner. My heart always thumped and my legs sagged under me whenever I saw them. This shortage of physical courage was my overriding concern in those days. I was forever measuring risk. I blamed my father for it, as if it was something he had given me, like a slap to the face. I prayed the war would end before I was required to join it.

One day I tripped on a tarred landing rope I didn't see and the huddle of boys laughed.

"Hey *Inglese*! Careful you don't fall over."

"All you English will be falling over soon."

So I was abused as an Italian in England and as an *inglese* in Italy. It was around this time that I first became aware of Michante. He was known locally as the "*indiano*". He was taller than most of the men in the village. And there was something exotic about the cut of his eyes and the chiselled bone structure of his face. He was the most alone person I had ever seen. And this attracted me, this aloneness. We were fellow outcasts. That's how I felt. I never once saw him talk to anyone. I always wanted to say hello to him but he never raised his eyes. His eyes were always riveted to the ground as if the present moment held no interest for him.

There were flags and fascist uniforms everywhere. I was quickly made to learn Italian. I had private lessons with Ada's mother. Ada was often around while I had my lessons. By that time Jewish children were forbidden to attend state schools. I remember once we were sitting opposite each other at a table. When I rocked back on my chair I saw she had slipped off her shoes and was caressing one stockinged foot with the other. That was the first time I became aware of her sexually. The first time I was given a glimpse of a world in which there was a more courageous pulse in my blood. Or would be if I could inspire the love of such a beautiful girl. I fell in love with Ada. She was a year older than me. It was a hopeless love.

I was too shy, too nervous then to look at Ada with anything but stolen furtive glances.

I used to pretend I needed the bathroom often so as to be able to walk past her bedroom. I always hoped to spy something intimate and revealing – perhaps an item of clothing abandoned on the floor or a smudge of powder on her pillow, some folds on the sheet that mapped out where her body had slept. It occurred to me that she would enter this room when I left. Think her private thoughts there. Take off her clothes there. But the room I saw had always been tidied of all its secrets, cleansed of all its fingerprints and scents. It gave me no new knowledge of her mysteries. It offered up a blank face to the interrogation of my eye.

Before my first day at school it was discovered I had nits. I was taken to the barbershop where all my hair was shaved off. Even the man shaving my head was frosty with me and called me *inglese*. Three of the boys who always jeered at me were in my class at school. My chief tormentor was called Bobo. I was appointed the desk next to Ivo, a boy who had a birth mark on his face. My Italian was rudimentary and I found it difficult to pick up the local accent. The boys were quick to jeer when I made a mistake. Only Ivo was kind. He too an outcast.

I was bought a *Ballila* uniform which, I confess, I liked. It was one of the first things that gave me a sense of belonging. I especially liked the black fez with the tassel and the black cape. Membership was obligatory for all schoolchildren and on Saturdays we were forced to parade and sing songs. Although I liked the uniform I always felt I was betraying Ada by singing these songs.

Every time I saw Ada's black bike with the loose spoke propped up against a wall my heart began thumping.

If Ada told me to read a book I often began it the next day.

When she wasn't present I existed only as anticipation. When she was present she either raised expectation or flattened it.

I remember Ivo broke his ankle not long after I joined the school. We were in the playground. Bobo and his gang surrounded us and Bobo snatched away Ivo's crutches. Ivo was left hopping on one leg. Even Bobo's gang were taken aback by the dubious ethics of this act. There was a murmur of protest. Bobo, with his slicked back black hair, stared at his companions. Silently challenging any of them to question his authority. He visibly became more incited to violence. He swung back his fist and hit Ivo full in the face with a powerful right hook. Ivo collapsed in a heap, blood oozing from his nose. "For befriending the *inglese*," Bobo told Ivo. The janitor came over. I can't remember if it was the first time I realised Michante was the school janitor. He didn't say anything but Bobo and his gang walked away. It was the first time the "*indiano*" looked me in the eye and his eyes shone with what seemed the light from a dead star. I felt I could see the jumble of private sorrows and chaffing defeats which made up his inner life.

Ivo remained my friend which troubled me a little. I felt guilty for doing nothing while Bobo hit him and felt he ought to feel betrayed by my cowardice. I was sometimes jealous of Ivo because Ada was so fond of him. Ivo and I became good friends. Ivo was at his happiest in water. He swam with his face down. Some of the boys at school said his face looked like raw liver, like scar tissue, because his mother had slept with the devil. I knew Ivo hated mirrors, hated glass. That he felt his appearance created a disturbance, like that of a latecomer in a darkened cinema who makes everyone look up.

But otherwise the fishing village remained a sleepy world, even though, beyond the smell of gutted fish and brine and pine resin, beyond the jumbled tiers of pastel coloured houses, beyond the enclosing wooded hills, beyond the wandering finger of the lighthouse across the bay, momentous things were happening in the world.

*

Time has now been shifted about in my mind as happens in the layers of soil of an archaeological site. But at some point I was slapped in the face by a young man wearing the ubiquitous black shirt for failing to salute some fascist official. I felt sullied and belittled for months after. Felt that what I needed to do was to get up at dawn and tramp through early morning mist and dew - from field to field with the innocence of sheep and cows as company,

One time Ivo and I went to the cinema, the Goldoni. I saw footage from the air of the German bombing of London. Whole streets reduced to flattened wastelands of smoking rubble. The Italian commentator gloated over the destruction. When the film finished the fascists all stood up, saluted and began chanting the name of the Duce. The purpose of this saluting and chanting was to identify any detractors in the audience. If you didn't join in you were abused and physically assaulted. You had to put on an act. I enjoyed telling the occasional lie though. To tell a lie is to risk being caught out and there's excitement in avoiding traps: it was an aspect of my childhood I was perhaps averse to relinquishing. So every time I went to the cinema I pretended to be a fervent fascist, except one time when I went with Ada and we were both abused for refusing to perform the fascist salute and sing the fascist songs.

Ada's face always creased into a mask of scorn when she saw fascist militia. These were often men who had been refused by the army on medical grounds. They tended to overcompensate for this slight to their manhood by becoming bullies. They took things from shops without paying; they constantly harassed people in the streets, demanded to see papers and often the contents of bags. I already knew, of course, how much Ada loathed fascism but I had no idea how bold, how foolhardy she could be in her defiance. She was as easily moved to anger as she was to pity. Any man in uniform now reminded me of the slap I had received, triggered off a reflex mechanism of the humiliation of that event. Surprisingly they always pretended not to notice Ada's provocative distaste and walked past us.

There was propaganda everywhere. We were told what to think and feel. There was only ever one side to every story. The billboards were mostly splashed with fascist slogans. The only pledge of allegiance I had made was to Ada. I was happiest when all other thoughts were driven from my mind except the thought of her.

Ada had beautiful hands, long slender tapering fingers charged with sensitivity. There was a lively nervous eagerness in her touch as if she was poised on the tips of her toes.

I had imaginary conversations with her all the time – monologues rather than dialogues. I carried her voice around inside me as if she were a ghost. I was constantly tormented by the idea that I had given her the wrong impression every time we met and was frantic for another opportunity to exonerate myself in her eyes.

I rarely saw Ada's father. He was a chemist and worked in La Spezia. His name was Ettore and he always smelled of the brilliantine he lavished on his thinning hair. In appearance he looked like a fascist – which simply meant he was always immaculately groomed. He didn't seem as fond of Ada as he was of his younger daughters. His coldness towards her made me dislike him a bit. He was fascinated by antique maps. There was always a collection of folded old maps on the table next to the red leather armchair where he most often sat.

I had a favourite hiding place, among the rocks at the end of the wharf, where I'd gaze at the white script of surf. Imagining it was a letter the sea was writing to me. Telling me to be brave, telling me Ada would be my wife one day.

I began to see how certain clothes she wore reflected her mood. There was a black blouse of a stiff unyielding material that she buttoned up to the neck which became my enemy. She was always forbidding and intolerant when she wore what I jokingly called her fascist shirt.

*

Late at night on July 25th 1943, Mussolini's fall was announced on the radio. The family in the apartment downstairs told us the news. Everyone in the building was out on the stairwell, some in their pyjamas. They were like excited children at Christmas. It was almost midnight when I ventured outside. The streets were full of people as if it were the middle of the day. They were cycling in groups or striding with purpose and exuberance towards Piazza Garibaldi. I was touched, hugged and kissed by a host of people I didn't know. I noticed someone had torn up their ration book whose pieces lay scattered in the gutter. People were smiling and talking openly again. Faces looked more humane, more trusting. Everyone wanted to be outside again, everyone wanted to be together.

It was Bobo who scaled a ladder the day after the armistice was signed when everyone was happy to have finally lost the war; Bobo, to cheers and jokes, who smashed the stone head of Mussolini on the plinth outside our old school, smashed it with a hammer. Bobo embraced me during the celebrations. In that instant I forgave my former persecutor all his sins. Bobo now liked the *inglesi*. It was the fascists he and everyone else hated. During the month of August the number of young Italian men in the town had noticeably increased. The number wearing uniforms significantly decreased. My father returned from France. My father was always badmouthing our neighbours as if they were of a lower breed and his support of the fascists was a constant source of embarrassment to me. He was quiet after the armistice but when, by early September, the Germans arrived, in khaki shorts and shirts, his support for the fascists grew more raucous. Bobo too became a fascist again.

One day I was walking with Ada along the seafront and Bobo and a group of his fascist cronies came over to us. He called Ada a Jewish pig and spat in her face. I should have hit him but I didn't. I changed that day. I shrank. I was ashamed of myself that I didn't hit him. Even if it meant getting beaten to a pulp I should have hit him. And I got the feeling Ada never really respected me afterwards. He spat in her face because he wanted me to fight with him. And I walked away. I told Ada to ignore them. I realised that day how cowed she too had become by the regime. She took the abuse in silence; not something she would have done before the Nazis arrived. For years I wished I could have that moment again. It became my most urgent wish. You have no idea how many times in imagination I've landed a punch on that bastard's chin. I imagined it more times than I imagined making love to Ada.

We were sitting in a moored fishing boat when she told me Ettore wasn't her father. I remember she was wearing a silvery grey dress, a black cardigan with a pearl brooch. The moon broke up and reassembled on the black water.

"You mustn't tell anyone this," she said. "My real father is Michante."

Truth be told I had heard this rumour. Heard it at school where I was mocked for courting the janitor's bastard daughter. Nevertheless I feigned surprise as best I could.

"His first name was Smoking Earth. Then he was called Michante. When he was taken off to boarding school in America he was renamed George. He changed his name back to Michante when he came to Italy. He was part of a wild west circus. His father was white but he never knew him. Which probably means he, my grandfather, was a rapist. His mother was killed at a place called Wounded Knee. He was orphaned at the place called Wounded Knee. I'd like to go there one day."

"How did your mother meet him?"

"My mother was a dancer when she was young. She had the idea of incorporating Lakota dance steps into a choreography. He taught her steps he told her were from a dance called the ghost dance. The choreography never saw the light of day; instead I did. He still loves my mother now. I've seen the way he looks at her. It always used to frighten me the way he looked at me. The intensity in his eyes. And even as a child I sensed how much my father disliked him."

"Have you ever spoken to him?"

"No. Mum only told me all this recently. Mum says he wants to talk to me. I'm going to see him. When I can pluck up the courage. Mum said she couldn't build a life with him because he was too intense. So she married the man I thought was my father."

I couldn't see Ada at the other end of the boat. But I could feel how fervently her secret had heated up her body. Betraying a secret is an irreverent act; both a declaration of independence and a provocative challenge to unseen higher powers, like breaking a rule in church.

Earlier American bombers had attacked the harbour at La Spezia. When searchlights suddenly flared up across the bay the nakedness of Ada's face was startling. I too felt exposed, as if I were under the scrutiny of a large audience. The three smoky prongs swivelled about, illuminating the undersides of clouds. Before long the distant wail of sirens could be heard.

The tide seemed to grow more restless. I felt the pull of the dark sea beneath me, an increased urgency in its swell. I steeled myself against this hated timidity in my nature for which I couldn't help blaming my father. Soon we could hear the low growl of the approaching bombers. It was like a cold breath shimmying down my spine. My chest tightened as a cluster of black silhouettes appeared to the north. I got to my feet but Ada told me to sit down. She wanted to stay in the boat and watch.

On the far side of the bay chained red comets shot up into the sky, the darkness as if sewn with jewels. Now and again the searchlights, ghostly with pale reds and blues, briefly picked out a plane, pinioning it to the dark fabric of sky like a pinned butterfly. Explosions sent up white flashes. A splintering flash of light momentarily brightened the unripe oranges on the trees along the promenade. Soon the colours were dirtied by clouds of rising black smoke caught in the white light. Some of the bombers were now directly overhead, faint black smudges whose engine noise sent vibrations down into the wooden frame of the boat. I heard a whistling noise and then it was as if someone had torn the world in half.

The bomb missed any houses but left a bald patch on the hillside where it had ripped up lots of trees.

The next time I saw Ada I forgot to ask if she had met up with Michante. She was in bed with a fever. I was allowed to sit at her bedside for a short while. It was the first time I had seen her in bed. She was wearing an embroidered white nightdress. Once or twice I saw her bare bronzed shoulders and the imprint of the black spidery lace of her bra on the white cotton.

It was becoming increasingly dangerous for Jews now. At first the Germans deployed most of their resources in hunting for fugitive Italian soldiers and renowned antifascists. But rumours began to circulate of Jews who had been arrested. At this time I heard the story of how Ada's youngest sister, Chasya had asked a German soldier if she could look through his binoculars. Not only did he let her look through his binoculars, he also lifted her onto his shoulders and ran with her down to the sea. But I remember the fear in Ada's eyes when an armoured vehicle passed by outside her house, rattling the glass in its window frames. During the war it was often an overheard noise that didn't quite belong to the familiar rhythm of the day that made you realise how much tension you were always carrying about in your body. Abrupt transitions of expectation were common in those days: one minute you were contemplating the idea of your imminent arrest or death; the next, without any jarring or exuberant gear change, you were washing dishes or chopping an onion.

I blame the sight of her in bed and the mad old woman called Medea for what happened next. Medea stopped me near Shelley's old house in San Terenzo with a big knowing grin on her face. She did a little jig in front of me. The movement of her hips was shockingly fluid. "You've got to find her rhythm," she said, showing her gums and the missing teeth in her smile. "If you can find her rhythm you'll make her happy." I felt afterwards that the entire town knew about my feelings for Ada and was mocking me for my inability to act on them.

So, one evening, I tried to kiss Ada. She refused me. She told me I didn't attract her physically. She was wearing a darker shade of red lipstick, a cotton blouse and green and gold skirt; her black hair was gathered up at the back with a comb and hairpins.

Sometimes, especially when you're young, you can't help simplifying the nature of boundaries. I would look at Ada with all her sophisticated gestures and words, her pretty clothes and realise it was all essentially window dressing. At root she was a vagina and I was a penis and we were enacting the biological imperative of all life, the mating ritual. Or that's how it seemed to me. In the mating ritual it's generally the female who has the last word. The male does his dance and it's the female who decides what happens next. Ada rejected my penis. My penis didn't attract her vagina. And changed my fate. What though is fate if not attraction?

I wanted to hurt her for rejecting me, for making me feel I was ugly. So I ignored her when we passed each other in the town. I began treating her how the fascists treated all the Jews. I was deeply unhappy and my only desire was to make her equally unhappy. I could see how much my shunning of her hurt her. I thought if she discovered how much she missed me she might change her mind.

When I walked past her house, which, stealthily, like a spy, I did often, the last thing I wanted was to see her but it was also the thing I most wanted in the world. Soon it became clear no one was living in her house anymore. I began to worry she and her family had been arrested. No one knew where they were. Then I discovered her family had gone into hiding. It was Ivo who told me. They had moved to a house in the countryside outside Sarzana. First he made me swear I would tell no one. "Especially not your father," he said. "There's a reward now for information leading to the arrest of Jews."

I was annoyed by his implication my father wasn't trustworthy.

I still wasn't getting on with him but blood is thicker than water and I rose to his defence.

"My father's got nothing against Jews," I said. This was a lie. He was incensed I spent all my time with that "Jewish girl". His reasoning was I was threatening the security of my entire family by frequenting Jews.

I put off going to see her. I still wanted to make her pay for rejecting me. I held to the belief that emotionally she was like a fascist. She had treated me like my papers weren't in order.

When I finally did cycle to Sarzana I was still determined to show Ada a cold front. Inside though I was hot and nervous. Chasya was spinning about on the flagstones by the door when I arrived. She was reciting to herself some kind of singsong incantation. She was buttoned up inside a red coat and had a white ribbon in her long dark hair. Ada's two little sisters were very much part of my feeling for Ada. They showed me what Ada must have been like at five and nine. I took more pleasure in interesting and amusing them than just about anything else. Except for interesting and amusing Ada herself of course. They were always making me promise things, especially Chasya. Something Ada never did but I wished she would. Also I loved how much they loved their father. They showed me how attractive it was to be the father of girls who loved and worshipped you. I picked Chasya up and carried her into the house. For protection, to advertise my winning ways.

The kitchen was lit by the fire and two gas lamps which gave off no more light than a pair of struck matches. The windows, in accordance with regulations, were blacked-out with a frayed sheet that been dyed a metallic grey colour. The first thing I learned was that Michante had kidnapped Ada. That's how her father put it. Ettore had to be dissuaded from reporting Michante to the police. His face had a sharp, hounded look in the heavily shadowed light. Most people at that time had an air of not being quite as clean as they would wish, as if they were being forced to wear someone else's clothes. And this is how Ada's mother and father appeared. That said, as a result of the restrictions in our diet, Marisa's face had a pale chalkiness to it that made her look more beautiful. She was wearing a pair of silver earrings, shaped like tears. I always had difficulty in imagining her as the lover of Michante but I could never now forget it every time I saw her. I felt she knew I was privy to her secret. It was how I explained her recent discomfort in my presence.

Sitting in that kitchen I remembered a time when I had watched Ada rinse the earth from some leeks under the tap with her sleeves rolled up and her long black hair tied back and realised it was probably something I would never see again. I felt no gratitude towards Michante for helping her to escape to safety. In fact, for the first time, I disliked him.

Before leaving I offered to bring them anything they needed. Ada's mother gave me a list and the key to their house in San Terenzo.

I cycled back to Lerici and followed the coast road around the bay to San Terenzo. For a while I sat on the rocks by the sea. Children were playing in the piazza; the voices of women leaning out of windows echoed in the darkening air. There were discarded fishing nets on the wharf and a collection of fishing boats moored at the water's edge. The waves uncoiled with a serpent hiss over the fossilised rocks below me. Sometimes the high tumble of clouds blown in across the sea looked like an army of avenging angels. Other times like a new plague of demons. I felt guilty, resentful, confused and angry. But most of all I felt sad. Ada was my best friend. Her company gave me courage and the freedom to be myself. When she left it was as though some kind of new force took possession of me, attracting and kindling negative energy.

I waited until the streets had emptied just before curfew. A bright, almost full moon sketched my shadow on the doorstep of Ada's house as I inserted the key. My heart was thumping when I opened the front door. The photo of Marisa and Ettore in their wedding clothes was still tucked in the frame of the hallway mirror. Otherwise though everything had been turned upside down. There were broken bits of crockery and extinguished cigarettes on the flagstones in the kitchen. I noticed the shards of Chesya's favourite yellow and green mug. She had always refused to drink from any other cup. I froze for a moment. I thought I heard a noise upstairs. I strained my ears for sounds of movement in the house. The house, though, already had an atmosphere of dispossession. I could feel its new atmosphere of desolation on my skin. Never before had I experienced such a stark severance dividing one day from another – it seemed as though a decade of grief had passed since I was last here.

Most of the rooms upstairs were in a state of disarray. Drawers and wardrobes had been emptied and clothes and personal belongings were strewn over the floors. Beds stripped and mattresses slit open. None of these things looked like they would ever be reclaimed by their owners. There was a finality about their abandonment.

When I entered Ada's bedroom the white sheet on the floor shone like snow in the darkness. There was a blue jug and a candle on the bedside table. A purple shawl slung over an over-turned chair. I picked up a pair of stockings. The seamed black material bore a faint smell of her body's secretions and scent. Ada's clothes were strewn all over the floor. Each item carried memories for me. And then there were the things I had never seen – the soft silk, lace and cotton of her underclothes, materials that knew the press of her naked flesh. Her perfume made her seem further away instead of closer. The wardrobe door creaked when I opened it and it was strange to realise how familiar this noise must have been to Ada. How familiar to her was the weight of this door in her hand. The wardrobe was empty.

Finally, that night, I slept in Ada's bed. It didn't smell of her though; it smelt of mildew.

I was wretched for months after Ada left. Feelings are like waves; they require a shore to break on. With Ada gone I had lost my shore. All my young life I had sought an idea of action to attach myself to. The only idea I was able to find was Ada. When I looked at myself in the mirror one day I no longer looked like a boy. And I can't tell you how much that scared me. I didn't feel ready to be a man. You know when a candle throws your shadow huge on a wall and you don't recognise it as yourself? Well, that's how I felt. My legs felt heavier. Food didn't taste the way it used to taste. There was a constant disturbance in my field of vision, as if a vase was about to topple from a shelf. I felt unsteady on my feet, irresolute, as if I was standing in a gale and my hair was flapping and my clothes ballooning out.

Now that I knew I wouldn't be losing my virginity to Ada, that never would I see the mist of surrender in her eyes, I sought out more cynical means of getting rid of it. I still wanted to hurt her. Even though I knew she was in Switzerland or England and what I did had no relevance for her whatsoever. I turned my attention to whores.

I was working occasionally as a nightporter at a hotel on the seafront between Lerici and San Terenzo. The hotel was full of Germans and fascist officials. The five banknotes in my pocket made my heart skip occasional beats. It was more money than I had ever had. The world had got bigger. My role in it more influential.

For once I wasn't frightened of the men in uniform. The fear I felt tonight had a different source.

Then I saw Father Ruggiero walking towards me. My first thought was to suspect a divine plan to thwart me in my sinful intent. Father Ruggiero walked with flatfooted urgency as though his presence was demanded elsewhere. I felt the familiar sludge of guilt shifting darkness around in my mind. I had committed the same sin many times today – but so far only in my imagination.

"What is this light if not divine?" said the priest, gesturing towards the sea, though there was little of the implied wonder in his dry croaking voice. He stood blocking my way. "When you're as ancient as me you never know if you're not seeing this or that something for the last time. But I suppose war makes even the young feel old. Won't you be up for the next draft?"

I nodded. My eighteenth birthday was only three weeks away. I nodded but found it difficult to talk to Father Ruggiero. The priest made me feel I was still a child with little of any interest to say for myself.

"Make the most of your time, Max. You never know how much you've got left."

Was he encouraging me in my sin?

"And tell your mother I shall call round next week to perform the annual exorcism of your home. The world abounds with evil spirits at this present time. It's already that time of year again."

The whorehouse was inland, half way up a narrow cobbled street that sloped up the hill. I had walked past it countless times. Rehearsing the revolutionary dare of crossing its threshold. I had never been able to pull off the nonchalant entrance I craved even in imagination. I always felt winded at the thought of inside. Was pleasure always to be paid for with this sickening fear beforehand?

When I entered the street of my desire and my dread I saw three Nazi soldiers hovering outside the building. I could hear their insolent laughter. Then a blood-red spill stained the pavement and they were sucked inside. I envied them the facility with which they performed this action. It was nothing to them, I realised. No more nerve-racking than entering a shop.

I then began to worry about my lack of carnal knowledge. I also wondered if I would be expected to have a condom. On a piece of wasteland in Leeds I once saw a used condom in the grass. A dead and sordid thing. And yet to my thirteen year old mind the whole mystery of life seemed to stream through it. Nothing I've seen since has been so eloquent of the thrilling and terrifying mysteries of life.

I found myself inside the building without memory of how I achieved my entrance. Ninety seconds of my life were missing.

As I stood on the threshold of the large many-mirrored room with its divans and alcoves and open stairway I was shocked by my audacity. I had become a stranger to myself.

On the surface everything corresponded to my imaginings – scantily clad girls with painted sticky faces, raucous soldiers in uniform, swirls of smoke, insistent hectic piano music, a jostling underworld of scents, a floating membrane of coloured lights, glittering bottles and glasses on crowded tables. But there was also something I hadn't foreseen, something disarming and forbiddingly adult that I couldn't quite put my finger on. It had something to do with the languid rhythms of the bodies of all these men and women. They all seemed to bask in a medium that was foreign to me. There was a knowledge and a freedom in these bodies that I didn't possess. Almost immediately I realised I was out of my depth here. I was still a boy with grazes on my knees, toys in my room, who obeyed the orders of adults and who needed his mother's embraces and caresses when he was misunderstood. I felt my indecision made me suddenly glow with visibility.

And yet no one seemed to take any notice of me. The mirrors on the walls multiplied and crisscrossed every event in the room. One woman, I noticed, was naked. I was shocked by the isthmus of frizzy dark hair between her legs. I had no idea women had hair there. That's how naïve I was. I recognised a man descending the stairs, tucking his shirt into his breeches, the braces hanging limp. An acquaintance of my father. There was no one friendly. No one to guide me through this bright clutter of terrors. This was a mistake. This was a world I wasn't ready for. I backed out, past the counter with the rows of twinkling bottles behind it and the older woman in garish silks, toying with her bracelets, sitting there laughing with two German soldiers. I was about to leave when a woman called me dearie. At that moment the acquaintance of my father caught my eye. The man grinned.

As I was about to open the door to leave a young man flung it open and pushed past me in a fluster of impatience. Almost in the same instant the same young man shoved me aside in his hurry to leave. I thought of him as a kindred spirit. Someone else as terrified as I was.

I was back out on the pavement for five or six heartbeats when I was hurled to the ground by a gusting torrent of hot wind. Air was squeezed out of my lungs. A force that sucked at my eyeballs as if to pop them from their sockets. There was an explosion of light. The ground shifted and cleaved beneath my feet. I was struck by a flurry of sharp small missiles. Then everything went dark.

Sprawled in the gutter I opened my sore eyes to a new silent world of dust and oily smoke. I was beneath a shroud of tiles and shards of stone. My clothes perforated by pellets of glass. People were staggering out onto the pavement with torn clothes and white matted hair with bloody gashes and masks of speechless terror instead of faces. There was a girl whose petticoat was on fire. She took it off, screaming.

I sat up. Brushed the detritus from my clothes. Gingerly tested various joints in my body. I heard one distant ringing note in my ears. I wanted to say something. To hear the sound of my voice. I knew what I wanted to say but I couldn't say it. No sound emerged from my vocal chords. Above my head a white sheet was flapping from a high window, like a sail.

I found I could get to my feet without pain. But when I stood up I was knocked back down again.

"This is one of them. This kid here."


I was interrogated by a man who had the physique and attendant vanity of the ageing sportsman. There were three other men in the room. A small angry man with a neatly groomed moustache was the one who most frequently punched me. His centre-parted dark hair was shaved above the ears. Every time he shouted at me he sprayed me with his spit. My hands were cuffed behind my back. The metal clasps so tight they were like rodent teeth chewing into my tendons. My clothes were heaped up by one of the shuttered windows. I was wearing only shorts. Twice now I had urinated down my leg from the terror I felt. Both times I was punched and kicked afterwards. There were grazes and cuts all over my body where glass and shrapnel from the bomb blast had hit me. I was so full of anxiety that everything these men said to me sounded like wind rattling a window.

The interrogator kept asking the same two questions.

"Are you a communist?"

"Who was your accomplice tonight?"

The anger he vented on me was entirely personal, as if he had a secret wound I had touched and he was now intent on avenging. The political ambition of these men seemed to amount to little more than a desire to inflict physical harm. I realised that night there is no greater difference between people than the sources from which they derive self-importance and wellbeing.

"You will find us to be reasonable, even generous, if you tell us the truth," he said. "I don't want to have to hurt you, Max. You understand this, don't you?"

I nodded.

"You only have to give us the name of your accomplice tonight and we'll let you go."

"I don't know what you mean."

"I think you're lying to me," he said. "Why did you go to the whorehouse? You didn't go there for a whore. You were seen leaving three minutes after you arrived. Thirty seconds before the bomb went off."

"I was looking for a friend of mine," I said.

The small angry man with the neatly groomed moustache landed a ferocious punch to my groin.

"What's the name of this friend?"

"Ivo," I said. I was still too embarrassed to admit the truth. That my intention was to lose my virginity but that I lost my nerve.

"Ivo? Ivo what?"

"Lechese."

"Address?"

"I'm not sure exactly where he lives," I lied, appalled at myself for naming Ivo. They were all pleased I had snitched. It seemed to endorse the contempt in which they held me. Finally the insane hatred with which they all shouted at me, punched and kicked me abated. They almost began to look like ordinary men who might sing to themselves while shaving.

"Find out where Ivo Lechese lives and arrest him."

"Ivo didn't do anything."

"Only the guilty tell lies. What was the name of your accomplice tonight? The man who threw the bomb. Is he Ivo?"

"No. I don't know the man who threw the bomb. He just appeared out of nowhere when I was leaving."

"Liar!" He motioned towards the fireplace. Another man removed the iron poker. He held the glowing tip to within an inch of my eye.

"I wasn't looking for a friend. I did go for a whore but I lost my nerve."

I was taken down some stairs by a guard with a torch. In the basement we passed small closed doors on either side. The guard opened one of these doors with a large rusted key. He directed the beam of the torch inside. There was a girl sitting with raised knees against the wall. The girl looked up at me. I was shoved inside and the door was locked behind me.

"Was it you who threw the bomb?" she asked excitedly. She reached out a hand and it made contact with my bare calf.

I jolted at the contact. Its warmth and tenderness after so much brutality.

"No."

"But you know who did? A friend of yours?"

"No. I don't know who threw the bomb. He nearly knocked me over when he was in such a hurry to leave."

"What were you doing there then?"

"I don't know. It was a stupid idea."

"Did they hurt you upstairs? They do unspeakably horrible things to people, you know. I'm frightened. I've heard stories at the brothel. Burning men's genitals with a blowtorch, using pliers to crush a man's testicles, forcing men to swallow razorblades, prising out men's eyeballs with toothpicks. If I were you I would tell them the truth."

"I did tell them the truth but they wouldn't believe me."

I could smell the urine on my leg. I moved my legs away from the girl because I didn't want her to smell it. I was ashamed of naming Ivo.

A blood-curdling scream arrived from upstairs. She pressed her face to my neck in the dark. Her hand was suddenly feeling its way over my body, it left a warm imprint on my shorts, moved up my naval to my chest. She was little more than a scented outline in the damp darkness but she pulsed with all the thrilling mysteries of her sex. Her hair smelt of the world I dreamt of in bed at night.

"You can tell me," she said.

"Tell you what?"

"Who threw the bomb?"

"I don't know who threw the bomb."

Then there were footsteps outside and the door opened.

"Your turn," the guard said to the girl.

Throughout the night the screams and wailings did not cease. The girl did not return. Every time I dropped off to sleep I was awoken by a still more piercing and horrifying cry.

I was so thirsty I could no longer produce spittle to swallow.

I thought of the girl's hand moving over my body. I did this instead of praying.

The next day they brought someone else into my cell. A young man with a disfigured face. One of his eyes has closed up behind a swollen lump.

We listened to a muffled distant voice pleading. And then shrieking out in pain.

They arrested people for all kinds of preposterous reasons.

For smoking American cigarettes, for killing livestock, for listening to the wrong radio station, for greeting someone with a handshake instead of the fascist salute, for a loose word, an eccentric item of clothing. The rules had become so absurd it was like we were all participating in a childhood game formulated by a bully.

I was taken back upstairs. I was terrified. My legs sagging under me. I was taken to a different room. Then they brought Ivo into the room. He looked with displeasure at me. His cheek was swollen and blood was black on his face.

We were both marched outside. Both of us wearing only shorts. There was a palm tree, vivid beneath the bright moon. Someone turned on the headlights of a car. A ghost tunnel of light appeared along the gravel drive in which large moths or bats cavorted. There were half a dozen men. Some dressed in olive green tunics and ballooning trousers with a black shirt and a revolver in a holster at the hip. The death head badge on their caps. They shared bottles of alcohol.

"First one to the gate. Winner goes free; loser is shot."

Ivo and I exchanged glances. The dislike for me I saw in his eyes hurt me. Ivo had always been kind to me when other boys taunted me. I had betrayed Ivo. I knew I ought to let Ivo win the race. Even though I knew I could run faster than him. But I knew I didn't have the courage to let Ivo win.

We were lined up side by side, with our hands cuffed behind our backs. Our shorts were tugged down around our ankles. We were taunted and mocked by the guards who made bets. They called Ivo *Faccia di Fegato* - Liver Face.

"Ready…. steady…go!" The man fired off his pistol. As we began to run more pistol shots were fired. Almost immediately Ivo tripped and struggled to get back on his feet. It was hard to run with my shorts twisted around my ankles and my hands cuffed behind my back. Soon I was fifteen yards ahead. I slowed down but the pistol shots frightened me and I knew I didn't have the courage to deliberately lose the race.

I won the race. Ivo was crying. Ivo refused to look at me. The guards were all laughing and exchanging money. I was patted on the back. My cuffs were removed. Then they removed Ivo's cuffs too and pushed us both out of the gate. They threw our clothes out afterwards. There was a black car parked outside and two more guards. They both looked us over, interested in our physical afflictions, our wounds – our lacerated swollen wrists, the dried blood between our top lip and nose.

"You fucking dickhead," said Ivo and shoved me in the chest. We were standing in a deserted road that twisted downhill in the midst of olive groves and vineyards and a green valley. "Why did you tell them you had an appointment to meet me at a fucking whorehouse?"

"I'm sorry, Ivo. I was frightened. They started hitting me before they even asked any questions."

"Don't you ever talk to me again. Okay?"

He got dressed and marched off. I watched him get smaller and smaller. I sat on a wall. The sun was rising over the line of hills. A man was singing down in the vineyards. But the peaceful innocence of the stirring countryside was a lie. I was safe while I sat on the wall - there is almost always a protection of sorts in the present moment - but I knew the minute I jumped down there would be no way back to the innocence of my past.


I didn't know it at the time but I was now under surveillance by the Italian secret police. People I knew were wary of me. I sometimes thought about all the bureaucracy of the war. My name on lists mysterious people were studying and passing back and forth. Ada's name was on a list too. The other thing I didn't know was that people suspected I had given the secret police the address of Ada's family's hiding place because, not long after I was released, they were arrested. I think it was Ivo who spread this rumour. Only Ettore escaped arrest. He was in Genoa, working for an organisation called DELASEM who, together with the

Catholic Church, helped hide Jews, procure them false identity papers and sometimes escape to Switzerland. I found out after the war that Ettore had eventually been arrested because of the naivety of a Jewish woman he was helping. She had gone to see her husband in prison and the Gestapo had followed her after she left. She had an appointment to meet Ettore. Without knowing he died in the same gas chamber as his wife and two children.

While listening to the narrative of the war I began to feel the first stirrings of shame about my situation, especially after my eighteenth birthday. I was contributing nothing. There were deprivations in my life, the occasional moment of fear, but essentially I was able to drift through my days with a certain languor, a ghostly sense of immunity. Not only did this incur a feeling of guilt in me, it also created a vortex of confusion from which I was unable to liberate myself. The responsibility of having to think and act for myself became oppressive. Everyone else in the world was following orders. They had been liberated of the responsibility of making decisions. I was acting in a vacuum. Or so it seemed. Also, my freedom seemed more and more a temporary respite, as if I had committed a crime for which I was waiting to be caught. I began to feel it would be both shameful and disastrous for me to continue hiding from the war. War was a social event, not a private one. I was becoming invisible to myself. Anticipation and memory were my cherished mediums. There life couldn't touch me in the raw. I think Ada was quite similar.

I was constantly hungry, my trousers riding ever more loosely on my hips, and hunger brings irritability. I was often irritable. At this time the roundups began. The fascist militia would suddenly appear, block either end of a street and cart off all able-bodied men to send to Germany to work in factories. It became dangerous to be out on the streets. Then my draft papers arrived. I was still working as a nightporter. The hotel had mostly Nazi residents, including an SS Untersturmführer who was always driven there in a black car. The cleaner had seen a photograph in his room. The photo showed a naked woman holding a child and kneeling before the Untersturmführer in his SS uniform. He was pointing a pistol at her. Behind the woman were several heaped naked bodies. Rumour was this Untersturmführer had personally killed over a hundred Jews in a prison in Trieste. He was always in full SS uniform. I was struck by how confident, how committed to his elegant uniform he was. He terrified me. There was a nervous unpredictable energy around this man like static. Whenever I had to deal with him my hands trembled. His expression was a cross between a smirk and a grimace. I always found it hard to retain my equilibrium in the face of his skewering stare. His name was Kurt Allers.

One night I was sitting at the desk when there was a tap on the glass. Inside the lobby there was a faint light behind the blackout curtain. It was unusual for anyone to arrive back this late because of the curfew. Only Kurt Allers and his entourage ever appeared at this time of night but I knew he was already in his room tonight. When I pulled aside the drape I could only see my own face on the glass until I peered closer. Then I recognised Ivo. He still hadn't spoken to me since I gave his name to the fascist secret police. In fact I rarely saw him. He was smiling but there was something strained about his expression. The moment I unlocked the door another man appeared. He was pointing a gun at me. He was twitchy with nervous tension. He asked me quietly if the SS officer was in his room. Ivo meanwhile had slipped away. The man kept clenching and unclenching the fist of his free hand. He motioned me over to the desk and asked what room the SS officer was sleeping in. He took the key off the hook.

"Okay, I have to hurt you. It's for your own good. Otherwise they will think you were involved." And he struck me hard in the face with the butt of his pistol. I was unconscious for a few moments, until I heard the muffled crack of gunshots upstairs. Blood was streaming from my nose. I expected to hear the footsteps of the assassin hurriedly descend the stairs. But there was an eerie silence. Something had clearly gone wrong. (I learned later the assassin had both shot and been shot by the SS officer's bodyguard.) I panicked. I reasoned I would be arrested and this time I wouldn't be let off. Blood was dripping from my nose when I opened the door. I plunged blindly out into the black night. The darkness seemed to rush out to meet me, to swell up inside me. The blackout meant the sky, the sea and the earth were all one engulfing blackness with no dividing lines. Just flickers of guttering filament and braid when the moon appeared from behind clouds. The wind off the sea stung my eyes, salted my lips. I stumbled through the smoky black swell of the blustering night, falling over twice. All the time feeling I was on the verge of some crumbling precipice. The trees in the dark took on human shapes. The only sounds were the tinkling of anchored boats eddied by the tidal swell and the hiss of the waves washing over the rocks.

Out of breath, I stopped and leant against the wall of an alley. It smelt of cat urine. I ran my fingers over the powdery masonry and damp moss. For a while I could hear nothing but my own heartbeat drumming in my ears. Then I could hear the wind whipping at the tarpaulin covers of the boats in the bay. My eyes began to accustom themselves to the dark. I decided to make for Ada's house. I still had the keys in my pocket. I began to creep slowly, keeping close to walls. It was like there was a tense delay between every tremor of movement and the effect it had on me, creating a suspense in which I felt myself exposed. My body had not been so tensely alert since childhood. I imagined tracker dogs on my trail. Stupidly I gave no thought to the trail of blood I was leaving in my wake.

It took what seemed ages for me to insert the key into the lock. My hands were shaking. I wasn't prepared for what greeted me in the living room. A candle was burning on the octagonal table of inlaid wood at the centre of the room. Michante was sitting on the sofa. He had a dress draped over his lap and photographs scattered by his side. His eyes were moist. If he was surprised by my intrusion he barely showed it. At the best of times there were depths of mystery in his eyes that frightened me. A fierceness too, like a wild creature. He was silent for a while. Blood was still dripping from my nose. Then he said something in his native tongue. It sounded like he was putting a curse on me.

"You were cruel to Ada." These were the first Italian words he had ever spoken to me. The protective intimacy with which he released her name reminded me of the night Ada told me about Michante and how he had never stopped loving her mother. I realised then it was one of Marisa's dresses he had draped over his lap.

"I know. I'm sorry." I began to cry. I couldn't stop myself.

Michante's hands were clasped in his lap as if tied together by a rope. I found it difficult to meet his gaze.

"You upset her. She told me she deliberately rode her bike recklessly after you began ignoring her because she thought if she had an accident and was taken to hospital then you'd have to come and see her, you'd have to talk to her."

It was strange to hear him speak. He had a deep resonant voice. I had always warmed to Michante's acute shyness. I liked his isolation, his singleness, his refusal to have any connection with people, his self-containment, his air of creating wholly from within the atmosphere he carried around with him. It was like he wished himself invisible and yet, paradoxically, was the most charismatic and therefore most visible figure in the town. For all his loneliness Michante had always evoked an air of accomplishment, like someone tired after performing some lengthy and admirable task. For the first time I perceived how much frailty and uncertainty there was inside him.

I saw there were lots of photos of Ada. Ada in a bathing costume. Ada holding up her skirt and running towards the camera. Ada sitting in the crook of a tree she had climbed. Ada sitting on the seawall with her sisters. I was struck by how far away she looked in all these pictures, as if she and I were now separated by a medium far more conclusive than distance.

"Thank you for accompanying Ada to safety."

Michante looked down at the cigarette he was rolling.

"Ada returned to me the sound of my laughter. I hadn't laughed for a long time. Only one thing worries me. The guide I paid to escort Ada the last part of the journey originally asked for 2,000 lire. When he met us he looked me in the eye and asked how much I could afford. The question threw me off balance. I thought he was going to try to extort more money out of me. And yet there was an amused kindness in the man's eyes. "I'll tell you what," the man said and he handed me back all but 500 lire. This meant Ada had more money to bribe the border guards. This act of kindness moved me. And yet afterwards I had to keep convincing myself the man was being kind because a suspicion took root that the man gave me back the money out of guilt, knowing he was going to betray Ada to the Germans for the reward."

"How do you know he didn't betray Ada to the Germans?"

"I don't. But I trusted the man. Instinctively. I can still see his face. A kind face. I'll always remember his face. You need to clean up your face. Why are you bleeding?"

While I was telling him what had happened there were footsteps outside. It was Italians who came to arrest me, not Germans. The trail of my blood had led them to Ada's house. And, of course, they arrested Michante as well. Ironically, it began to lash down with rain while Michante and I were being handcuffed and abused. The trail of my blood was swiftly washed away.

The windscreen wipers sluiced a monotonous stream of rainwater and the inside of the car smelt of all the dead kilometres it had clocked up in its lifetime. I was sitting in the back with Michante. A man with a pink mole on his forehead sat between us. His thigh pressed against my thigh. The intimacy of his blood warmth troubled me. It was at odds with the hatred he showed me. The headlights of the car forged a tunnel of light through the unlit coastal road. That road had become my native ground. Every scent and sight here was connected to a cherished intimate moment of my life. It was the tiny stretch of the world that best knew me, to which I most belonged. The lizard prints in the blown sand by the esplanade wall, the wistful smell of pine resin, the shadows thrown by the orange trees, the heat rising up through the paving stones, the sight of fishermen eating lunch on their boats or mending their nets, the unruly clamber of the pastel houses up the hillside. I felt sure this was the last time I would ever see it.

I think they believed neither I nor Michante had anything to do with the attempted assassination of the SS officer. However, that didn't mean they were going to release us. And that didn't stop them from arresting my father. He joined me in the cell. Hollow cheeked, unshaven, cowered. I already felt guilty for being responsible for Michante's arrest. Now I had to feel guilty on behalf of my father, too. There was no end to my guilt. And I didn't expect forgiveness from any of them. I expected my father to be angry with me. Instead he seemed contrite. I soon found out why. He confessed it had been him who had given the address of Ada's family to the secret police. He told me he had followed me there on his bicycle. "I didn't do it for the money. I didn't want the money. I did it because you were putting the whole family in jeopardy by spending so much time with that family. They were Jews. Enemies of the state."

It was the first and last time I saw my father cry.

Thankfully Michante was in a different cell when my father made his confession. I couldn't feel anger for very long. In fact I began to feel a protective tenderness for him. I remembered when I practiced long jump in the garden in Leeds, to develop my muscles, and my father used a tape measure to tell me how far I had jumped; I remembered when he helped me set up my Hornby train set in the attic. I remembered my father as an ally and a friend. Later he was to say, "I didn't understand what a vile regime this is until they put me in here. And we Italians are as bad as the Germans. You know the Italians here all show off to the Germans, like kids trying to impress older kids."

On our second night of incarceration all three of us were taken outside to the forecourt where I had been forced to race with Ivo. The scene was similar. It pained me to see Michante hurt and subjugated. As if a fundamental law of life had been broken. I looked up at the stars, trying to find a reassuring connection between my terrifying predicament and their expiring glitter. Then I noticed the young man who had arrived with Ivo. The failed assassin. His name was Piero. At first I didn't recognise him. His disfigured face. His bare chest was bandaged. Blood had seeped through and blackened on the bandages. The SS officer he had meant to kill was standing over him. He dragged him by the foot onto the gravel path where he was lit up in stabbing detail by the headlights of a truck. His cries took away what little courage I had. When he was lying in a heap on the gravel the German poured petrol over him. Then ordered one of the men to start up the truck. The man was reluctant. He suddenly looked more like a prisoner than a guard. The German yelled at him. I closed my eyes. To escape a moment I felt I was unable to endure. The German lit a match and tossed it down onto Piero. The flames leapt up pale in the bright glare of the headlights. The screaming of Piero opened up a terrifying devouring void under the stars. I tried not to breathe in the stink of burning hair and flesh carried by the breeze. The German ordered the driver to reverse over the burning legs of Piero. I felt the same howling noise Piero was making rise up inside me. My legs were buckling under me. I could taste vomit in my mouth. I retched when the truck reversed over Piero's legs.

We were soon transferred by bus to a prison in Genoa and from there herded onto a cattle train. I caught sight of Michante on the platform. He was shoved into a different boxcar. My father was with me. The fear in his eyes increased my own nervous tension. As soon I heard the bolt slide into place on the other side of the door of the cattle truck I felt the first stirrings of panic. I had to take deep breaths to calm myself. The train didn't move for ages. There was no room to sit. When finally the train set off I was rocked from side to side. Keeping one's balance was a constant strain. Whenever someone toppled over it caused an avalanche of falling bodies. To begin with this was a source of amusement, like a children's game. People laughing as they fell down on each other. But soon there was no more laughter. The slop pail overflowed and stank. Bad breath from thirst and body odour from sweating bodies. One of the worst moments was urinating into the full bucket. The shame of it. Your urine spitting up onto the clothes of those nearby. I spent hours fearing the arrival of the need to shit. Or that I might have to witness my father perform the act. My hips and legs soon began to ache. Thirst crusted my tongue like a swelling fungus. Hunger like a shoal of fish in my belly feeding on my insides. I become more and more irritated. Everyone began annoying me.

People fell asleep on their feet. They woke with a start when they began to topple. The children's game again. Except there was no longer any mirth. The deep grinding relentless iron on iron noise beneath my feet. The landsliding knowledge I was standing still but being conveyed across a continent. A taste in my mouth of rust. The rust I imagined on the metal parts of the train. I remember there was a deposit of sand in my trouser pockets. It was like the heartbreaking memento of a world lost forever. I spent almost the entire journey rubbing the grains between my fingers.

Deep into the second night a young man lost all understanding of where he was. He attempted to express what was going through his mind with his hands. It was as if he was holding a snake in his hands that was trying to whip itself free of his grasp. The effort of struggling with a more elemental and superior force twisting all kinds of grotesque contortions from his body. A space cleared around him. As if he was infected with a contagious virus. His agitation was like a dangerous electrical charge.

When the train finally grinded to a halt and the door was opened I can't remember ever knowing such a deep draught of relief. It didn't matter that my bloodshot eyes were assaulted by searing white floodlights, that SS guards were yelling and beating prisoners with sticks, that dogs were straining on leashes and showing their teeth. Didn't matter that we were called *schwein*. It was still so much better to be under the moon than inside the stinking airless claustrophobia of the boxcar. I took a deep breath of clean air. My breath joining the smoke swirling in the floodlights.

The mad boy began running as soon as he left the carriage. He touched one SS guard on the back. Made cascading hand signals in the air while the guard watched. It was like he was performing some elaborate spell on the guard. He then ran off, cartwheeling his arms like an exuberant child. A dog snapped at him. He had attracted the attention of several guards. He ran up to another guard. The guard hit him with the butt of his rifle. The blow knocked him to the ground, bloodied his face but he barely appeared to notice. He got to his feet and ran towards another guard. This guard shot him in the face.

We were lined up six abreast. I noticed the torn muddied page of a calendar down by my feet. I couldn't work out what the picture was of. It reminded me of a piece of bleached white bark. For a moment I remembered the garden of our house in England. The tree I used to climb to get into Rose's garden. I could hardly believe that tree still existed in the same world as where I now found myself. I touched the two weeks of growth on my chin. To remind myself I was no longer a little boy, that I was a man now. I overheard that we were in a place called Buchenwald. Someone translated the sign we were marched past. *To each his own.* In the near distance a square grey chimney belching out smoke. There was the Nazi eagle carved out of a block of white granite. The sight of Michante up ahead in the column heartened me a little. My father's low spirits were sapping my resolve. My father seemed on the verge of collapsing. I had to keep giving him words of encouragement. As if our roles of father and son had been reversed. It was almost impossible to accept what was happening. My eyes hurt from my mind's unwillingness to believe what they were seeing. We were made to jog towards a metal gate. There was a high watchtower with searchlights and machine guns trained down on us. We were made to kneel on the ground. Hands on head. There was a smell like burning leaves in the air. An officer gave a speech that was translated into Italian. It was all about work and obedience and the Reich. Several times an SS soldier stepped forward and struck someone with the butt of his rifle, the victim chosen at random. My father began violently trembling. I almost expected him to leap to his feet at any moment and begin running. This was the compulsion I felt clamouring for expression in my own body.

There were tubs full of water between the electric fence and the barracks. We were allowed to drink our fill. It seemed almost like an act of kindness on the part of the SS. Even my father regained some fighting spirit after relieving his thirst. Then we were made to run to the disinfection hut. Ordered to take off our clothes. I was embarrassed to witness my father naked. Looking back now that was one of the most painful moments. To witness the humiliation of my father. My father's mouth had tightened so much his whole face looked different, closer to death. The stench of the disinfectant was overpowering. The hairs on my arms stood up in anticipation of its horror. We had to climb into the huge tank and put our heads under the liquid. Kapos with truncheons struck anyone who didn't disappear beneath the cloudy stinking water. Then we were shaved brusquely by a barber. All body hair was removed. Then we were given work clothes. Blue and grey striped cotton uniforms. And my father and I were handed a triangle of red cloth with the letter *I* imprinted on it for Italian and a number. We had to learn our number in German so as to be able to call it out at roll call. We were all photographed in our new uniform.

Buchenwald was a work camp rather than a death camp. Which is to say no one was immediately gassed there; instead we were worked to death. After a month of quarantine my father and I were sent to work in one of the quarries. My father didn't survive very long. He was whipped twice for muddling up his German numbers at roll call. He had to count each stroke in German and every time he made a mistake the count began again from zero. He soon caught typhus and died.

We were woken at four every morning. I remember how grotesquely beautiful the feathery patterns of frost were on the window. It was emotionally painful to look at this reminder of the world's natural beauty. I wasn't surprised when my eyesight began to deteriorate. My eyes were tired of what they saw every day.

Sometimes roll call would be prolonged for hours, especially when the temperature dropped below freezing. Then the powerful crossbeams of the searchlights would be trained on us and flurries of snow would flicker across their scouring light. We stood there in our flimsy clothes, our disintegrating boots, trying to lean closer to the body warmth of the person standing beside us without being seen to do so.

Every morning I had to remind myself who I was.

It began to pain me that I had created nothing which would survive my death – a child, or even a painting or a diary.

To begin with I worked in the quarries (later I was transferred to an armament factory). I used to fantasise that at a designated moment all us prisoners attacked the guards with rocks. Then we would have guns. Guns were all you needed to eliminate the colossal divide between us and them. It all seemed so simple. When I was able to imagine myself shooting those guards I was reminded of how much exhilaration the body is capable of, like running at full speed down a slope with a friend.

Even in a nightmare scenario like this, where our tormentors acted like they shared one mind, I felt some compulsion to distinguish one guard from another. There was one Nazi guard I quite liked. I saw in his eyes this was a living hell for him too. There was also one particular guard who hated Michante, a bullish thug of a man who had copied Hitler's haircut. He was always on the lookout for signs of companionship between prisoners. Every time he spotted what he thought was an alliance he would drag the two men from the work detail, hand one of them a kapo's truncheon and tell him to beat the other man to death. If he refused the truncheon would be given to the other man. Nothing was harder to watch than the spectacle of a man forced to beat his best friend to death. This guard relentlessly tormented and provoked Michante. He always made Red Indian noises, slapping his palm to his mouth, after saying anything to Michante. Michante took every blow the man dealt him in silence. One day, even though Michante and I rarely spoke, this guard pulled me and him out of the work detail and gave the truncheon to Michante. He looked me in the eye for a moment. I will never forget that look he gave me. Then, with a dazzling speed of movement, Michante struck the guard in the face with the truncheon. His cap flew high in the air, his legs collapsed under him and his black uniform was spattered in blood. The impulse to cheer was almost overwhelming. Michante threw down the truncheon. The other guards didn't shoot him. They set upon him and beat him to a bloody pulp.

The next day we were all made to line up in front of the gallows. Michante's face was almost unrecognisable so badly had he been beaten. He sang a mournful song in his own language while the noose was put around his neck. I remembered the motes dancing in a shaft of light above his sleeping body when we were in a cell together and I remembered his moist eyes when he sat with Ada's mother's dress in his lap. Behind him I could see the smoke from a train crossing the plain and then the distant glittering of its windows; the rails on the embankment transformed by sunlight into shafts of molten mercury. I kept my eyes fixed on those rails when the box was kicked away from under his feet even though the punishment for averting your eyes was a pistol shot to the back of the neck. Not that I'm claiming to be brave. I wasn't. But that was one atrocity I could not look at.

I remember reading once that without the binding of plants

thin soil soon turns to dust and blows away. I couldn't help applying that image to Michante. I couldn't understand how Michante had sustained so much loneliness in his life without being blown away.

Bobo became a partisan. He survived the war. In fact we became friends of sorts. He once spoke about Ada and told me spitting in her face was the act he was most ashamed of in his life. "She had always been kind to me. I didn't know who I was in those days. I couldn't keep my identity separate from the crowd."

Ivo too joined the partisans. He was captured and executed.

When the war was over I weighed 69 pounds. For years afterwards I still felt I had Buchenwald's smoke and ashes in my hair, on my clothes, furring the hairs on my arms. For years afterwards I felt guilty and ashamed that I had survived while braver and better men had died. I didn't want Ada to see me so belittled and sullied so I made no attempt to get in touch with her. But I remember one day when I was walking up in the hills I saw chalked in large letters in the middle of the road, *Ti amo, Ada* and all of a sudden I was able to cry again. My favourite picture of her was restored to me. Of her holding up her skirt and running barefoot down the slope of an olive grove overlooking the sea. Her windswept hair, her peach pink skirt, her high notes of laughter.

# Part Four

## 1890

There they are. Dancing in a circle. Shadows swinging over the snow. Calling upon the ancestors. Each wearing the sacred shirt. Side stepping to the left in time to the urgent heartbeat of the drums and the urgent yearning of the songs. There they are. Shadows swinging over the firelit snow. Calling upon the ancestors. Expecting something wonderful to happen. There they are.

*Pine Ridge Agency. November 12, 1890. We need protection. And we need it now. Indians are dancing in the snow and are wild and crazy. The leader should be arrested and confined at some military post until the matter is quieted. And this should be done at once.*

Washington dispatches General Nelson A Miles with 5,000 troops, including the 7th cavalry, Custer's old command.

At the Standing Rock reservation in North Dakota there is a rumour Sitting Bull is about to join the ghost dancers. Forty-three Lakota policeman are dispatched to bring Sitting Bull in. Two troops of US cavalry follow at a distance. Before dawn on December 15, Sitting Bull is fatally shot by one of his own people, as happened to Crazy Horse. Sitting Bull's people, fearful for their safety, put their children on the few horses they now own and set out for Si Tanka's camp on the Cheyenne River reservation. Mourning the death of their spiritual leader. Michante's mother is among the mourners walking to Si Tanka's camp. There she is.

There they are. Dancing in a circle. Shadows swinging over the snow. Calling upon the ancestors. Each wearing the sacred shirt. There they are. Side stepping to the left in time to the urgent heartbeat of the drums and the urgent yearning of the songs. Dancing in a circle to call upon the ancestors. Expecting something wonderful to happen. Michante's mother is one of the dancers in the circle. One of the shadows swinging over the snow. There are four painted handprints, two green and two red, on the beaded and tasselled dress she wears. There she is. Dancing in a circle to call upon the ancestors. She is called Weayaya.

When Si Tanka learns of Sitting Bull's murder he fears the soldiers are coming to attack the ghost dancers and sets out for Pine Ridge, Red Cloud's reservation. Weayaya and Michante are among the frightened band of refugees. Weayaya can see her son's breath on the air. It gets colder and colder. There are 120 men and 230 women and children. Three days after Christmas, Si Tanka and his people are intercepted by four troops of cavalry. Si Tanka is sick with pneumonia. He travels in a wagon. He is too ill to stand up but he raises the white flag. He and his people are led by the soldiers to their camp, in a small creek and told to settle here for the night. The place is called Chankpe Opi Wakpala. Wounded Knee. The soldiers distribute rations. Some seem kind. Others not so kind. The soldiers post four canon on a rise overlooking the camp.

Weayaya puts up the tepee with her sister Winona. Most of the things owned by Weayaya's family have been lost during the fighting of recent years, the constant uprooting. All the sacred objects, most of the clothes, almost all the memories are gone, destroyed or left behind when the soldiers attacked one village after another.

Some of the people have no tepee. The soldiers give them tents. Weayaya helps build a fire inside the tepee. Michante, her five year old son, helps. He wears the grey school uniform of the reservation. Weayaya and Winona sing a song as they make the fire. They don't talk of the fear they feel. They don't talk of their mistrust of the soldiers.

"There are seven directions of the circle – the north, the east, the west, the south, as well as up and down, and the most important direction is within, and within the spirits of our ancestors are always going to be there for us."

Weayaya makes her son a bed. She gives her son the one buffalo hide she owns and soon Michante is asleep. Weayaya boils water in a bowl on the fire. She adds peppermint leaves from a pouch and she and her sister share the bowl of tea.

Weayaya is woken up the following morning by a bugle call. When she looks outside she sees the soldiers are mounted on their horses, sees the soldiers are surrounding the camp. The half breed translator shouts out that all the men of Si Tanka's band are to gather outside Si Tanka's tent where they will be required to hand over their weapons. The women become restless. Weayaya returns to the tepee and tells her son to wear her ghost shirt underneath his clothes. The holy men say the ghost shirts will stop bullets.

Outside again Weayaya watches a group of young Lakota boys playing leapfrog. Michante stands by her side. He wears the ghost shirt beneath his clothes and blanket. He wants to join the young boys playing leapfrog. His friend Zuya is one of the exuberant carefree boys. Like Michante, Zuya is wearing the grey uniform all the children are made to wear to the white man's school on the reservation.

Si Tanka has been carried outside on a stretcher. The Lakota men, uncertain, fearful, are handing over their weapons. The soldier chiefs believe there are many hidden weapons. They order mounted soldiers to enter the camp. A soldier wearing a beaver hat with snot running from his nose pushes Weayaya aside and enters her tepee. Soldiers enter all the tepees and tents and emerge holding knives and axes and bows and arrows. They rip open sacred bundles and throw the contents to the ground. There are scuffles between the soldiers and the Lakota women.

A holy man called Yellow Bird begins to dance the ghost dance and sing in front of the soldier chiefs. He picks up a handful of dust and throws it in the air. He asks the Great Spirit to scatter the soldiers as the dust has been scattered. Soldiers ready their rifles. Not far away soldiers are trying to disarm a Lakota man, Black Coyote, who is deaf. Who doesn't understand what is being asked of him. He refuses to relinquish his rifle. In the struggle his rifle goes off. There is a moment's silence as the echo of the gunshot dies in the cold morning air. Then the soldiers begin opening fire. They open fire and keep firing. With rifles, with revolvers and finally with the canons on the rise above the camp. Soon shells are exploding in the midst of the camp. Bursts of dirty fiery smoke hang a fog over the camp. Weayaya takes Michante's hand and begins running. Following the other running and screaming Lakota women. Running towards a ravine. A few of the Lakota men have retrieved their rifles and are fighting back. They are soon shot down. Tepees are on fire. The air thickens with powder smoke. Soldiers on horseback are shooting running women and children in the back. Weayaya runs past the spot where the boys were playing leapfrog. They have all been scythed down by bullets. They are all dead. A line of soldiers appear on the rise before her. A bullet cracks close to Weayaya's ear. And then another knocks the breath out of her.

When the shooting stops it is estimated that 300 of the 350 members of Si Tanka's band have been shot down and killed, including many of the children.

Michante has been wounded in the arm. He is taken along with the other wounded to Pine Ridge reservation. He is left in a wagon the first night and almost freezes to death. Then he is taken to the candlelit Holy Cross Episcopal Church where Christmas decorations still hang. Over the altar is a crudely lettered message: *Peace on earth, good will to all men.*

There they were. Dancing in a circle. Shadows swinging over the snow. Calling upon the ancestors. Each wearing the sacred shirt. Side stepping to the left in time to the echoing heartbeat of the drums and the echoing yearning of the songs. Dancing in a circle. Shadows swinging over the firelit snow. Calling upon the ancestors. Expecting something wonderful to happen. Everyone singing. We will live again. We will live again.

# Part Five

## 2052

A specialist has told him his mother is succumbing to the early stages of dementia. Usually so groomed, so merchandised in lacquers, dyes and powders his mother is unadorned and emaciated. Her hair is tangled and grey. Her expression is that of a woman running uphill in driving rain. During the three years he hasn't seen her it's as if she has shed all his complacent ideas about her. As if she has reinvented herself as a stranger, someone who plays no part in his memories.

Felix delivers his rehearsed speech.

"Look, Mum. I'm sorry we fell out. I behaved badly. I see that now. I was angry you left it so long to tell me who my real father was. And that consequently I only got to see him once before he died. I was angry you went back to Josh. Especially after my father told me he tried to win you back after we saw him in Italy."

*I did try to win her back after those few days in Italy. I remember she told me the same thing she told me when we were young. That I'd get bored with her if we became lovers. She seemed to think I was easily bored. Too much of a changeling. And yet I don't think I've changed one iota in the past twenty years. I don't know, Felix. Maybe love is essentially a story we make up about a person in our mind. But whenever I have something urgent to say it's always your mother I most want to share it with.*

Zinnia puts her finger to her lips. She looks over at the

wall. "Don't say anything," she hisses. "They listen. The room's bugged."

Felix isn't sure if he smiles or frowns. The room she refers to is a model of hygiene, a square white room afloat in glare. There are no photographs, no personal mementoes of any description. It is a room bleached of memory.

"Do you want some money?" she whispers. "I can give you some money if you want. It's best I give it to you before they take it. They might already have taken it."

"We don't need to worry about money, Mum."

Zinnia appears to be looking beyond him, fearfully studying something he can't see. Her expression is still that of a woman running uphill in driving rain.

It pains Felix that neither of his parents are aware of his success. *The Memory Tree* is a global success. The virtual world he has scripted which creates an interactive documentary of every user's lineage. Everyone's family is magical if its archives are investigated. Felix has always believed that if there is one thing in life that is fated it is our birth, that far-fetched conspiracy of circumstances which have to occur in order for us to get born.

Felix knows he will never have a child of his own. He knows that he will never have a flesh and blood child in the traditional time-honoured manner. But it's looking more likely he may help spawn a different kind of offspring. The recent breakthroughs he and his colleague Dr Mika Yasin have made on the creation of artificial intelligence systems are mouth-watering.

"Let's go outside," his mother says.

She ignores all the other elderly residents of the nursing home. They, in turn, seem to view her with circumspection as if she has a reputation. For what, Felix isn't sure. Muffled alarms can repeatedly be heard from behind closed doors.

A specialist has told him his mother is succumbing to the early stages of dementia. He expected to find her listless, vacated, ghostly, like an empty stage. Instead she is like an exposed tangle of electrical wires through which sizzles an overcharged current.

"They're after my money," she says outside in the enclosed garden. Then she suddenly increases her pace. Hurries off and disappears behind a vine of bougainvillea. When he catches up with her she says, "Every night they torture me. They want my passwords. Last night they played me recordings of you screaming. They said, under torture, you had told them all my passwords."

"I don't know any of your passwords."

"They strap me to a bed and cover me with sheets smeared with shit. And they insert needles into me. Look over there. That spot behind the bench. That's where they bury the people they kill. They say that's where they will bury me."

"Who?"

"The cult. I never heard him come in. He was always there at night. Creeping around. But I never heard him come in. That's why I had to leave. It was him. The hissing on the phone. He comes into my room when I'm asleep. Do you believe me?" she asks, suddenly appearing as vulnerable as an abandoned little girl.

"It all sounds a bit far-fetched," he says. It's the first time it has ever occurred to Felix that the silent stretches of his mother's mind might be more charged with heightened drama, with complex conflict than his own. He has never tried to follow her outside the realm of closeted domesticity before. On some deep level, it's as if she is mocking his complacent idea of her.

"He comes into my room when I'm asleep," she says. "He inserts needles into me. You have to get into the house. You have to go on my computer and change all my passwords before it's too late. Some of your father's relatives are evil people."

"Which father are we talking about?"

"I think he's going to come tonight in his mask and gloves and kill me. You've got to change all my passwords."

Felix feels a twinge of guilt for finding something attractive about his mother's madness.

"Have you got the keys to your house?"

"No. They stole them. They're probably there now. Waiting for you."

Felix can forge no connection with his mother. So much of her is missing, so much of her has shut down, that it's like she wants him to join her on a narrow crumbling mountain pass overlooking an abyss. Her paranoia though, her preoccupation with sinister hidden designs, reminds him of his father, the last time he saw him, when he told Felix what he thought really happened on 9/11. *Follow the money.* When he predicted all form of protest would soon be criminalised as economic terrorism. When he predicted the beneficiaries of the environmental catastrophes befalling the world. Turns out he was right about lots of things. Climate change and wars on terrorism have reaped whirlwinds of destruction. Turned a large part of the world's population into a caravanserai of homeless migrants. Which, in turn, has paved the way for homogenous militarised police states all over the planet. To quell the bitter divides, the social unrest. An elite secret cartel does now control nearly all the planet's dwindling resources. And elephants, along with dozens of other animal species, are now virtually extinct.

When he enters the small garden with its magnolia tree and overgrown and nettled lawn it is dark. He passes an overhead security camera attached to a post and for a moment the cult leader his mother spoke of takes on a momentary flare of credibility. He pictures a man in shadow watching him on a screen inside the house. He remembers the fixed haunted expression on his mother's face. The expression of a woman running uphill in driving rain.

His intention is to break a window at the back of the house. The nearest other home is about one hundred yards away. Nevertheless he is nervous about breaking glass. The violation of it. The resounding noise of it. He remembers when, in his teens, a friend of his had dared him to throw a stone at the window of a random house. His friend was one of those people who always had to up the stakes. It was night and light from a television screen flickered over the drawn curtains of the window. It has frequently troubled him that he performed this dare. It was so unlike him. He and his friend began running as soon as the stone left his hand. When the crescendo of shattered glass arrived he had never felt so ashamed of himself. He lived in fear the subsequent days. In his imagination a shard of broken glass had embedded itself in a member of that unknown family's face and he was wanted for murder. And yet breaking that window became a watershed moment in his life. He found he was emboldened afterwards. He can trace back to that night the advent of the man he became. Never again would he suffer bullies, never again would he shrink in front of obstacles. He began to stand his ground, get his own way in life, even if that way turned out to be a lonely and loveless way. He became a success, at least in the eyes of the world.

It takes him several attempts before he succeeds in hoisting his weight up onto the top of the side gate. He perches there for a moment, listening. Suddenly experiencing himself as an intruder, a fugitive, a guilty man. He is smiling to himself when he jumps down.

He doesn't have to break any glass. The back door latch yields to the pressure of his hand. He knows the same blend of bowel-loosening excitement and apprehension he felt as a child when left alone in a house. There is no electricity. He finds a candle. He walks with his flame into the sitting room. There laying over the sofa is the ghost dance shirt. And by its side a photograph of Milo and himself in Italy.

Felix likes to think she used the ghost dance shirt and the photograph as the final amulets to ward off the tide of fear and forgetting swamping her mind. That they brought her some light, some respite.

# Part Six

## 2084

### 1

The first thing Solstice does when he hears the gunshots is to search for Mitakuye Oyasin. She is nowhere to be found. Without her he is clueless. Soldiers are pouring down the slopes in the early morning mist. Bullets whistle and crack in the chill air. The warriors, some still in their sleeping robes, are mounting their war ponies. He has no war pony. He still hasn't learned how to ride a horse. He will have to follow the women and children who are running down towards the stream and the belt of timber beyond. The willows, the aspen, the oak scrub and the sage brush. First he sees the dead body of No Laughter No Pain. By his side are the scattered contents of a medicine bundle – two eagle bone whistles, a paint bag, two snake vertebrae, a black squirrel skin, eagle claws, a broken red garlanded healing pipe. Only now does Solstice realise how fond he was of No Laughter No Pain. Then he sees Alowa. She is standing motionless. He realises he has left her memories in the tepee. He is so nervous he has only a child's vocabulary at his disposal, rudimentary verbs and adjectives, as if the stark nature of his emotion has yet to evolve a sophisticated language. He takes her by the hand. He tugs at her hand. He runs with her down towards the water.

Even amidst the chaos he is more alert to the sensation of her wrist enclosed in his hand, her pulse, than anything else. *The Ancestor taught you and Alowa the ghost dance. Only when you join hands will you both remember it in its entirety.*

"Alowa, it's me, Solstice," he says but sees only a blankness in her eyes. It's as if, in her mind, she is warily circling around a forbidden zone. "Do you remember the ghost dance? We're supposed to remember a dance when we touch hands. We've touched hands. Do you remember a dance?"

"Can you see Enapay? I can't see Enapay."

Solstice hides his irritation that she's thinking of Enapay. Eight hundred yards away elders, women and children are being massacred and yet his prevalent emotion is irritation. *You should be ashamed of yourself.*

"Perhaps holding hands was a metaphor? Perhaps we've got to go a few steps further than holding hands. What do you think? I've got your memories but I left them in the tepee. Alowa, you must remember me. I'm Solstice. We've known each other forever. We were soulmates. Then you rejected me as your infant provider. I used to make you laugh. You saw me naked. You must remember. It's me, Solstice."

He cannot attract Alowa's attention away from the battle. He is desperate to tell Mitakuye Oyasin he can't get Alowa to recognise him, to remember him. He turns his attention to the battle.

"Have you spotted Enapay yet?" he asks. "Isn't that him? The cowardly one who's hanging back? I think it is, you know."

"Why aren't you fighting?"

Solstice flinches from the scorn in her eyes.

The Sa'i Tor Shyela warriors make relentless counter charges. *Hiyupo! Follow me!* Guiding their horses with their knees while stringing arrows to bows. The yellowstripes are either drunk or frightened because they are disorganised and fight badly. They make stupid decisions. And their horses are tired. Their horses slip and stumble on the icy slopes. The yellowstripes seem to fear fighting the Sa'i Tor Shyela in close combat. As if they attribute supernatural powers to the singing and painted warriors. So they dismount and form skirmish lines, firing from kneeling positions. A stupid decision. Even Solstice can see that's a stupid decision. More yellowstripes have appeared on the ridge to the east. But so too does there seem to be an endless stream of warriors entering the fray. *Hiyupo! Follow me!* Some have painted themselves in the sacred way as instructed in their dream quests; some have quickly braided their hair with eagle feathers. Face paint running down their faces. Solstice watches one warrior on a white pony painted with black and red zig-zags ride back and forth along a skirmish line of yellowstripes. He is wearing buffalo horns. He is shaking a rattle at the soldiers. He is singing his death song. But he doesn't die. Solstice is thankful it isn't Enapay. The last thing he wants to believe is that his rival will be honoured with bravery songs.

There is a confusion of many different battles. The whistle and crack of bullets. The twang and whistle of feathered arrows. Pony nostrils wide with fright. The higher frequency of screams. The mist and the smoke. The shouts and the cries. The drumming of hooves. The puffs of blue smoke. The neighing of wounded horses. The bucking and rearing of frightened horses. The trilling of the women. The tide of each battle shifts this way and that. This way and that. Then the tide turns. The ice turns to sleet. The mist and smoke lift. And out of the smoke and out of the mist Solstice sees Enapay appear on his painted war pony. Alowa, next to him, in the grass, rasps out a faint sighing sea note. Solstice is struck by the vulnerability of her veins, the delicacy of her bones, this sudden flare of heat and arousal of which her body is capable.

The yellowstripes are on the run. *Hiyupo! Follow me!*

Solstice asks a white-haired old woman if she has seen Mitakuye Oyasin.

The woman frowns at him. "Mitakuye Oyasin went to the spirit world seven sleeps ago," she says.

## 2

The drums, the fires, the dancing. The shrill eagle bone whistles looping in and out of the rhythm of the medicine drums, the war drums. The deep throaty voices of the men. The haunting refrains of the singing women. The honouring songs. The lamentations and the celebrations. The mourning for the dead, the honouring of the brave. The war cries. *Oyate kin ninpi kta ca lecamu. I do this so that the people will live.*

Enapay is one of a dozen dancers inside the circle. But Alowa sees only him. *Who I am. Hiding in his blood, flowing through his veins, pumping in his heart.* The green branches pop and flare up on the fires. Huge otherworldly shadows flit over the tepee walls. There is a red stripe of paint across Enapay's eyes. Half his face is painted black, like all the warriors who have performed brave deeds. A bonnet of eagle feathers on his back. His bare chest a network of scars. His moccasins designed with a pattern shown to him in a dream. He stamps the ground. He turns in circles. A red feathered shield on his arm. He crouches down low. He sweeps the ground with a club. He points up at the stars. Alowa is part of the big circle surrounding the dancers. Alowa feels the rhythm of the big drum enter her blood. Alowa too wants to dance. She has difficulty restraining her body.

Then there is a dance for young girls. They all wear deerskin dresses with beaded red and green strips and a soft robe of elkskin. The men beating the drums wear buffalo horns and look fierce and frightening in the uncertain light of the fires. The girls sing while lightly pawing the ground. All the girls take the beaver skins they are holding and pass them over their bodies, underneath their skirts. At the end of the dance each girl passes her song over to a warrior and gives him the beaver skin with the scent of her skin on it. One girl gives her song and beaver skin to Enapay. Alowa is furious. Alowa is mortified. Until she sees Enapay cast her an apologetic look. *Who I am. Hiding in his blood, flowing through his veins, pumping in his heart.*

A holy man steps forward. He is wearing the entire skin of an antelope. The drums are silenced. The whistles are silenced. The singing stops.

"I was wide awake when the dream came to me. I heard a gathering of powers song. The song told me that to stop the yellowstripe bullets, to save the elephants and the rivers and the green grass, there is a dance we must all learn. A song we must all learn. The custodians of this dance, this song are here. They have a hidden place within where the memory of the song and the dance is stored. To trigger the memory they must join as one. Then they will teach us the sacred dance and the sacred song."

Alowa realises he is looking at her. Everyone is looking at her. *Look at the flames, Alowa. Aren't they beautiful? Look at the smoke. I'm dancing in the smoke, Alowa.* The holy man walks over and takes her hand. Leads her into the centre of the circle. He then leads the boy Solstice into the centre of the circle. "You will now teach us the dance and the song," he says. Alowa looks into the boy Solstice's eyes. She has a momentary sensation of grass beneath her bare feet. Of smoke arising around her. Of smoke seeping into her clothes. Of smoke making her eyes water. Of smoke moving with her as she moved. The sensations intensify as the boy Solstice begins singing. She sees he is shy. She sees he is nervous. But as he gains in confidence the song becomes beautiful. The song begins to touch her. She is confused. *The things I have thought. Gone. The things I have seen. Gone. The things I have done. Gone.* She feels she is betraying Enapay by allowing this song to enter her. She seeks him out in the crowd of faces.

## 3

Solstice and Alowa have been put together in a tepee. There is a solitary bullet hole in the fabric. They are alone.

"I don't remember a dance," she tells him. "I don't really remember you either. Sometimes I see you in smoke and you take off your clothes and then you disappear."

Solstice doesn't understand why she's so harsh, so icy with him. He doesn't recognise her. She is not the Alowa he knows. She is wearing a skirt made of buckskin, sown with sinew, dyed blue and golden yellow and decorated with white painted stars and the fringes are trimmed with mescal seeds and ermine tails and feet. He is surprised he knows all these details.

A small wood fire surrounded by a circle of stones is smoking at the centre of the circular floor. Robes and blankets lay strewn over the ground. The walls are covered in brightly painted buffalo hides, shields, beaded painted bags and strange bundles from which feathers and animal tails hang. Beaded and quilled clothes hang from the lodge poles. There are backrests made of willow wood arranged around the walls.

Outside he hears the laughter of girls, the singing of two women, the neighing of horses and the slow pounding of the medicine drum.

"Don't you remember the janitor? I think he taught you the dance."

"You knew the janitor?"

He can see he is interesting her now.

"We both did. But he's dead now."

"How do you know he's dead?"

"We both saw his dead body. You must remember that. Not long after we saw his dead body together they took you away. You were taken away to become a dispenser."

"I did become a dispenser."

"I know."

"And then I met the janitor. He helped me. But he didn't teach me a dance. He taught me how to change my dreams."

"How could you meet the janitor if he's dead? Let's think about this, Alowa. The janitor gave you a shirt. Do you remember the shirt? It's one of your memories that I've brought with me. Not that I've opened your memory bundle. The shirt is connected to the dance. And the memory of the dance is stored in that shirt and in your body. That's why they want us to mate. That's why they've put us in here together. There's a connection between us, Alowa. The touch of our bodies will trigger the memory in you."

"I don't want to mate with you."

Her icy defiance hurts him less than he would have expected.

"I've got your memories, Alowa. Surely you want them back. The shirt is one of your memories. Shall I go and get them?"

"Yes."

"Okay. I will. In a minute."

"Anyway, how can a dance stop bullets? It's stupid."

Solstice is braiding a handful of sweetgrass. He doesn't know how he knows how to do this but it comes naturally. He lights the braid and ushers the smoke up towards his face and then over towards her face. Alowa's face, which he knows better than any face in the world.

"Don't you sometimes get vivid outbursts of memory, Alowa? Pictures rising up out of darkness, flickering on and off? See faces you know but can't place in space or time? Remember things that you can't recall ever happening to you? Like you're in a dream being dreamed by someone else. Don't you remember when we discovered the dead janitor? I think we're immigrants, Alowa. You and me and everyone here. And I think we've got some kind of override function built into our lifecycle. An invulnerability program. And to trigger the source code we all have to dance as one. Mitakuye Oyasin told me we have a memory encrypted into our circuitry. That must have been what she meant. The janitor is dead, Alowa. And yet you've been talking to him. Mitakuye Oyasin is dead and yet I've been talking to her. How is it possible we're able to commune with the dead? It must be some kind of programme installed in us that allows us to reactivate the teachings we have received, to bring back the past as if it's happening now. We can resurrect the dead. I think the janitor and Mitakuye Oyasin created us, Alowa. I think they were renegade scientists. And I think us immigrants are programmed to save the planet. And it's up to you and me to begin the process. Only we know the triggering dance and song."

Solstice is astounded by what he's just said. Never has he thought these ideas before. It's as if the sweet smoke has ushered them out of his mouth. For a moment he feels a yearning for the company of Mitakuye Oyasin. He wants to feel she might finally be proud of him.

Then there is a rumpus outside. Enapay appears at the entrance. His face is still half painted black with the red stripe across his eyes. He wears a shirt decorated with his deeds in battle. Shells tied into his braids. He frowns at Solstice. Holds out his hand to Alowa.

"We will go to the government reservation," he says. "We will learn the ways of the yellowstripes. You are the woman of my heart. That is all I have to say."

# 4

Alowa sits astride the pony. Holding onto Enapay's waist. It is her favourite time of day. Darkness is draining out of the sky and the earth. Everything seems to quiver with the expectation of light. The hoofs of the horse kick up beads of dew. Webs strung between branches glisten with tiny beads of water. This is Alowa's favourite time of day. Every memory of yesterday as if erased. Everything about to begin again.

*Who I am. Hiding in my blood, flowing through my veins, pumping in my heart.*

The drums are silent now. The sweet smelling incense gone. The vibrant colours of the village a memory. They ride alongside a waterway. There are rainbow oil slicks on the water; deposits of black sludge on the banks. Dead trees like the skeletons of arrested dancers.

She looks at the ring Solstice gave her before she left.

*Look at the flames, Alowa. Aren't they beautiful? Look at the smoke. I'm dancing in the smoke, Alowa.*

A scouring cold wind peppered with dust catches in Alowa's throat. The wind whips her clothes against her body. She has the feeling it is blowing her back to where she came from.

*Back again. To the time of forgetting. To the time of darkness.*

Then Alowa sees the herd of elephants. They look exhausted. They look famished. Their coats sheened in hoarfrost. The largest elephant stops in its tracks and looks over at her. The gentleness in its eyes makes her fearful for its safety.

It begins snowing. The snow reminds her of the lions and

her friend Nya and the three executive sons in the dome. The Unity collar is again a ghostly echo around her neck. Enapay doesn't talk. His silence makes her more uncomfortably vivid to herself. She hides behind him from the gale blowing snow and sleet across their path. The thickening snow begins to erase the world around her. Her own outlines though become clearer. The elk teeth of her ankle bracelet seem to heat up, send a stream of warmth up through her body. Then there's a displacement in the air, a heightening of atmospheric pressure. She is aware of the flapping of large silvered wings, like a disturbance deep down in her being. The bird descends and settles on the ground to her left.

*Say hello to Esawa, Alowa.*

The bird gives Alowa a piercing knowing look. For a moment it's as if the janitor is looking at her again. As if he has returned to reprimand her. She notices now that smoke seems to lift off the falling snow. Her heartbeat is loud in her ears. It becomes a pulsing drum that enters her bloodflow as a kind of entreaty. It's all she can do not to sway her body in time to the hypnotic rhythm of the drum. The hypnotic heartbeat rhythm of the drum. She wants to respond to a memory of a dance in her feet, in her hips and in the muscles of her legs.

*I think the janitor and Mitakuye Oyasin created us, Alowa. I think they were renegade scientists. And I think us immigrants are programmed to save the planet.*

"I want to go back," she tells Enapay.

# Acknowledgements

**For inspiration, sustenance and feedback, thanks to:**

Charles Cecil, Freddie de Rougemont, Georgiana Calthorpe, Emily Pennock, VJ Keegan, Rupert Alexander, Vanessa Garwood, Antonia Barclay, Justin Sparrow, Anna von Kanitz, Jessica St. James, Lucy Corbett, Tom Lumley, Talitha Stevenson, Charlie Warde, Paola Rosà, Gina Monaco, Tim Binding, Alex Preston, Judith Kinghorn, Annabel Merullo, Charlie Campbell, Hamid Khanbhai, Christabel Brudnell-Bruce, Charlotte Raymond, David Flusfeder, Tim Atkins, Tiarnan McCarthy, Sarah Haybittle, Chiara De Cabarrus, Lisa Andris, Kim Macconnell, Rachel Webster, Stuart Bridgeman, Linda Fleischman, Hugo Wilson, Eloise Anson, Caroline Scott, Marc Dalessio, Paolo Cristellotti, Mark Roberts, Richard Burton, Katie St. George, Charlotte Cecil, Josephine Rea, Bill Liesegang, Ebba Heuman, Cristina Zamagni.

www.ingramcontent.com/pod-product-compliance
Lightning Source LLC
Chambersburg PA
CBHW061023120726
47910CB00006B/2081